TH
ASH MOON

MICHELLE DARE

The Ariane Trilogy
Book 1

The Ash Moon

Cover Design & Photography by ©MaeIDesign and Photography
Interior Design by Down Write Nuts
Editing by Barren Acres Editing
Proofreading by Landers Editorial Services, Tiffany Landers

A kept secret. A life altered. A new journey.

Ariane lived her life one book at a time. She would never have guessed those books were about to change everything.

They led her to Orion.

Tall, dark, with eyes only for her. The rest of the world ceased to exist when Orion was around. But during a fateful ash moon, he shifted into a wolf. Ari thought she was dreaming, but she'd recognize those eyes anywhere.

Fiction became reality. Fantasy was actually history. And soon, Ari would learn her role in it.

A pack war was on the horizon, and she was the only one who could stop it.

Nothing would ever be as it once was, because Ariane was now part of the Avynwood Pack.

CONTENTS

ONE

"WE'VE BEEN STANDING HERE FOR THREE hours," Paige says, while leaning against the golden-colored walls outside the hotel ballroom.

I check my phone. "We've only been here thirty minutes."

"Same thing."

"Paige is right," Brayden chimes in. "I think we should go. This is a waste of time." He's only here because Paige is. He doesn't care about the author we're waiting in line to see. Paige does, though. We're both hooked on her books. I would gladly stand here for hours waiting to see her.

"You two are more than welcome to go, but I'm not moving. I have a pile of books with me and they're all getting signed," I state, crossing my arms.

Paige pushes off the wall and wiggles her arm through mine. "Ari's right. We aren't going anywhere until Lealla Raines signs our books." I give a sharp nod, happy to have her on my side. My nickname is Ari. My full name is Ariane, pronounced Ar-ee-ann.

Letting out a long sigh, Bray goes back to people watching. There's plenty of it to do. So many are waiting with us. Lealla is huge in the paranormal romance world. Her books are on the steamy side and geared more toward adults. I just turned eighteen. Mom doesn't care what I read anymore, so long as I stay out of trouble.

"The doors are opening!" Paige squeals beside me. She grips my arm tight as I roll the small piece of luggage behind me. That's right. I have enough books to get signed to warrant a carry-on size suitcase. Paige only brought two books with her, which she stuffed in my luggage.

One by one, people walk into the large room. This is an event only for Lealla. She does these four times a year, each one in a different part of the world, two of which are usually overseas. Each year they are in different places, so she is always meeting new readers. We lucked out having this one only two towns over from us. Paige, Bray, and I take turns showing the printed tickets we bought online six months ago and then we're let inside.

The ballroom is enormous. The kind big wedding receptions are held in. The walls are a soft ivory, and the carpet is a muted beige with swirls of mocha throughout. Rows of white folding chairs are set up before us, with a broad aisle down the middle. There are tables in the front of the room and along one side. Each has a rich, emerald green tablecloth draped over it, embroidered with Lealla's logo—an L and an R intertwined in front of a full moon.

The tables off to the side are stacked with her books, which are available for purchase. Six tall banners stand behind the tables at the front of the room. Each one is a different book cover in the series, though there are more than six books in the series. I can't imagine them trying to squeeze all of them in that row.

Lealla hasn't entered yet. With every step I take, my excitement goes up a notch. I can't believe I'll finally get to see her. Meet the woman whose stories I go to bed at night reading.

The three of us follow those who were in front of us in line and end up sitting only three rows away from the tables where the author will be. I luck out and get an aisle seat. The tall person in front of me won't be able to block my view completely. I can lean out to my right to see.

Tucking my luggage in front of me, I glance around and notice I'm not the only one with a suitcase of books. I'm among my fellow book lovers, and everything feels right in my world.

Brayden sits between Paige and me as we marvel at the crowd and how close we got to the front. We talk about our favorite characters and hope the cover models of the books we love will be here. Poor Bray. He's in a special form of hell right now, and I can't help but smile. The things he does for his friends.

A hush falls over the crowd. I turn my head, surveying the room. There are easily three hundred people sitting and standing in the back along the walls, waiting to meet the author. When my eyes reach the front of the room again, I notice a tall man standing off to the left of the tables. The dark jeans he's wearing don't leave much room over his thick legs. His emerald T-shirt has Lealla's logo on it with a wolf underneath, howling at the moon. Black, military-style boots complete his look. I need one of those shirts. I'd wear it all the time. The man widens his stance and crosses his muscular arms like he's inviting all of us to try and take him on. Cocky much? It's a book signing. This guy needs to get a grip. I doubt any of us are here to harm Lealla.

Two more men enter, each in similar clothing. I immediately recognize them from Lealla's covers. The crowd starts going wild when they see the men who have taken on the image of the characters we love.

Paige reaches for my hand, squeezing it tight. “It's Aries and Cace!” she exclaims in a loud whisper. “Can you believe this?” Her excitement matches my own. I can barely keep my butt in the seat.

Then Lealla enters. Her chestnut hair falls in soft waves over her shoulders and down her back. She's tall and slender. The noise of the crowd becomes deafening at this point. I'm not sure if they're happier to see Lealla or the models. One man, I don't recognize as one of the cover models, walks to the end of the tables opposite the other guy and stands the same way—arms crossed, legs wide. These two must be security.

Aries and Cace sit on either side of Lealla. I have no idea what their real names are. Anytime Lealla mentions her models, she always calls them by the characters they represent. I once looked them up on the internet. Each has their own social media page with their character name on it and Lealla's last name as theirs. I couldn't find their real names anywhere. I even did a reverse image search. Nothing. Yes, I know. Stalker much? I couldn't help it. I'm single and don't have a job since my parents want me concentrating on school. A girl gets bored.

Lealla makes herself comfortable and takes a sip of water before waving to the crowd. There's a small microphone clipped to her black, V-neck, sleeveless shirt, which she adjusts. I didn't miss the jeans she's wearing, nor the black high heels. Every time I get to the end of one of her books, I see her picture. She's the definition of beautiful. Her makeup isn't too heavy, only accentuating her eyes. Her skin is flawless.

“Thank you for coming,” she greets, and the crowd quiets down to hear her speak. “I'm Lealla Raines. It's a pleasure to meet you.” I clap along with everyone else. “You already know the two men beside me,” she says with a wink, which causes cheering from the crowd. She waits for us to calm again. “Let's get started.”

Over the next half hour, she tells us about herself. There are a few things I already know from her biography and others I had no clue about. She talks about her writing and how it's her passion. How, when she was little, her dad worked two jobs to keep a roof over their heads so her mom could stay home and take care of her. A strong work ethic was ingrained in her from the start. Lealla worked a lot of different jobs, sometimes two and three at a time, while writing late into the night, getting little sleep. Every time she was finished writing and editing a book, she independently published it, hoping it would be the one to get her noticed. It wasn't until her fifth book in the series before she was able to quit her job and write full-time. By then, her books had taken off and she never looked back.

I sit in awe of her. She's a true inspiration. Hard work and determination got her where she is today. We could all be so lucky to have jobs we love as much as she loves writing.

A question and answer session follows. Almost everyone raises their hand in anticipation of asking Lealla, or one of her models, a question. One of the men, who stands off to the side of the table, has a microphone and walks down one side of the rows, picking random readers to speak, then he comes up the side where I sit.

Unfortunately, I'm looked over. Something I'm very used to. I'm on the shorter side, with pitch-black hair and hazel eyes. Standing next to Paige, most of the time, I don't exist. Her fiery red hair makes her stand out everywhere she goes. Of course, the guy with the microphone chooses her.

Paige stands and smiles up at him with perfect white teeth and smoothes her hand down the curve of her slim waist to the slight flair of her hips. She knows exactly what she's doing. Even at eighteen, she can probably get the guy standing beside me to go out with her. He's almost too muscular, if that makes sense. Too jacked up for me, but Paige is loving his looks.

"Thank you," she says to the guy then turns toward the front. "Hi, Lealla, nice to meet you." Lealla returns the sentiment. "I was wondering where you find such sexy men for your covers." Poor Brayden is scowling between us at Paige's use of the word sexy, while the guys behind the table smile at the compliment.

Lealla responds, "Believe it or not, some of these men found me. Others I've literally run in to when I've been out at other events or running errands near home."

Paige still grips the microphone. "Where do you live? I think it's time for me to relocate." Laughter rings out through the crowd. Lealla even smiles.

"I have a few homes spread across the country. The closest is about an hour from here. It's a quiet little town. None of my guys came from there, though. It would have been easier if they had."

Paige smiles and takes her seat. I'm envious of her

being able to ask a question. I wish he would have picked me.

More readers get to ask her questions, then row by row, we're called forward to get our books signed. This is what will take the most time, but luckily, we get our turn sooner than most. Once all the books are signed, the event is over.

I'm relieved by how quickly the line moves. When our row is up, we stand in line, slowly making our way to Lealla. I'm ahead of Bray and Paige. The male models are helping this move smoothly by opening the books for Lealla so she can sign each one efficiently as she talks with every reader.

Everyone has smiles on their faces after meeting her. Lealla is truly loved, and she seems to return that love to her readers. No one is rushed along. She listens as each person talks to her and replies with kindness in her voice.

Moving forward, I'm in front of Aries. He smiles as I lift my carry-on suitcase onto the table to pull all the books free. Who knows when I'll have the chance to meet Lealla again? I need to get all these babies signed.

“I'm so sorry. I'm a bit of a book whore,” I tell him. “I'd love Lealla to sign the whole series.”

“She'd be happy to,” he replies in a deep timbre. Holy hotness. I think I’m going to melt into a puddle in front of him.

I hand Paige her two books as Bray's eyes go wide at the number of books I have stacked on the table. “Damn, Ari, did you need to bring all of them?”

“No one’s forcing you to be here,” I reply as I pull the book with Aries on the cover free. Setting it on top of the pile, I ask, “Would you mind signing it, too?” His is the first book in the series. The one that hooked me on Lealla's writing.

“Not at all.” He smiles again and quickly scrolls his name on the title page. He even puts a smiley face under it. I let out a breathy sigh before snapping out of my daze. My cheeks flush. I hope he didn't hear me.

Quickly, I move along. Cace is now next to Aries to help keep things moving. I ask him to sign his book as well. He draws wolf ears over his name. The whole series is based on wolf shifters. Could he be any cuter? He's got this whole boyish charm thing down pat.

After a couple of minutes waiting for my turn to meet Lealla, I finally step in front of her. Cace took the time to open all of my books to the title page so they would be ready for Lealla. She's in front of me, and I'm having a hard time forming words.

“It's such a pleasure to meet you,” I eventually get out. “I'm a huge fan. Sevan’s book is my favorite so far, but then again, I say that about every new book you release.”

“Thank you,” she says as she smiles up at me. “What's your name?”

“Oh, sorry. I should have told you. I'm Ariane, but you can make the books out to Ari.” She nods and, one by one, signs each of the books. Twelve in all, so far.

When she finishes, she stands, which catches me off guard. From what I've seen, every reader in front of me asked for their picture with her and she’s gladly obliged. I'm too nervous to do so.

“Would you like a picture?” she asks.

“Yes, that would be great.” I turn and give Bray my phone, my hand shaking as I do so. I warn him, “You mess up taking this picture, and you'll see rage like you never have in all your life.” He rolls his eyes, brushing off my threat. Lealla chuckles, causing my cheeks to heat with embarrassment. I didn't even think of her overhearing me when I said it.

I walk between two of the tables and stand beside her. She's a solid six inches taller than me. Then again, she also has on heels. She puts her arm behind me, resting her hand on my hip as I smile like a fool for the picture.

Back on the other side of the table, I gather my books and put them in the suitcase. “Thank you so much for signing these and for the picture. You have no idea how much this means to me.”

She picks up one of her business cards and writes something on the back. When finished, she hands it to me and leans in close. “Come to this address tonight for an after-party. I'm only inviting my biggest fans and would love to have you join us.”

My eyes widen as I stutter out, “R-really?” She nods, smiling.

That's when Paige leans forward and loudly whispers, “We'd love to come.” This girl has supersonic hearing.

If I'm not mistaken, Lealla's smile falters for a split second before firmly going back in place. “Your friends are more than welcome to join, but no one else,” she says pointedly, glancing between the three of us. “It's invite only, and you'll need that card to get in.” I nod, still beaming at her invitation. It's like Christmas and my birthday rolled into one.

TWO

PAIGE LIES ON HER BED WITH her phone in her hand, texting someone, while I obsess over how I look. "Are you sure this looks okay?" I ask and spin so she gets the full effect.

"I told you," she glances my way. "You look great. Besides, I don't know what you're so worried about. It's just an after-party. All the guys are way out of our league. We'll probably just be relaxing with the author."

Sweeping my hair up off my neck, I cock my head to the side. It looks better down. Definitely. "I still can't believe she invited us."

She waves her hand dismissively and keeps typing on her phone with her other one. "She probably handed out a hundred of those cards."

"Way to ruin the moment," I pout. Grabbing a pair of socks from the folded pile of clothes on her dresser, I throw them at her.

"Only being realistic," she says, catching them. "We live in two different worlds, you and me."

I place my hands on my hips. "What's that supposed to mean?"

Paige places her phone on the nightstand and sits up to give me her full attention. "I'm a realist, while you fantasize all day. You live and breathe the books you read like one day it's all going to come true and you're going to live the life of the heroine."

"You love those books as much as I do!"

"I do, but I know where to draw the line. Sure, it's nice to escape into a good book, but when you're reading or thinking about the books you've read, nothing else exists. It's only the books for you, Ari."

"Sorry for getting wrapped up in the story and liking the world I get pulled into." I can't believe she's getting on me about reading. I don't give her grief about any of the things she loves.

"All I'm saying is don't get your hopes up for some magical party tonight. The author is a regular person, just like you and me. The models are only that—men who are on book covers, paid to model and interact with readers. They aren't really the characters."

"Whatever." I roll my eyes and brush her comments off. I won't let her bring me down tonight. "Are you ready? I don't want to be late."

She stands and shakes out her long locks with her fingers. "I'm ready. Wait, lipstick."

I borrow one of her lip glosses and apply it. I rarely

wear makeup, but tonight I put on mascara and lip gloss. My mom always tells me how naturally beautiful I am and that I don't need makeup. She said one day someone special is going to notice. I'm still waiting for that to happen.

Paige and I stand side by side in front of the full-length mirror on her closet door. We're both wearing dark jeans. I have on a black tank top with lace trimming. Paige has on a navy, sleeveless blouse. I borrowed the tank from her. Her clothes are much nicer than mine. Hell, her whole house is, for that matter.

Her parents are wealthy and rarely around. Paige does whatever she wants, whenever she wants. As long as she gets good grades, they leave her alone.

Since it's Saturday night, my parents know I'm staying at Paige's. I do almost every weekend. They trust me. I'm also not one to get into trouble. They don't need to know every time I go out. Every once in a while, Paige will lure me out. I never tell my parents. I don't want them asking a ton of questions. I don't lie. I only omit certain aspects of the weekend.

Brayden is downstairs waiting for us when we're done. "Took you two long enough," he huffs and stands from the couch. His eyes rake over every inch of Paige's body. Lovely. I get to watch him drool over her all night. Make no mistake, I don't have any feelings for Bray outside of friendship, but it gets to be a little much how he fawns all over Paige. She's completely oblivious to it. I've tried telling her, but she dismisses me and laughs.

"I'll drive," Paige says.

Out in the garage, her silver BMW coupe is waiting for us. She got it for her seventeenth birthday. I received my mom's old Buick Skylark when I turned seventeen. Lucky me.

After a little over an hour of driving, we finally get close to the address Lealla had written down. The trees seem to grow taller, blocking out most of the moonlight. It's as if they are stretching before my eyes. I rub them and look again. No way did the trees move like that. This time, I see nothing but trees that aren't moving at all.

We stop when we reach two tall, stone pillars and an iron gate. Atop each pillar is a light, casting its glow over the gates and stone drive below it. The top of the gate has silver points, almost like tiny arrows pointing toward the sky. As I glance to the left, I notice the arrows running the length of the fence. I pity whoever tries to scale this thing. They'd get an arrow in an unpleasant place.

Paige rolls down her window. "Weird. There's no intercom. No button to press. How do we get in?"

"I say we don't. We turn around and go back home," Bray states from the back seat. "This place gives me the creeps."

"Man up," Paige replies. "It's just trees and a fence. You aren't afraid of trees and fences, are you?"

"No, but the tall dude who just appeared from the shadows is frightening. Put it in reverse. Let's get out of here."

I squint my eyes in the direction of Bray's gaze. Sure enough, someone is coming toward us and isn't giving off a warm and friendly vibe, thanks to his scowl and the way his fists are clenched by his side. No, this is the kind of situation where you expect to be on the evening news after all is said and done.

He stops a foot from Paige's window and bends down. His hair is cut close to his head. I don't miss the color of it even in the dark. It's bright white. It's in stark contrast to the black clothes he's wearing. "Why are you here?" he asks in a gruff voice.

Paige speaks up before Bray or I get the chance to. "Why are you here?"

"Excuse me?"

I grip her arm. "What are you doing?" I whisper.

She shakes me off. "You heard me," she replies. "You're out here like some kind of creeper, and you expect me to give you information. I don't think so."

"Listen, little girl. If you want to get past those gates," he points ahead of us, "then I'm going to need to know why you're here."

Anger rises in her voice. "Did you just call me little girl?"

He stands and grumbles so low I can't make out what he says. I decide to speak up since Paige is getting us nowhere. "We're here for a party." Leaning over, I hand the guy the card Lealla gave me. He glances at it, then back at us, before his eyes settle on me. From his pocket he pulls out a phone. A second later, the gates begin to open. Now we're getting somewhere.

"Follow the driveway to the right. You'll reach a large, grey stone house. That's where you need to go. Don't drive anywhere else." I hear the warning in his tone and don't want to find out what would happen if we ignore it. Luckily, Paige stays quiet but rolls up her window as soon as the guy stops talking.

She drives ahead slowly. Little lights line either side of the light grey pavers, which make up the drive. "Who did that guy think he was? Little girl. He's lucky I didn't get out of the car and knee him right in the crotch."

"I'm glad you didn't act on that," I say. "He looked like he could do some serious damage, given the size of him."

"Oh, please. Every guy has the same weak point—right between the legs. Tall or short. Thin or stocky. They all go down when you knee them in the junk."

I glance out the window of the car. The trees are thinning. Moonlight begins to filter through. The house comes into view. If you could even call it that. Grey stone, three stories as long as four ranch homes combined. It's huge.

Paige parks near the front door on the semicircle drive. A slender man in a tuxedo gives her a small, white ticket with a number on it as she exits the car. As soon as we're all out, he drives the car out of sight. Let's hope we make it out of here alive and get her car back. Although, if I'm listening to my gut, I need to relax a little. No alarms are going off in my body. Only butterflies in my stomach from the anticipation of what is behind the emerald green, double doors in front of us.

One of the doors swings in wide before we have a chance to knock. Another man in a tux is inside, holding it open for us. He sweeps his arm out to welcome us in. After thanking him, he asks us to follow him. We walk through the open entryway with its beige marble floor and stairs that curve down on either side of a massive crystal chandelier. I've never seen a house so grand. Even the stairs are marble.

We turn left and pass a kitchen, but we move at such a clip I can't make out anything about it, outside of ivory cabinets. The sounds of food being stirred and lids being placed on pots filters to me as we walk past. The aroma stays with me. Rich, hearty fragrances like my mom's beef stew, but better, have me faltering in my steps as I pull the scent in. It smells like home.

Then it's the bass thumping loudly that draws my attention while it begins to vibrate through my body as we get closer to where the party must be going on. The farther we walk down the hall, the louder the music gets. I lose count of how many closed doors we walk by before we reach a massive ballroom. It rivals the size of the room we were in for the signing.

Strobe lights bounce off the walls as bodies dance to the beat. There's a DJ on a raised stage at one end of the room. A bartender isn't far from him, tossing bottles in the air and easily catching them as he makes drinks. The dance floor is packed. So many men and women. Some men are shirtless, while others are not. I can tell the women love every second of the ones without their shirts on, as some skate their hands up and down the bare chests of the men they're dancing with. I've never seen anything like it. Then again, I don't exactly get out much.

The man who escorted us points to the far wall, where Lealla is talking with a small group of two men and two women. I recognize the men as models from covers of her series. They each have their arms protectively looped around one of the women's backs beside them. We thank the man and make our way through the crowd toward Lealla. Paige's hand slips into mine as we weave through the room. She's smarter than me. With all the hot men in here, my brain checked out and was focused on them, not losing my friends in the chaos of the party. I hope she has a hold of Bray's hand as well.

When we finally reach Lealla, we stand just outside the small circle of people talking with her. I want to offer my thanks for inviting us, but she's in the middle of a conversation and I don't want to interrupt. Instead, I hang back with my friends.

We each lean on the wall to take in the people here. I hadn't noticed until now, but everyone seems older than us. Early twenties through their early forties, if I had to guess. I'm not the best judge of age. If I'm right, however, we are the youngest people in the room. I try to see if I can find any other readers here, but all I see are couples dancing, talking, and drinking. And they all look at home. Not on the sidelines like us. I wish there were more people our age here. It would help me relax a little. Maybe coming tonight wasn't the best idea.

I hear my name called over the music. Turning to my right, I see Lealla waving for us to join her group. We push from the wall and join her as they part to make room for us. "I'm so glad you could make it," she says with a smile. "How do you like the party so far?"

"It's a little overwhelming," I reply and duck my head in embarrassment. I shouldn't have said that. I really need to think before I speak. Here I am, standing with people I don't even know, and I feel like a lost child.

"Yes, it can be. Once you've been here for a while, you tend to block out most of the noise. My guys love the music, though. It gives them a chance to let loose and have fun with their mates."

My head snaps up. "Mates?"

She waves dismissively. "Girlfriends and wives, I mean. I get so wrapped up in my own world sometimes that I use terminology from my books."

I smile. "I can understand that."

She peers over my head and waves someone over. "I want to introduce you to my newest Avynwood model.

He'll be on the cover of an upcoming book. At nineteen, he's my youngest model yet, but he's perfect for the story." Avynwood is the name of a forest about four hours from here. Lealla titled her series and pack after it. When I first read the books, I did some research. There are some crazy tales about what took place there.

When I turn in the direction she's looking, all the breath leaves my lungs in a silent *whoosh*. Walking toward us is hands down the hottest guy I've ever seen, and that's saying a lot, considering my current environment. He's wearing a shirt, thankfully. If not, I'd probably lose all capability to speak. The shirt he's wearing clings to him like a second skin, showcasing his muscular arms. He's lean, not broad. His dark hair is neatly combed back from his face. It's hard to tell the exact color in the semi-dark room, especially with the lights bouncing around.

Jeans slung low on his hips pull me to the way he walks. With every step, his body moves and flexes with the grace of a predator. Each step is exact and full of purpose. When my eyes finally make their way up to his face, I expect a cocky grin from him realizing I was checking him out, but what I get is a smile and dimples. Dimples!

He stops mere inches from me. There's a good six-inch difference in our height. And this close, I notice the crystal blue color of his eyes. My lips part, but no words form, not even a sound. His eyes drop to my mouth as the color of those beautiful eyes flash briefly from blue to a deeper hue that's hard to make out in the darkened room. I blink a few times. His eyes are blue. It must have been the lights playing tricks on me.

Lealla steps forward and places her hand on his shoulder. "Ariane, I'd like to introduce you to Orion."

I can't help the laugh that bursts from me. "Orion? That's seriously your name?"

He crosses his arms over his chest, his biceps bulging. "Yes, little mouse, it is." I can't place his accent. Something exotic and unlike anything I've ever heard before. The way he accentuated the t's in little—it's very sexy. Wait. Did he just call me a mouse?

THREE

"EXCUSE ME, BUT I AM NO mouse," I reply.

"Aren't you? You're small in height and can't weigh much," he says while looking me over. "Your hair is black like some of the pet mice I've seen, and your voice is sweet. Although, not squeaky like a mouse, so maybe there is a slight difference."

Paige leans in front of me to get in Orion's line of sight and snaps her fingers to get his attention. "She may be short, but she's got plenty of fire in her, unlike an ordinary, timid mouse." Why does everyone have to keep pointing out how short I am?

He looks past her, his eyes never leaving mine. Cocking his head to the side, he says, "Fire isn't the right word."

I pull back my arm. "Keep talking about me like that

and my fist is going to meet your face." I'm unsure where this violent streak is coming from. I've never hit anyone before, yet this guy has me all riled up. I've been called much worse than a mouse. In fact, I've been picked on often throughout high school. It was only when the most popular girl moved away last year that I finally got some peace. Her little clan disbanded without their leader.

"Bite," he adds.

"Huh?" What is he talking about?

"You don't have fire within you, little mouse. It's bite. I bet if I tried to touch you right now, you'd hurt me."

"Why don't you find out?"

"Okay, enough," Lealla laughs from my side. I forgot she was there. "You two sure have some chemistry between you already, but I'm not surprised." What is she talking about?

I turn to her. "I'm sorry. I'm a little confused."

"Not to worry, dear. There's plenty of time."

"Plenty of time for what?" Why were we talking in circles?

Lealla lifts her hand high in the air and waves to someone across the room. "If you'll excuse me. Have fun, but don't go wandering off without Orion."

"There's no way I'm going anywhere with him."

She smiles. "So much to learn. This is going to be fun." Then she's off, walking through the throng of dancers, garnering the attention of everyone she passes.

"What the hell was that about?" I ask Paige and Bray.

"I told you we should have turned back. You two never listen to me," Bray mutters as his eyes stay focused on Orion. "Hey, what's your problem, man? Quit looking at Ari. She's with us." He slings his arm across my shoulder.

I'm taken aback. He's never been possessive of me before. Well, except outside of the jerk jocks in school, who tease me every now and then. He always stands up for me. Other than that, I'm mostly invisible to him when Paige is around. Now, if someone were staring at her, he'd probably get in a fight with them. He'd most likely lose, however. Bray isn't the most muscular guy. Okay, he has some muscle in his legs. He's a runner on track at school.

Orion glances over at Bray before those blue eyes of his land back on me. "Is this your boyfriend?"

I try hard not to laugh. "Hardly. He's just a friend."

"Jeez, Ari, say how you really feel." Oh, please. Like Bray is truly hurt over me telling the truth.

"Quit it. You and I both know we're only friends. Besides, it's not me you're interested in." His eyes narrow and his lips form a thin line. The whole world sees how badly he crushes on Paige, yet he tries hard to hide it from her.

"You'll dance with me, then?" Orion asks, his voice pulling me from my conversation with Bray. Orion's arm is extended, his palm facing up, waiting for me to accept his invitation.

For a moment, I can't move. I simply stare at his proffered hand.

"I didn't think it was a difficult question," he states with a quirk of his lips. Why is he so arrogant?

"Oh, I'm sorry. I'm just a little mouse. I'm not smart enough to answer your question." I roll my eyes.

He laughs and damn if it doesn't do something to my insides. Those butterflies I felt earlier were tame in comparison to what's going on now. There's a wildness inside me that wants to keep challenging him. Wants to push every button he has, to make him push me in return. I like the challenge.

His hand wraps around mine. Something zips through me at the contact. Like a little jolt of electricity. What's going on? Orion is smiling like he just won the lottery. Did he feel it, too, or is he just a guy who is trying to win over a girl so she'll dance with him?

Scanning the room, I notice everyone dancing. Even Paige and Bray have stepped into the throng of people. When did that happen? Deserters. Orion and I are the only two not having fun. But why did he ask me? There are drop-dead gorgeous women all over the place. I'm nothing special.

"What's wrong?" he asks. When my eyes land back on him, I notice the way his brow is furrowed. Is he genuinely concerned for me?

I've got nothing to lose at this point, so I'm going to ask him what I'm thinking. "Why did you ask me to dance?"

"Why not?"

I shake my head. "I'm serious. There are far more attractive women out on the dance floor. I'm sure you could dance with any of them."

"Most are with their mates." Here we go with the mates talk again. Does everyone involved in this book series say that? "The ones who aren't, I don't desire. You're who I want to spend time with."

"Say what now?" Did he just choose me over all the other women here?

"Let's go, little mouse," he chuckles as he tugs me into the middle of the crowd. He finds a small spot for us to dance and pulls me close to him, his strong arms wrapping around my waist.

I'm dazed, unable to move. The guy before me looks like he fell from the heavens, and I'm ordinary Ariane. I don't get it.

When he starts swaying his hips in time with the music, all coherent thought leaves my head. And then I'm moving with him in perfect synchronization. How? I don't know. I've never been a good dancer. Not like Paige. Yet, with Orion, I'm graceful. I don't step on his toes or stumble. We flow as one.

He leans in close, his breath caressing my cheek. “There's no one else I could move like this with.”

“I don't understand.” I'm not sure what he's saying. He's an amazing dancer. Why can't he dance this way with someone else?

“Don't think. Only feel.” So I do.

Song after song plays as I stay in his arms, the most relaxed and content I've ever been in my life. I'm not sure how long we dance. Paige taps me on the shoulder, saying it's late and we should probably head back. She yawns. Reaching into my pocket, I pull out my phone and see it's three in the morning. How long was I dancing with Orion?

The light lands on Orion. For a moment, his eyes flash to a brilliant emerald green. But as soon as it’s there, it’s gone again—back to their normal crystal blue. I pull back from him and the trance breaks. I study him, trying to figure out if I’m seeing things again or if his eyes did change colors. No green remains now. Only that gorgeous blue.

“I should go. I didn't realize how late it was.” Orion nods stiffly.

The crowd has thinned significantly. The people who are left dancing look like they are about to do a lot more than sway to the music and don't seem to care who is around to watch.

Ducking my head, I walk toward the doorway. Orion's hand finds mine and I'm zapped again at the initial touch. Once his fingers thread through mine, it dulls but doesn't disappear completely. It's a low flow of energy, like it was while we were dancing. If only I knew what was causing it or what it means. I peer up at him to ask, but he shakes his head and smiles. This evening has left me with so many questions.

He leads us through the mansion until the four of us are standing outside. His hand tightens on mine as Paige's car pulls up. I step forward, but Orion doesn't move or release me. Paige lifts an eyebrow then ushers Bray to the car where they wait for me.

"I don't want you to leave," Orion softly says.

"This night… I've never had one like it or met anyone like you." I need to ask if he feels what I do when we touch. I think he does, but if he says no, then I'll know it's all in my head. I lift our joined hands. "Do you feel something when you touch me?"

"How much do you know about the Avynwood shifters?" Why are we talking about Lealla's books?

"I've read each book in the series, some twice. Why?"

His thumb gently rubs the back of my hand. "I want you to read Aries' book again. Think about everything you felt tonight while you read it."

"I'm not sure what that has to do with anything. I asked you a question and you start talking about books instead."

"Take my advice, little mouse. Read it again."

I stiffen. "If you call me little mouse one more time..."

He steps closer, only a breath away. I notice the rise and fall of his chest. "What, Ariane? What will you do about the name I've given you?"

Shaking his hand free, I turn toward the car. Orion catches my elbow. That zip is back, racing up my arm, causing the hair on it to stand on end. I freeze.

He steps around me and cups my face in his hands. "Don't leave angry. I didn't mean it as a negative thing. Every animal in our world has a purpose and does something extraordinary. Mice, they're sensible and resourceful. They're fast and agile. They're able to slip from a room with no one noticing they're gone. Though," he continues as he leans down, his lips mere inches from mine, "I'll always know where you are."

My eyes flutter closed, waiting for him to kiss me. When he doesn't, I open them and find him standing straight again, no longer so close. My cheeks quickly warm. That's not embarrassing at all. I must look like a complete fool.

"Ari, let's go!" Bray yells out the open window of Paige's car.

"I should go. I guess I'll see you never." I offer a small smile and open the door to the car.

"Never say never, little mouse."

I take one last look at him and climb inside. Paige wastes no time pulling away from the mansion.

"What was that, Ari?" Bray asks. "You don't even know him. You spent all night dancing with a complete stranger."

I spin in my seat. "What's your problem, anyway? I'm surprised you even noticed where I was."

"Oh, right. Like I didn't see where my best friend spent her night. Or how every time I looked in your direction, you had this stupid look on your face. It was like he drugged you."

"I don't know what you're talking about," I huff and cross my arms, facing forward again.

"Come on," Paige cuts in. "Orion is hot as sin, and he didn't care about anyone else in that room but you. If I were you, I would've stayed wrapped up in him all night, too. I couldn't get any guy in there to pay attention to me. They were all paired up. What kind of party has no single men?"

"It's like I'm not even here," Bray mumbles from the back seat.

"I saw you," Paige states. "We danced. However, I was looking for some action, and we're only friends. I love you like a brother, Bray, and that's not a line I'm going to cross with you."

He leans forward between the front seats. "One day, P, you're going to realize what's right in front of you, and it's going to be too late."

She pats him on the cheek while one hand remains on the steering wheel. "You're so cute."

"Cute. I don't want to be cute!"

I'm unsure if the day will ever come when Paige sees him differently. I do wish Bray would move on, though. He deserves to be with someone who sees how wonderful he is and only has eyes for him. He won't find that in this car, however.

FOUR

BRAY PASSES OUT ON PAIGE'S COUCH, and I take my usual room in her house. It's technically a guest room, but no one sleeps here but Bray and me, and he's always on the couch. There's another guest room. For some reason, Bray has always liked sleeping downstairs. I have no idea why.

Orion's words keep playing through my head about how I need to read Aries' book again. I dig my tablet out of my bag and find his book. Yes, I always have my tablet with me when I'm sleeping over at Paige's house.

It's not until chapter three when I find something that has me pausing. When Aries first met Cassandra, and his hand touched her arm, he felt a spark. He didn't know what to make of it, but the longer his hand remained on Cassandra's arm, the happier he became. His body was recognizing something in hers.

I read this section over and over, shaking my head—this can't be real. Orion and I shared this lightning bolt of something between us. But I'm not a shifter. He's not a shifter. We're just people. Maybe it was all in my head. Maybe I wanted this connection with him to be more than it was. I need sleep. Turning my tablet off, I roll over and eventually drift into a peaceful slumber.

By the time I crawl out of bed, it's one in the afternoon. I go to Paige's room and wake her. We were all up late, so it's not uncommon for us to sleep in. Bray is downstairs cooking for us. I keep telling him to go to culinary school after we graduate, but he always waves me off.

A rich aroma greets me as I stumble into the kitchen. Cinnamon, bacon, vanilla, you name it. Food is spread out on the table.

Paige sits down and dives in. "Seriously, Bray," she says, with a mouthful of food. "No one cooks like you do."

"You only keep me around for my cooking," he replies while setting down a plate of scrambled eggs. Paige winks at him but doesn't stop eating to say more.

I flip my phone over on the table and start scrolling through messages. Most are social media notifications. It seems Paige posted about our night out. I decide to click on one of her posts and find a picture of me dancing with Orion. He's giving me an intense look. One I'm not sure how to decipher. Maybe it's desire. That thought has me almost choking on the food in my mouth. I cough and sputter, gasping for air.

Bray pats me on the back. "Are you okay?"

"Yeah," I rasp and turn the phone to Paige. "Why did you post this?"

She smiles around a piece of bacon. This girl can eat anything she wants and never gain a single pound. "How could I not post that? Look at him, Ari! He's gorgeous and obviously in to you. Why wouldn't I show the world just how desirable you are? Those jocks in our high school can suck it. Orion could wipe the floor with all of them."

I bury my face in my free hand. "Why are you creating problems for me?"

"Not a problem. A solution. Did you read the caption?" Oh, no. What did she write?

Looks like Ariane Sanderly is officially off the market.

"Paige," I groan.

She pats me on the shoulder. "Chin up. Any of the girls in school would have loved to trade places with you last night. You'll be the talk of the senior class."

I ignore the fact that what she posted is a lie and address what she just said. "I don't want to be the talk of anything. I want to finish the final months of high school and never look back. You know I don't like anyone at school outside of you and Bray. They all hate me. I've accepted that."

Bray drops down in the chair opposite me and points at me with his fork. "You may have, but Paige and I haven't. You don't deserve any of the grief they give you. If they'd stop for one second and have a conversation with you, they'd see how amazing you are."

"I don't want to talk to them. I have zero desire in creating more friendships. And now people are going to be talking about me for a whole other reason." I don't need this. I don't like everyone's attention on me. I could throttle

Paige for posting what she did. Though, I do like the picture. If only she reserved it for me and had not shown it to everyone else.

Paige's phone vibrates on the table. She lifts it and yells, "Ari, look!"

I take her phone from her. What in the ever-loving...? "How did he...? Why did he...? Paige!"

"What are you two reading?" Bray asks.

Paige smiles like she's very proud of herself. "Orion Raines liked and commented on my post."

"Who?"

"The guy from last night. Jeez, Bray, were you even there?"

"You mean the crazy guy who wouldn't leave Ari alone?"

Paige quirks an eyebrow. "There was a mutual attraction there, and now Mr. Raines wants the world to know about our Ari. He shared my post." What has she gotten me into? More importantly, why would Orion share her post? Maybe he wants to show Lealla's readers what fun we had at the party last night. Strictly for marketing reasons, of course, since he's on the cover of an upcoming book.

My phone vibrates in my palm. When I look at the screen, I nearly drop the phone. "He just sent me a friend request."

"Quick, accept it!" Paige yells. "Maybe he'll message you. You two didn't exchange numbers last night, did you?"

"No." I shake my head. "I didn't think to ask."

I click on his name and scroll his profile. All the pictures of him are model photos where he's posing. But there is one casual picture of him and Aries. The caption beneath it reads, *I owe everything to this man.*

"Did you accept it?" Paige asks. I glance up from my phone and find her practically bouncing in her chair.

I started to go down the social media rabbit hole. There will be time for that later, when Paige and Bray aren't around to ask me questions and distract me.

I click a button and say, "Accepted." Then I find Paige's post and start reading the comments—the many, many comments. The only one I care about is Orion's, though. He wrote, *Best night of my life, with the most beautiful girl I've ever laid eyes on.* He can't be serious, can he?

"You just read his comment, didn't you?"

I look up and find Paige staring at me, smiling. "You're in so much trouble. I still can't believe you posted this." I shake my phone at her.

She winks. "You're going to thank me for it. Wait and see."

"He just sent me a private message!" What is happening to me right now? How did this become my reality? The hottest guy I've ever seen called me beautiful and is now messaging me. If I were alone, I'd be screaming in joy.

"Read it out loud so the rest of us know what he says."

"I will not." She's crazy if she thinks I'm telling Bray whatever this message says. They both might be my best friends, but this conversation stays firmly in the girl-talk category. Besides, Bray doesn't seem too warm and fuzzy in the Orion department.

She winks again. "Whatever you say." She knows me too well.

I stand from the table, having taken only a few bites of French toast, and I walk into the living room to sit on the couch. I open Orion's message.

Orion: Hello, little mouse. How did you sleep? Any dreams about big, bad wolves?

Me: If you're referring to Aries' book, I wouldn't call him that. He's more like a protective, butt-kicking wolf.

Orion: I like how you see us.

Me: Us?

Orion: Do you have plans for dinner?

Why is he so evasive? I ask a question, he asks another to redirect the conversation. So frustrating.

Me: Yes, I need to be home for dinner with my parents.

Orion: What about tomorrow after school? I can pick you up when you get out.

Me: How do you even know what school I go to?

Orion: Your profile.

Now I feel stupid. I have what high school I attend on my page.

Me: Isn't it a far drive?

Not that I know where he lives. He could be hours away from Lealla's home, for all I know.

Orion: No drive is too far to get to you.

Boy, does he know the right thing to say. If I weren't already sitting down, I'd need to be.

Me: Okay.

Orion: It's a date. Wear something comfortable.

Me: Will do.

I can't believe I just agreed to go out with someone I hardly know. This could be the most foolish thing I've ever done. I wonder if I can rope Paige and Bray to come with me?

Orion: Oh, and no friends this time.

Me: How do I know you aren't a serial killer?

Orion: If I were going to kill you, I would have done it last night when everyone else was preoccupied. You have nothing to fear around me. I promise.

Me: We'll see.

Orion: Did you finish reading the book?

Me: No, I passed out.

Orion: Finish before I see you.

Me: You're awfully demanding for someone I barely know.

Orion: Don't you?

Riddles. I feel like we're talking in riddles.

Me: Gotta go. I'll try and do my "homework."

Orion: Have a good day and stay out of the woods.

Me: You're so weird.

Orion: And you are very many things.

I don't respond. What do I even say to that? It's all confusing and cryptic. Who talks like that anyway?

"Ari, would you get back in here and eat?" Bray calls.

Standing, I make my way back to the table and eat slowly while Paige and Bray talk about who knows what. I'm not paying attention to them. Instead, I'm going over everything in my head that Orion said to me as notifications keep popping up on my phone. Most are messages from classmates asking how I met him and if he has any friends. Girls who have never said one nice thing to me. I'm tempted to reply to each one of them with the middle finger emoticon, but instead, I ignore them.

I'm the last one at the table. I dive back down the rabbit hole and try to find any information I can about Orion. It's not much. Everything about him is tied directly to Lealla and her books.

A new message pops up from him.

Orion: Your friends won't leave me alone. I'm getting a lot of requests to be friends with them.

Me: They aren't my friends. They're trolls who think you have guy friends for them.

Orion: They aren't nice to you?

Me: Nope. My only true friends are Paige and Brayden.

Orion: Noted.

Me: I don't mind if you're friends with them.

That's a flat-out lie, but I'm trying to stay casual and not think about the worry coursing through me that once he sees those attractive girls, he won't want anything to do with me.

Orion: I won't be friends with anyone who treats you badly.

Me: Your call.

He doesn't say anything else. I decide to be nosy and click on his profile to see if he accepted any of the requests. We have no mutual friends. Not even Paige or Bray. There are a few girls at school I keep on my friend's list. They are the ones who aren't jerks to me. Yet, others keep messaging me.

Overall, I'm not big on social media. Not like Paige is. She's always scrolling or posting. Always has the newest app and begging me to join. I'm good without it. I'd rather read than be immersed in gossip and drama. I get that every day I go to school.

Paige sits back down next to me. "Bray left. Are you going to tell me what happened with Orion? What did he say?"

I show her our messages. She tells me how the girls on

her post, who are all drooling over him, are saying how hot he is. I haven't read any of the recent comments. They'll just make me angry.

Paige thinks Orion has a serious thing for me. When I told her he was picking me up after school tomorrow, she literally screamed. Right in my ear. It's still ringing.

She laughed when I suggested he was a serial killer and told me I need to relax; not everyone out there has bad motives. She obviously hasn't absorbed books as I have. There's always a bad guy. At the same point, there's always a hero. The one who saves the day and rescues the damsel in distress. Now to wait and find out which one Orion is.

FIVE

SCHOOL ON MONDAY CONSISTED OF ME fielding questions from girls I've rarely spoken to about the mysterious Orion. They wanted to know how I got him to go out with me, and if he has any friends. Is it that hard to believe I can get a guy like him? Who am I kidding? I can't even believe it. He's so far out of my league. We aren't even in the same galaxy.

There were also the guys who suddenly showed an interest in me. Ones who teased me in the past, now looked at me like I was fresh meat. I hate high school. So very much.

I'm currently leaning against a tall oak tree, along the walkway to the main entrance of the school, waiting for Orion to appear. I shooed Paige and Bray away so I could leave when Orion gets here. At this point, I'll take my chances he's a serial killer instead of having to deal with this high school stuff.

"Ari!" I turn and find none other than the captain of the football team walking toward me. A guy who had never said two words to me yet felt it appropriate to laugh along with the other jerks when they were teasing me. Lovely. This is just the icing on my horrible day.

He jogs over to me. "I've been looking for you."

I quirk an eyebrow. "Really? Why?"

"I wanted to see if you have any plans."

Pushing off from the tree, I step closer to him. "Let me get this straight. I've been going to this high school for four years. Not once have you talked to me. Now you decide to ask me out? Where's your team of groupies who usually follow you around? I'm sure one of them would be quick to jump in your car."

He smiles and even appears a little embarrassed. Did I step into another dimension and not realize it? "I'm sorry for not talking to you sooner. I've been busy with football and school work—"

"And other girls."

"Yeah, but I'm not seeing anyone and would love to take you out."

"I'm going to level with you, Chad. The chances of me going anywhere with you are zilch. Besides, I'm waiting for someone to pick me up. Someone who noticed me immediately and didn't wait until a hotter guy paid attention to me."

"That's not why I asked you."

"Of course it is. You didn't pay any attention to me until the most attractive man in the universe was interested in me and our picture was posted on social media. Sorry, but I'm in to genuine people."

As the last word leaves my lips, I hear someone rev an engine nearby. I peer around Chad to find the sleekest car I've ever seen. Black, two doors, and expensive.

Then Orion steps out. Long legs clad in dark denim. A hunter green shirt with the sleeves bunched up at his elbows. And the look he's sporting screams murder.

He strides over to us quickly, his arm immediately going around my waist to pull me close to his side. "And you are?" he growls at Chad. Like, it legit sounds like a dog growl.

Chad straightens his spine to appear taller. It doesn't work. Orion is still bigger than him. I'm barely holding back a laugh at the display. "I'm Chad. I was talking to Ari, not that it's any concern of yours." What the…?

"If it concerns Ariane, then it concerns me," Orion bites back.

"Listen, I don't know who you are, or where you came from, but I've known her a lot longer than you have."

Orion releases me and takes a step forward. I move as well, putting myself between the two of them.

"That's enough out of both of you," I say, my gaze bouncing between them. "Chad, you and I aren't friends. Why you're challenging Orion is beyond me. I'm sure there is a harem of women somewhere waiting for you." I put my hands on Orion's chest and gently push him back a little. He lets me. Although, I bet if he wanted to hold his ground, a big rig couldn't move him. He continues to peer over me at Chad.

"I'm ready," I state, trying to get him to move. "We can go now." I glance around and notice we're drawing a crowd.

I'm going to kill Paige. She started this by posting that freaking picture. While I'm happy about seeing Orion, I don't need all this other craziness at school. Is it June yet?

Orion relaxes. Chad must have wandered off. Peering down at me, Orion reaches for my hands and holds them to his chest. That zap of electricity is back the moment our skin touches. “I didn't give you a proper greeting. Hi, Ariane. Did you have a nice day?”

“Can we just get in the car and away from here?”

“As you wish.”

He holds one of my hands, threading our fingers together. When we reach his car, he opens the door for me. I get in and the first thing I notice is the scent of leather and sandalwood. It wraps around me in the most soothing way. It’s then I remember Orion smelled of sandalwood the night we met. He closes my door, securing me in his fully tinted car, then walks around to get in the driver’s seat. The entire world slips away when we’re alone.

“Buckle up, little mouse.” I do as he asks. There is no compromise when it comes to safety in a car. I've been in one while Bray drives. Seat belts are a must.

The steering wheel has a jaguar on it and the soft, quilted leather seat cups my body.

“What kind of car is this?” I ask as he pulls away from the school. “I mean, I know it's a Jag, but what is it? I've never seen anything like it.”

“It's an F-Type SVR.”

“Ah,” I reply, like I have a clue. I want to know so I can search it on the internet and find out how much it costs. My curiosity is getting the better of me. Pulling out my phone, I do a quick search. My eyes almost pop out of my head when I see the price. “You paid a hundred and twenty-two thousand dollars for this car! Are you insane?"

"Give or take. It's just a car." He shrugs and smiles.

"Sure, because most nineteen year olds can afford a car like this. Do you make that much modeling for Lealla?"

"No. I inherited most of my money after my parents' deaths." Now I feel like a jerk.

"I'm sorry."

"Don't be. You didn't know. They died when I was very young."

I wait for him to say more; he doesn't. I decide to change the subject. "Where are we going?"

"Did you read the rest of Aries' book?" We're back to evading questions and him asking me more. Two can play at this game.

"Is there someplace specific you're taking me?"

"Why aren't you answering my question?"

"Why aren't you?"

He chuckles. "Touché. Okay, I'll go first, but then you have to answer me." He stops at a traffic light. "We're going to visit Aries."

"The model?"

"Yes. He's also my uncle."

The light turns green. He hits the gas and takes the next right to get onto the highway. The Jag glides smoothly over the pavement. I could get used to riding in this car. I focus back on the conversation at hand.

"Where does he live?" I ask.

"You didn't answer me." I don't think I'll ever get over how much I love his accent. I still can't place it. It does something to me; warms me up in all the right places when he speaks.

"I got halfway through the book and passed out. I did

have school today, you know. I can't stay up all night reading." He gives me a knowing look. "Okay, so I stay up most nights reading, but I was actually tired last night."

"Aries and Cassandra live near Lealla's home."

"Hold on. His wife's name is Cassandra?"

He turns to give me a brief, confused look. "Did you think it was something else? It's in the book."

"It's a book. A fictional book."

"Or so you believe." Why does he have to be so frustrating?

"Could you stop talking in riddles? If it's not fictional, then what is it? Last time I checked, paranormal romance wasn't real."

"Do you remember the epilogue when a baby was brought to their home?"

"Yes, but that baby wasn't mentioned again in any of the other books unless I forgot about it." What's he getting at?

"What was the baby's name, Ariane?"

I think back, rattle my brain. I remember the baby but can't remember its name. I search the internet and sure enough, there's a page with details from the book. And the baby's name—Orion.

"Were you named after the baby in the book?" One day, hopefully soon, I won't be so confused.

"They aren't just books. They're our lives."

"I don't believe you. You're playing a part. The role you were hired to play as the model for Lealla. Does she make all of you constantly stay in character? She must pay you a lot to do that." What is going on right now?

"Feel free to ask my uncle when we get there."

I cross my arms and look out the windshield, trying to

avoid the man next to me. Could he be serious, or am I trapped in some kind of warped game? I don't understand this at all.

Minutes tick by, as does the landscape. Neither of us says more. At this point, I'm not sure what I'd say. I feel like I've barely got a grasp on reality. Or maybe it's Orion who doesn't.

We turn off the highway and start driving through dense woods. I remember this part from when we went to Lealla's. It looks a little different in the light of day. The trees are still thick, but they don't seem to stretch as they once did. They are just ordinary trees.

Orion comes to a stop and reaches for my hand. "Are you okay?" The familiar zip is back, racing up my arm.

I ignore his question. "Do you feel that?"

"Feel what?"

It's my turn to growl at him. "You're infuriating sometimes. You know that, right?"

He laughs. "I like being around you. I never know what you're going to say."

"I know what's going to come out of your mouth—more questions." I look away from him, needing to focus on something else.

Before us is a big log cabin: three stories, a wraparound deck on the second level, balconies off the third level's rooms. In the center is a high peak with large, glass windows. The bottom level has rock facing. It's absolutely stunning. There is a firepit off to one side with wooden Adirondack chairs around it. Flowers are blooming along a grassy hill. It's like the perfect mountain retreat.

Orion shuts off the engine. "I'd like you to do something for me." I nod, uncertainty taking bloom in my stomach. "Okay, two things. One, call me Rion." He says it like the name Ryan, though I'm almost certain that's not how he'd spell it. "Two, keep an open mind."

"I always have an open mind."

"You're going to need to broaden it for this. Forget everything you know of the outside world. Also, please remember that whatever you learn must never be repeated. You can't tell a soul what you hear."

"Okay, now you're scaring me." I'm back to thinking Orion might be a serial killer.

"There's nothing to be scared of, little mouse. I would never bring you to a place where you'd be in danger."

"That's what serial killers say," I mumble.

He chuckles. "I'm not a serial killer."

"So you say."

"Come on. They're waiting for us."

I unbuckle my seat belt and open the door. My stomach is twisting and I'm starting to sweat. Nothing like anxiety to make this a special day.

Orion…Rion comes up beside me and takes my hand. The zap is back. I'm starting to get used to this feeling when we touch. If only I knew what it was. I glance up at him and he smiles warmly.

"Did you do that?"

"Do what?"

I try to shake him off out of frustration. Must he make everything so difficult? Can't he tell me what this is that happens between us when we touch?

"You have a lot to learn. I'm happy to be your teacher."

"You?" I scoff. "You're a year older than me."

"And all the wiser." He smiles his gorgeous dimpled smile and tugs me toward a set of stairs that curve up to the second level of the cabin.

Aries opens the door before we can knock. He ignores Rion and steps up to me. "Ariane, so happy you came. We've wanted to spend more time with you." Really, why? Maybe I'm going to wake up soon and realize this has all been some sort of crazy dream.

For now, I'll be polite in case it isn't. "Thank you for having me to your home."

"Of course. Come in. Cassie is in the kitchen making us a snack."

Inside, the house is as beautiful as the outside. A tall, stone fireplace is on one wall in an open living and kitchen area. It's the total mountain oasis package. Warm, wooden floors, black suede couches, and a massive television give it a relaxed vibe. The kitchen has black cabinets and ivory marble countertops. I think I could live here.

SIX

CASSANDRA IS CUTTING UP VEGETABLES WHEN she notices us enter. She stops what she's doing to come over and greet me. Her smile is kind, instantly putting me at ease.

"Ari, I'm so happy to meet you finally. I didn't get to do so at the party. I'm Cassie, Aries' wife. Please, make yourself comfortable."

Aries leans over and kisses her cheek. Where Aries has light blond hair and the same crystal eyes as Rion, Cassandra's hair is a rich chestnut. Her hazel eyes seem to be assessing me the same way. I duck my head, wanting to draw the attention away from me. She's stunning, after all, and I'm over here in a pair of sneakers, jeans with a hole in the knee, and an off the shoulder T-shirt. Rion said to dress comfortably. Why? I don't know. Maybe he didn't want me to think I had to dress up to come to his uncle's house. But he's not only his uncle. He's a freaking model.

Rion walks with me over to the couch. We sit, him beside me—but not too close—yet near enough where we can keep our hands connected. Aries sits down opposite of us, his smile broad. "Tell me, Ariane, what did your friends think of you spending time with Rion today?"

"Paige was excited." I chuckle nervously. "I'm sure she'll be texting soon, asking what's going on."

"It's nice that you have a friend who cares about you."

"Yeah, all two of them."

"I'm sure you have more friends than that."

"Not really," I say honestly. "I'm kind of a loner. I keep my head down, do my work, and look forward to leaving school every day."

"No one bothers you, do they?" Rion asks.

"Define bother."

"Ari, you must tell me if someone is giving you trouble."

I wave him off. "It's fine. I can handle them. I have been for almost four years. I'll deal with it until graduation. Although," I turn to face him, "now that Paige posted a picture of us together, I seem to be more popular."

"Is that why Chad was talking to you?" I don't miss the way he growls his name.

"Yup. He's never talked to me before today. Seems being with you makes me appealing."

"I'll snap the neck of any male who comes near you."

"I think you can take it down a notch." He barely knows me yet is so possessive. What is that?

Cassandra steps in front of us with a plate of veggies and dip. "Here we go. Help yourself. Ari, what would like to drink?"

"Water is fine, thank you."

Once she steps back into the kitchen, Aries speaks up. "How much has Rion told you?"

"Told me about what?"

"You've read all the books, correct?"

"Oh, no. Not you, too?" He cocks his head at me. "Sorry, Rion told me to reread your book. Then, on the way here, told me it's about your life. I think he hit his head before getting to my school today."

"What he said about the book is true. It's about my life with Cassie. How we met. What we went through. Almost everything in that book is factual." Maybe I'm the one who hit my head and forgot about it.

"Okay, say I believe that. Am I also to believe you can shift into a wolf?"

"If you don't believe the rest of the story, why would you believe I can shift?"

I look at Rion. "What's going on?"

"I told you to keep an open mind."

"An open mind is one thing. What you're both talking about, it's not logical. I'm all for the romance and mystical things that happen in books, but it's fiction—not real."

Cassandra returns with drinks for all of us and sits down beside Aries. "Why don't you boys go out and play and let me talk to Ari. I don't think either of you know what you're doing." She gives Aries a knowing look.

"That's a good idea," he states. "I have some wood that needs splitting. Rion can help me." He kisses her on the cheek and stands.

Rion releases my hand. "I'll be right outside if you need me." I nod. What could I need him for? A sanity check? It wouldn't come from him. That would come from a shrink.

Cassandra gets up to come over and sit beside me. "Let me tell you a little story. Once upon a time, there was a woman who lived a lonely life. Her family moved across the country, and her friends had all gotten married and started having kids. She didn't think she'd ever find someone to love her. Then, one day, while she was at the home improvement store in the plumbing aisle, she saw a handsome man in a pair of grease-streaked jeans and a plain grey sweatshirt. She fell in love at first sight."

"That was you and Aries." I remember it from the book.

She nods. "It was. Our story is real, Ari. I met him that way. I lived every day of those pages. Aries showed me how unconditional love could be. These men, these models of Lealla's, when they find the woman they are meant to be with, their souls sing in joy. They see no one else but her. I've seen it happen with every pairing in the pack. When Orion comes back into the house, I want you to watch him. Really take in his movements and the way he analyzes things. The way his eyes are either on you or scanning the area around you. You're ahead of the curve. You've read the books. All that's left is for you to truly absorb what they say."

The conversation lulls while we snack, then picks up again when she asks me about my parents and school. We avoid book talk. I'm not sure what to think about all this. Furthermore, what is this thing between Rion and me? We met, danced for hours, and now he's picking me up at school and taking me to meet his family. Are we a couple? I've never had a serious boyfriend before. The only thing left for me to do is ask him. But that pales in comparison to what Aries, Cassandra, and he are telling me. I'm not sure what to think anymore.

Aries and Orion come back inside, and it's then I realize what time it is.

I jump up. "I need to get home." If we leave now, I can get there before my parents do. I'm not ready to introduce them to Rion when I don't even know what we are.

We say goodbye and get back into the Jag.

"Is everything okay?" Rion asks.

"Yeah, I want to get home before my parents do."

"Do you not want them to see you with me?"

"I'm not sure. What is this, Rion? What are we?" One conversation at a time. That's how I'm going to take this. We can figure out what we are now and this whole other craziness later.

"I'm sorry. I have to remember how different things are in your world."

"My world? Last time I checked we live in the same state, not to mention planet."

"What did you and Cassie talk about?"

"Oh, no. You're not doing this to me again. Tell me what you mean."

He lets out a long breath. "I was hoping you'd read at least the rest of Aries' book first."

"Well, I haven't. I want answers. We have an hour in the car together."

"How about I make you a deal? You reread as many of the books in the series as you can by Friday. Then, Friday night, I'll take you out and answer any questions you have." Why is everyone so intent on me reading these books? I've read them; however, if it means I finally get the answers I've been seeking, then I'll read them again.

"Fine, but I still want to know what you and I are. What's going on between us?"

"I can answer part of that. The rest will have to wait until Friday."

I groan loudly. "Fine."

"I want to be with you, Ari. I want us to be exclusive." I wasn't quite expecting that. I figured he would ask if I wanted to date him, not be with him and only him. Though, given how protective he seems to be, it makes sense he'd want me to be with only him.

"You hardly know me."

He shrugs. "Sometimes you just know."

"After a few hours of dancing?"

He turns and smiles, then focuses back on the road. "I knew from the first moment I laid eyes on you that you were mine."

"I wish I had your kind of confidence."

"You deny you felt something for me when we first met?"

"I'm not sure if it was something I felt when I first saw you, but I thought you were attractive." Did I admit that out loud? I need to get home and out of this car.

"It was more than that for me. I saw you from across the room. You were this beautiful creature. It felt like no one else existed but you. The world fell away. What was left was a single path from me to you." If he keeps talking like this, I'm going to melt on his leather seat. I'll be nothing more than a puddle. "Then," he continues, "when we touched, I knew you were her."

"Her?"

"My...forever."

"Okay this is getting a little heavy. We just met. There's no way you know that already."

"In all the books in Lealla's series, there is one common factor—the men always knew when they found the person they were meant to be with." Here we go again.

"They are books. Nothing more. Of course they know. They're wolf shifters. They have this magic or something in them that lets them know when they've found their mate. Then they spend chapters making the woman understand she is it for them."

"Exactly."

"Huh?"

"Keep going." He's starting to make me crazy. Wait. Starting isn't the right word. He is making me crazy.

"Hold on. You're telling me you feel for me what all those men—in all those books—felt for their mates when they first met them? How everything in their life paled in comparison to that one moment when she appeared?"

"Yes."

"You need to drive faster."

"Why?" he asks.

"Because I need to get out of this car. It's a book! A fictional book! This is real life we're talking about."

"What if they were one and the same?"

"Enough. No more talking until you pull into my driveway."

"As you wish," he replies with mirth. I turn my body in the seat to look out the side window.

This is ridiculous. How can he possibly think our lives are like those in books? Okay, sure, Aries and Cassandra met the way that happened in the book, or at least she said they did. Maybe they were mere muses for Lealla. She loosely based their book on their real-life story. She took a real situation and adapted it, adding the paranormal element. That's possible and doesn't sound wildly insane, unlike all these men being wolf shifters. I can't even wrap my head around that.

I spend the rest of the drive trying to remember as much as I can about the books. Stuff that sticks out to me: traits, when the mates met, how the men behaved around them. It all makes my head spin. Rion is right about one thing: I need to read all the books in the series again. Underneath all this insanity, there's a part of me that wonders about everything he's saying. And that's the part that scares me. Nothing to do but read now. Considering there are twelve books in the series, it looks like I won't be getting much sleep this week.

SEVEN

RION PULLS INTO MY DRIVEWAY. I didn't realize we were back in my hometown. Hold on.

I turn to him. "How did you know where I lived?"

"All will be explained on Friday."

"You know you're bordering on creepy. Tell me how you knew, or I'm not going with you on Friday to wherever you're taking me."

"I followed you after the party. I wanted to make sure you got back safe."

My eyes narrow. "But we didn't go to my house. We went to Paige's."

"I kept watch over you until you got back home."

"I'm not sure whether to be flattered that you thought enough to want to keep me safe or completely freaked out that you stalked me for the night." I need to get a grip on my emotions. Something inside of me is rejoicing at the fact that he spent all night watching over me. Then again, why would he need to? The hesitation is there as to whether I should be happy about this.

“If it makes you feel better, I don't think I could have gone home without making sure you were safely in your house.”

“Why?”

His eyes soften and drop to my lips. “Because you’re mine, Ari. There's no one else for me. My life will be dedicated to making sure you're happy, protected, and never want for anything.”

“I don't know what to say.” Partially because he's leaned forward and his lips are a breath away from mine. What I wouldn’t give for him to close the remaining distance and press his lips to mine. Would the kiss be soft and sensual or hard and possessive? Maybe I’ll be the one to lean toward him and find out the answers to my questions.

A car horn blares behind us. I practically jump out of my seat. If not for the seat belt still covering me, I might have whacked my head on the roof of the car.

I spin in the seat to peer out the back window of the car. “Oh, no.” My mom is behind us and she's getting out of her car.

“It’ll be fine. You'll see.” He gets out of the car without another word. This could be horrible.

I jump out after him and round the back of the Jag to try and intercept him and my mom.

“Mrs. Sanderly, it's nice to meet you,” Rion greets with an outstretched hand.

She ignores him and focuses on me. “What's going

on?"

"Mom, this is Rion. He's, um... We're dating." My face flames with heat and is no doubt as red as a ripe tomato.

"Are you sure about that? Sounds like you're guessing." Then she's looking at him again. She takes his offered hand. "What's your name?"

"Orion Raines. It's a pleasure to meet you."

"Uh huh. How old are you?" My mom. Never one to beat around the bush. No wonder I have the attitude I do.

"Nineteen, ma'am."

"Don't call me ma'am. I hate that. How can you afford such an expensive car when you're only nineteen years old?"

"My parents were killed when I was very young. I inherited all their money when I turned eighteen."

"And you thought it wise to blow it all on a car?" If possible, her eyes keep getting narrower and narrower. Pretty soon she won't be able to see out of them.

Rion chuckles. "I haven't even come close to spending all of their money." I have to give him credit. He's fielding the questions just as easily as Mom's doling them out.

"Are you some kind of playboy? Like to prey on young girls and show off how rich you are?"

"You have me all wrong. In fact, I've never been in a relationship with anyone before. Ari is the first girl I've met who I've wanted to spend time with. Before her, I kept mostly to myself, only interacting with other members of my family."

"Where were you two?" Then she turns and her scrutinizing gaze is on me again. "And why didn't you tell me you were going somewhere, Ari?" I never tell her what I'm doing. For her to ask me, she must be very mad about what she's seeing in front of her.

“I was only gone for a little bit after school. I made sure all of my homework was done before I left. We went to visit his aunt and uncle. Nothing more. He wanted to introduce me to his family.”

Her eyes swing back to him. “How serious are you about my daughter? I don't like any of this. If you're really a stand-up guy, I'm going to need you to prove it. Ari isn't one of those girls who parties all the time and gets wooed by fancy cars. She's a girl of substance, who has a bright future ahead of her.” She's pulling out all the stops, especially since she knows I have no plans to go to college.

I never found anything I wanted to study and decided to take the summer to think about my options. The last thing I want to do is spend my parents’ hard-earned money on college when I don't know what I want to do with my future. They don't make a lot as it is. They'd have to take out loans to pay for it, and I don't want them going into debt for me.

“I have nothing but the best interests at heart where it pertains to Ari. I promise,” Rion says.

“You're a teenage boy. I have an idea what your interests are.” My mom tosses me her keys. “Move my car, Ari, so Rion can leave.”

I don't wait for her to say more. This could have gone a lot worse. On the other hand, it could have gone a whole lot better. I back her car out and wait for Rion to get in his. He says something to my mom before he does so. I hope it was nothing horrible. Though, I doubt he'd dig a deeper hole. He didn't say anything bad to start with. I bet that's why Mom doesn't believe him. He was saying exactly what he should.

Rion is driving out of sight as I pull my mom's Volvo

back into the driveway. It's seen better days, but it's reliable and takes her to and from her job as a nurse.

She's waiting for me when I get out of the car. "Ari, you could have warned me there'd be a random boy in my driveway when I got home."

"I'm sorry."

"You were hoping he'd leave before your dad or I got home, weren't you?" she asks, while slinging her arm over my shoulder.

"Kind of," I reply sheepishly.

"Well, just be thankful it was me and not your dad."

"Really? Because I think you were harder on him than Dad would have been."

She laughs. "Maybe. Now, tell me all about him."

We sit and talk while she makes dinner. I fill her in on how I met Orion through the author whose book signing I attended. I decide to leave out that I met him at the after-party. I say that Rion was at the signing with his uncle, who is one of the cover models on the book. Only part of that is a lie. Rion wasn't there; however, the rest is true. She asks what he does for a living. I tell her he's going to be a model for an upcoming book. I thought she'd flip, but instead she cocks her head, and says, "I could see that." She also told me she trusts me not to do anything foolish.

I let the conversation change to other things like school and Paige. I'll leave telling her I have another date with him on Friday until later in the week. No reason to pile that onto everything else I've said already.

My dad comes home just as dinner is being served. I'm dreading what my mom is going to tell him. They don't keep secrets from one another. Ever.

"Ari, how was school?" he asks as he starts to slice into

the food on his plate.

"Good. I'll be happy when I graduate."

"I bet."

"Ari met a boy," my mom adds casually.

This causes my dad to put down his knife and fork. There's a hard edge to his tone when he speaks. "And who is this boy?" He's looking at me, not Mom. I need to be selective with what I tell him and hope Mom doesn't fill in the rest.

"He's nineteen, and I met him over the weekend at a book signing. He's very nice. I met his aunt and uncle today."

"I met him, too," Mom states.

"Oh, you did? I missed out on meeting the first boy my daughter has ever brought home?"

"Hey, you've met Bray. He's over here a lot," I say.

"He doesn't count," my dad replies.

I roll my eyes. "Anyway, yes, Mom met Rion."

"And?" Dad asks. "What did you think of him?"

"He seems very nice. He was courteous to Ari and to me. I liked him." She says all this very nonchalantly as she's eating. I, on the other hand, sit with my mouth agape. I quickly close it before my dad notices. I'm so grateful Mom met Rion first and even more so that she hasn't said more. I'm sure if Dad knew he drives a car that cost more than half of what our house did, he'd have something to say about him. Hopefully, it will be dark on Friday night when he picks me up, and Dad won't be able to tell what kind of car he drives. I doubt I'll be able to get away with not introducing them, though.

After dinner, I help Mom with the dishes as a thank you for not spilling everything. She knows why I'm doing it, too. She winks as she hands me a clean dish so I can dry it. Once we're all done, I head upstairs to start my reading, grateful, once again, I got my homework done in school.

Hours tick by. I take small breaks here and there, but for the most part, I stay glued to my tablet. I finish Aries' book and move on to Dante's. With each page I turn, I highlight certain things that pop out at me. Like the way the man acts when he finally meets his mate. The way he watches her intently. How his thoughts are solely on her and wondering how he can convince her to be with him, even though he's not an average human. Aries' book was a little different. They were both wolf shifters, but they were each lone wolves. Dante is a wolf, but his mate is very human. He has to approach her differently—get her to accept him for what he is.

Page by page, I find more and more things to highlight. And with each one, I gain a little insight into Rion's behavior. Could it be that he and Cassandra were telling me the truth? That these stories are based on their real lives? But they can't mean the wolf part, right? That's absurd. Humans don't shift. Vampires and the fae aren't real. There are no mages. No one can actually perform magic.

Around two in the morning, I hear a noise outside. The house is eerily quiet as I tiptoe to the window in my bedroom, trying to avoid the creaky floorboards as I go. If my parents knew I was awake, they'd yell and take my tablet. They love that I read, but I learned last year that if they think I'm giving up sleep to read, they take my devices away. Nope. I don't want that to happen. Not now. Not when I feel like I'm finally on to something, although what, I'm not completely sure.

Parting the curtains, I glance out in the dense trees behind my house. They go for a while until they meet a river. Nothing stands out to me. Nothing that could have made a sound. It's only trees and darkness.

Then, as I'm about to close the curtains and go back to my book, I see a quick flash of something green standing out in the darkness. But before I can locate it again, it's gone. I sit, staring out the window for a few minutes. Nothing happens.

Back in bed, with my tablet glowing down on me, I turn a page and hear a howl outside. That's it. I have to put the book down. Now I'm hearing things. Enough wolves for tonight. They're getting too deep inside my head. I should be sleeping anyway.

EIGHT

I'D LIKE TO SAY THE NEXT four days at school went by fast, but that would be a lie. Each day went achingly slow. I was exhausted and barely able to keep my eyes open. By Friday, I'd read eight out of the twelve books in the series. Every night, I read until I passed out. I was hoping to read the whole series by our date, but no such luck. I also never saw that green flash outside my window again, nor did I hear anything else howl. I firmly believe it was all in my head. The books are to blame for that.

I didn't realize it until the next night when I was reading, but one of the traits of the wolf shifters is their eyes turn an emerald green when their wolf moves to the forefront. It either happens right before they shift, while they're in wolf form, or if the wolf is trying to take over the human. It is the same color I thought I saw Rion's eyes change to that night at the party. Although, I didn't see them do that the next day when we were at his uncle's place. I think I live too immersed in books. Maybe Paige was right. I have to remember they're fiction.

Rion and I have been messaging all week. We made plans for Friday night. I tried to tell my Mom I was spending the night at Paige's, but now, with a new guy in the picture, she wasn't having it. She told me he had to pick me up at home, and he had to meet Dad. She also told me I had a curfew of one in the morning. Lovely. Never before have I had one. She's looking out for me and I'm grateful for that. However, I'm eighteen. I would have thought I'd have more free rein at this point. Sometimes, I'm envious of the way Paige's parents let her do whatever she wants.

I'm sitting in my living room in a pair of jeans and a faded black T-shirt, waiting for my date. I didn't need to dress to impress Rion on Monday, so there's no reason to now. And then I hear it. The low rumble of his car. I don't move, not until the doorbell rings. When I stand, my dad gives me a look that has me staying in place. He wants to be the one to answer the door.

Swinging it wide, I don't get to see Rion, though I hear him. That rich, sexy sound of his voice. "Mr. Sanderly, I'm Orion Raines. It's nice to meet you."

My dad takes his hand. "It's nice to meet you as well. I want you to know that Ari is my only child. If anything were to happen to her, I would find you. The end result wouldn't be pretty." He went straight to the point. My dad isn't a small man. I get my shortness from my mom. But he's also not up to Rion's caliber. He might be near the same height, but Dad has let himself go. He's got a bit of a pot belly, and he hasn't worked out in a long time.

"I understand, sir. Your daughter will be safe with me," Rion states.

"I hope so." Dad looks over at me. That's my cue to grab my purse and head for the door. Mom had to work late tonight, so she isn't here to greet Rion.

I falter in my steps as I get a good look at the guy who came to pick me up. It's dark outside, but the light over the door casts a brilliant glow upon him. He has on his signature dark jeans. His shirt is white, making his eyes stand out more. His dark hair is neatly combed away from his face. And his smile at seeing me is something you read about in books.

My dad snaps me out of my trance. "One o'clock, Ari. Not a minute later."

"I know." I smile and wave as I practically skip out the door.

I didn't realize how much I was looking forward to seeing Rion again until he was at my doorstep. I've been so immersed in books and school; I didn't have much time to think about where we were going tonight or what we're going to do. He didn't give me any hints. Just told me to trust him. Still kind of hard to do when I don't know him that well.

Rion opens the car door for me like a perfect gentleman, tucking me safely inside before getting in the driver's seat. We both buckle our seat belts. He turns to me and tugs on my ponytail. My hair was not doing what it's supposed to today, so I swept it up to keep it out of my face.

"I like this," he says with another tug.

Suddenly, I'm self-conscious. "Yeah? I wasn't sure

what to do with it. It was a little frizzy today." My hair is straight on a good day. I shower and blow it out at night before bed. In the morning, I use a flat iron to get it looking how I want it. Today, even the flat iron couldn't tame the frizz. My hair is naturally wavy, but sometimes nothing seems to help.

"You're beautiful, Ariane."

I smile as my cheeks begin to heat, but this time I don't duck my head in embarrassment. "I like it when you say my name, Rion."

"And I like it when you say mine."

I'm seconds from leaning over the center console and kissing those gorgeous lips of his, but he starts the car and backs out of my driveway instead. Maybe by the end of the date I'll get to find out how he kisses.

"Where are we going?" I ask.

"Toward my uncle's house." Seriously? We're having a date with his uncle?

"Ummm...okay."

He chuckles. "We're not going to visit him. There's this large field that is perfect for looking at the night sky. I want to take you there."

"You promised you'd answer my questions, too." He probably thought I'd forgotten. Not. Going. To. Happen.

"I did and will hold true to my word. You can ask me anything now, if you'd like." Finally! I get to ask him the billion questions that have been flowing through my brain nonstop.

"Do you miss your parents?" I want to know more about Rion. Not just about the books and why he keeps pushing them on me, but about him.

"I do. I wish I would have gotten to know them. I was

only a year old when they died." I can't imagine growing up without parents. That must have been awful for him.

"What happened? If you don't mind me asking, that is."

"I don't. I told you I'd answer your questions."

"I know, but this is more personal."

He takes my hand in his while keeping his other firmly grasped to the steering wheel. The zip of electricity is there, shooting up my arm then slowly dulling to a low hum in my veins. "They were killed in battle."

"Like a war?"

"Yes, but probably not the kind you're thinking of. It was only briefly mentioned in Aries' book, but the year before I was born, a pack war broke out. My mom was pregnant with me, so my dad didn't want her anywhere near the fighting. They fled from their home and were able to find somewhere new to live, far enough away from the violence. It was quiet there for a while. Our side won the war. Then, the week of my first birthday, something happened." All this talk of a pack war has me confused. He's speaking as if shifters are real again, unless he's using the term to refer to something else. Pretty soon I'm going to start believing him.

"Aries and Cassandra were visiting from out of town for my birthday. They said they'd watch me so my parents could get a night out on their own. My parents were leaving a restaurant near our home when three men approached them. My dad immediately went on the defensive and pushed my mother behind him. The men attacked. While my dad was strong, he was no match for three of them. Aries heard the call." I wonder what he means by call. Did Rion's mom call them on the phone? I don't have a chance to ask. "He told Cassandra to get me in the car and drive to their home as fast as she could. He needed to know we were safe so he could search for my parents. He found their bodies in the woods, not far from the restaurant." My heart splinters in my chest. What a horrible thing to happen.

"Did the police catch who did it?"

He shakes his head. "No, but Aries knew who they were. Do you remember the fight scene in Dante's book where he and Aries took on three men?"

"Yes. All the men shifted. They fought as wolves. Aries and Dante killed them." My mind drifts to the book, to the words Aries said right before he killed them. *You took my brother from me. I will rid the world of you.* For some reason, those words have stuck with me since I first read Dante's book. "You're saying..."

"Aries and Dante killed the wolves who murdered my parents."

"Shifters aren't real, Rion. Maybe they told you that as a child to help you cope with the deaths of your parents so you knew vengeance was served."

He slows the car down and pulls onto a dirt drive. We've been driving a lot longer than I thought.

Rion parks the car, shuts it off, then turns to me. "It's no story, Ari. It's the truth about what happened. The pack war might have ended, but a new one has been on the horizon for almost two decades. Aries has been able to hold it off and try to make peace with the rival pack, but we're not sure how much longer it will be until they come for us again. It's only a matter of time before they're on our doorstep."

He opens his door before I can say anything and then comes to open my door as well. Reaching down, he helps me out, but I become dizzy upon standing and fall against his chest. Rion's strong arms wrap around me to hold me upright.

"Are you okay? Are you sick?" Concern is evident in his voice.

"No, I feel all right. Just a little lightheaded." I attempt to stand on my own. "It's a lot to take in. You're talking as if wolf shifters are real. I'm not sure what to do with that. Do I need to seek help for you?"

He peers down at me, his lips curving up ever so slightly. "You're the only one who can help me, little mouse." Bending, he places a chaste kiss on the tip of my nose. The dizziness starts all over but for a different reason. His arms hold me tight as I go lax. "Are you sure you're okay?"

"It's your fault, you know."

He chuckles. "How do you figure?"

"You have to be so sweet and kind and hot."

"Hot? You think I'm hot?"

"Oh, please. The entire world thinks you're hot."

"I don't care what everyone else thinks. Only you. Your opinion is all that matters, Ari."

"And there you go again, making me swoon."

"You read too much romance." If he only knew.

"Says the guy who practically shoved said romance books down my throat."

"For your own good." He laughs.

"That remains to be seen. I'm extremely sleep deprived, thanks to you." Which might also attribute to some of this dizziness I'm experiencing.

"Can I let you go? I want to show you something."

"Hmmm?" Can't I stay in his arms forever? His scent

of sandalwood wraps around me as I breathe him in. "You smell good," I murmur dreamily. His chest vibrates with laughter. It's then I realize I said that out loud. I immediately slap my hand over my mouth.

"All the more reason I need you to come with me." He drops his arms and takes my hand in his. Luckily, I'm able to stand on my own without swaying.

We start down a narrow path through very dense trees. I can barely see in front of me. Fortunately, Rion leads the way. He walks like it's broad daylight and he can see clearly. He holds branch after branch out of the way so I can step down the path safely without any of them smacking me in the face. That's just what I need. To be blindsided by a tree branch. I wish I had his eyesight.

Eventually, we break through the trees and emerge in a clearing. It's large and circular. The moon above shines down on us, illuminating the open area.

Rion walks behind me, slipping his arms around my waist. "Look up."

I do. The moon is stunning and seems so big in the sky. "It's a full moon."

"Not only that, it's an ash moon."

"I've never heard of that. What does it mean?"

"If you look closely at the moon, you'll notice it appears sooty, as if it's covered in ash. Most don't notice it, but we do. Legend says: *What happens beneath an ash moon will be life-altering.* Good or bad, the moon brings something which will change everything."

I turn slightly to peer up at him. His warm breath skates across my cheek. "And what will be life-altering about this date tonight?"

"I'm glad you asked."

Rion steps away from me and walks into the center of the clearing. Something in the air prickles my skin, causing goosebumps to break out all over and the hair on my arms to stand on end. I look around but see nothing other than Rion and me. Then his eyes flash emerald green a second before he turns into a wolf.

NINE

I STUMBLE BACK UNTIL I BUMP into a tree. The wolf before me doesn't move, only watches me with emerald eyes. His fur is black; his ears tipped in white. This can't be happening. Shifters aren't real. I'm dreaming. That's what's going on. This is a dream. I've been reading too much.

The wolf yips and sits down. I have no clue what that means. If I'm going off the dream theory, then it won't hurt to approach the wolf, right? I'm not actually awake. You can't get hurt in a dream.

Stepping forward hesitantly, I wait for the wolf to spring. He never does. I don't stop until I'm a few feet away. He's bigger up close. Much bigger than I would have thought a wolf would be.

The wolf tips his head back to peer up at me. His eyes

change to a crystal blue. My breath catches in my throat. This can't be happening.

"Are you... Are you Orion?"

He drops his head down and back up as if to say yes. As quickly as they changed, his eyes go back to green.

"You're a wolf."

He snorts as if to say, "Obviously."

I spin and walk back toward the path we took. "This can't be real," I say out loud, to no one in particular, since I'm alone with a wolf. "Shifters aren't real. They don't exist except in books, television, and movies. This is ridiculous."

The wolf, or Orion if you will, darts in front of me to stop me from walking away.

"Okay, I honestly don't know if I'm awake or dreaming, so if you're in there, can you come back? I'm having a hard time processing this and think you're going to need to take me to the emergency room for some strong meds."

Just like that, Rion is back in all his manly glory, fully clothed, and grinning like he did the first night I met him—like he won the lottery. I'm not smiling, however.

"What just happened?" I ask.

"I'm a wolf shifter."

"Uh huh. And when did you slip me the drugs?"

"I didn't slip you anything. This is what I've been trying to tell you all week by having you read Lealla's series."

"Yeah, I don't think so. I think I'm either having some sort of breakdown or I'm dreaming. I can't figure out which."

Rion steps closer, his crystal blue eyes staring intently at me. Then they flash emerald green. I shake my head and they're back to blue.

"The green you see in my eyes is my wolf. The color appears when he is rising to the surface. The blue is me in human form."

"Let's just assume I believe you. If you're in wolf form, can I pet you like a dog?" Of all the things for me to ask, this is what I choose. It's not logical by any sense. However, it's what slips past my lips.

"While my wolf doesn't like being compared to a dog, he would let you do anything you wanted to him. He'd never hurt you."

"Why is that?"

"You're my mate, Ariane."

"That's it. I'm out." I start down the path back to the car at a good clip, not caring that I trip repeatedly. I need to go to the hospital. This isn't normal. He said he didn't slip me any drugs. Now I need a professional, too. The good kind that makes me happy and stops me from freaking out.

"Ari, would you stop?"

"Nope. You're taking me to the hospital. This has to be a mental break. I don't know how else to explain all of this."

"I'm a shifter, and you're my mate."

I spin, stopping him in his tracks. "I asked one thing of you tonight, and that was to finally answer my questions. Instead, you tell me you're a wolf." Tell me, show me, same difference.

"I only want you to know the truth."

"I don't know what to believe."

"How can I convince you?"

"You think I have the answer to that?" I start laughing uncontrollably. "I'm losing my mind, Rion! You expect me to find a way for you to convince me? How about you make me believe I'm not dreaming or losing my mind? How about that?"

He stares at me intently for a moment before cupping my cheeks in his hands and pressing his lips to mine. I freeze, forget to breathe, and all I do is feel. Feel the heat of Rion's body pressed to mine. Feel the strength he possess as my hands rest on his chest then slide down to his hips.

Turning his head slightly, he deepens the kiss. Our tongues meet and it's as if a thousand fireworks are going off behind my eyes. Sparks like I've never known are lighting up my body. The jolt I get when we touch is nothing compared to what this kiss feels like.

He growls deep in his throat as he nips at my bottom lip. Before I have a chance to pull him closer, he's breaking our kiss.

"Would I do that to you in a dream?"

"In my dream you'd probably do a lot more."

He laughs and wraps his arms around me. Instinctively, I hold on to him, my hands fisting the shirt at his back, afraid at any second, he's going to disappear. Then I'm chanting in my head: *Please don't be a dream. Please don't be a dream.* As much as I thought I was dreaming before, the reality is, I want it to be real. Wolf or not, I never want this to end. The way I react to him is something of another world—something magical.

He rests his chin on top of my head. "I would never lie to you. I want you to know all of me. That means knowing my wolf, too. He and I are entwined. We're one."

Pulling back, I glance up into those blue eyes I easily get lost in. "Show me again."

"Are you sure? I don't think I could handle it if you tried to walk away from me again. I meant it when I said you're my mate, Ari. For me, there will only ever be you."

"I won't walk away. Promise." Maybe this time, if I'm ready for it, I won't freak out as much. Maybe. In reality, there's no telling how I'll react.

Rion leads us back to the circle. He leaves me off to the side and stands in the middle, where the moon is shining down on him. "You can come up to my wolf if you like. He won't hurt you. Introduce yourself. Talk to him. He's part of me."

"Can you hear me in there?"

"I can. When the eyes of my wolf are green, he's in control. When they're blue, that's me. I can take over at any time, though. We have a cohesive relationship. He doesn't rule me, and I don't rule him. Sometimes, the wolf can take people over who don't respect them. Then, you're dealing with a completely wild animal."

"All right," I say, rubbing my hands together. "Let's do this."

In the blink of an eye, Rion is gone and his wolf remains. Whoa, buddy. This is still a lot to take in. I mean, he's a wolf—a big freaking wolf.

He lets out a yip and sits down. Cautiously, I step forward. Rion said he'd never hurt me, but that doesn't stop my trepidation at approaching a wild animal. Well, not completely wild.

Reaching my hand forward, palm up, I come a little closer, stopping about a foot from him. He leans toward me and sniffs my hand. Those eyes of his are green, letting me know the wolf is in charge. I remember reading about their eyes changing in the series. It's all true, isn't it? All the books?

Rion, the wolf, stands and does a lazy circle around me,

sniffing my legs as he goes. He nudges me with his nose. I decide to pet him, though, I'm not sure if he likes to be petted. Only one way to find out.

His ears twitch and move as I run my hand over the soft fur on his head. Standing, the top of his back comes up to my waist. I stroke down his back as he walks by.

"You're not so bad, are you?" He sneezes and shakes his head. "I'm not sure who I like more—the man or the wolf." Orion's crystal blue eyes flash forward, making me laugh. "I knew that would get to you."

We spend a bit of time together—the wolf and me. I sit on the ground; he curls his body around me and rests his head in my lap.

"Mates, huh?" I ask, not expecting an answer. I can talk to him easily like this. It's probably because he can't talk back. "I'm not quite sure what to do with that information. Or any of this, for that matter. It's going to take a while for this to sink in. I'm only eighteen." That makes me pause and think back to something I read in the books. "Are you really nineteen, or are you like two hundred and fifty? I remember reading that you can live up to a thousand years. Maybe you like younger women."

My phone vibrates in my pocket, startling me. Orion jumps to his feet as I do the same. "It's only my phone."

I dig it out and see a text from Paige, asking how the date is going. Did she think I'd answer her while still on the date? She can wait. Checking the time, I still have two hours until I need to be home.

"Are you hungry? I could eat. Not you, the wolf, but the man. I think it's cool you're a wolf and all, but I don't want to see you hunting down a deer and ripping it to shreds in front of me."

In a flash, Rion is standing before me as a human. All his clothes just as they were.

"Hey, why don't your clothes get shredded when you shift?"

"Shifter magic."

"Thanks for your thorough explanation," I respond dryly. I'm not sure I'm fine with all of this, but I'm more relaxed about it.

He chuckles. "All shifters have magic within them. It's what allows us to shift in a flash, to keep our clothes on when we turn from our animal back to human."

"Is that why I get zapped every time we touch? Magic?"

"The magic, yes. But it has to do with you being my mate. I've never felt that with any other person—shifter or not. No one I've shaken hands with, or touched skin to skin, has given me shocks as you do." Wait, who else is he touching with only his skin? White-hot jealousy flares to life inside of me. Jealousy I didn't know existed within me. I push it aside. He said he's never been in a relationship. I have to trust him.

"So, you only feel that current of electricity, or whatever it is, with your mate?" He nods. "Is that why you lit up at the party when you first touched my hand? You were so happy."

"Wouldn't you be, if you were told your whole life there is only one woman out there for you, and when you meet her, you'll know for sure the second your skin touched?"

"I see your point." I smile. "So, you've never been with anyone else? Never dated, slept with, nothing?"

"No. Other shifters like to party their way through women until they find their mate. That was never me. I kept going to school, learning, and once I graduated, Lealla asked if I was interested in working with her."

"I'm going to need you to fill me in on Lealla and the role she plays in all of this. But not right now. I need food." My stomach growls on cue.

"Me, too. Come, let's go back to the car."

He leads us down the path to where he parked.

"Do your wolf senses work when you're not a wolf?"

"Yes."

"That explains how you can maneuver on this path so easily. If not for you, I'd have face-planted four times by now. I can't see anything." Too bad the trees are so dense; it would be nice if some of the moon's light could cut through to light my path.

"It certainly comes in handy. My wolf's night vision is far superior to mine."

"You're really nineteen?"

"Yes," he chuckles. "I'm certainly not two hundred and fifty."

I smile. "You never know. I needed to verify. I've read how old those other wolves are."

"Rest assured, little mouse, I'm only a year older than you."

TEN

AFTER WE ATE AT A LOCAL DINER, we started the drive back to my house so I wouldn't miss curfew.

"Tell me about Lealla," I say to him.

"What would you like to know?"

"What role does she play, except to write the books? And why write them?"

"Well, she writes them because she loves doing it. She started writing when she was younger but didn't discover the love she has for her current series until she met Aries. Then it was as if everything clicked into place for her. Before the Avynwood Pack, she wrote from dreams. Once Aries came around, she found a new purpose. You see, Lealla is psychic. She didn't realize she was one until she met Aries. Once she did, she knew she had to help him. He was a lost, lone wolf. He and my father weren't always close. There was a rift in the family and they didn't speak for many years. My father traveled a lot before settling down. It wasn't until a year or so before my mom got pregnant that they mended things."

"But that timeline doesn't make sense with the book and Aries and Cassandra getting custody of you at the end."

"The timelines in the books aren't always exact. The stories are true, but Lealla will rearrange things to make the most sense in each book. You have to remember, while they mostly are true, she has to spin things for entertainment purposes. For Aries and Cassandra, them getting me at the end of their book made more sense. And the series as a whole takes place over many years, when in reality, some of the stories overlapped or happened one right after the other. Lealla had to change things to make sense in the literary world of fiction."

"Okay, I can see that. So, she's a psychic?"

"Yes, she helps each wolf find their mate. With Aries, she wasn't sure what was happening since she'd never had a vision before him. She had dreams, yes, but none of them came true like her visions did. The first time she saw Cassandra, she knew she was meant for Aries. How do you think he ended up in the home improvement store that day and in that particular aisle?"

"Lealla," I say with certainty.

"Exactly." This is all fascinating. I can't believe Lealla is psychic.

"She wasn't able to predict the deaths of your parents so she could prevent it?" I ask, though I already know the answer.

"No. She doesn't see everything. She gets bits and

pieces. Only once in a great while does she get more."

"That's a shame. She might have been able to save their lives."

"She did save one. Mine."

"What happened? Did someone try to kill you, too?" I can't believe someone would want to hurt Rion. He's such a nice guy.

"No, little mouse. She told me about you. The moment I knew you were coming, my world brightened. I had a renewed purpose."

"Oh," I say quietly. My cheeks heat. I'm thankful for the darkness to conceal my blush.

"She knew she was going to meet you at the signing. That's why she invited you back to her house. She wanted us to meet."

"And here I thought it was fate."

"It was. Everything has to fall into place for things to happen a certain way. I went to live with Aries. He introduced me to Lealla. You bought tickets to her signing. She met you in person. It all put us on a path to each other. Lealla's vision helped us meet. Everything after is up to us. Although, I'd like to think, even if she hadn't intervened, we would have found each other somehow."

"Lealla doesn't see anything else about our future together?" A part of me wants to know what's going to happen, while the other loves the unknown.

"You're going to have to ask her. She does want to talk to you, but she needed to wait until you knew what I was." I wonder what she has to talk to me about. Is it something bad? Good? Something that could change the rest of my life? Then something comes back to me.

"Did you always plan to reveal yourself to me under

the ash moon?"

"Lealla told me to wait until then."

"Did she tell you I was going to freak out?" I smile.

"No, but she did say you'd accept me as I was. She saw how we'd connect, then it was a vision here or there. You have no clue how worried I was about tonight, Ari. I was afraid you'd get scared. Or hate me for what I am." While I was unsure about what our date would entail, Rion had been afraid I'd reject him. I'm not the only one nervous. Things could have gone differently tonight if I hadn't given him a chance to shift a second time.

"I couldn't hate you," I tell him. "You can't control who you are. Sure, it took me a bit to wrap my head around it. I'm still shocked and in disbelief, if I'm being honest, but after all you've said and the books I've reread, it's starting to make sense. Like pieces of a puzzle finally fitting together." Hopefully, with each day and each conversation with him and Lealla, more pieces align and I get a broader picture of everything.

"Why did you think I wanted you to read them?"

"Yeah, yeah, I get it." I smile.

Rion was right about the ash moon. Once he shifted to a wolf, everything changed. I might accept he's a wolf, but this whole mate thing is still throwing me for a loop. How can I be someone's forever when I've never dated before? Everything is on the fast track with us. It's a lot to take in.

Rion is a wolf. Shifters are real. There's a thing called an ash moon. Lealla is a psychic.

"Hey, are vampires real?" I ask. I need to know. I mean, if shifters are, does that mean there are different kinds of paranormals out there?

"Yes, as are the fae, mages, and other paranormals."

"Get out! Do you know any vampires? Can you introduce me to one? Do they really kill people? I have so many questions." I'm serious. Those are just the tip of the iceberg.

He laughs. "I do know some vampires. No, they don't kill people unless absolutely necessary. They don't drain humans dry for fun. They do drink blood, but mostly from other vampires or paranormals. I can introduce you to one, eventually. I want you to meet with Lealla and talk with her first. She'd like you to come over to dinner tomorrow night, if you're available."

"She would? In that huge mansion? Will the other shifters be there?" I may be freaking out all over again. Holy information overload. He better not forget that I still want to meet a vampire.

"It will just be me, you, and Lealla. She wants to talk with us; no one else. The rest of the pack does know about you, and all but Aries, Cassandra, and I live there. Lealla told everyone this week. Aries and Cassandra knew first because I told them. I can't hide much from them since I still live in their house."

"I'm surprised you haven't bought your own place yet, since you have all that money."

He takes my hand in his and kisses the back of it while driving. "I was waiting for you, Ari. I wouldn't buy a home without your input. It would be our home." And stop.

"Hold on there, wolf. I'm only eighteen. I'm still in high school. I can't move in with you or buy a house with you." Maybe going to the emergency room wasn't such a bad idea after all.

"Ari, I'm not asking you to come with me tomorrow to buy a house. I'm simply stating the truth. I will always be honest with you. It could be ten years from now. Time doesn't matter. I only want you in my life."

"Time may not matter to you, since you can live for a thousand years, but I don't have your genes." At least he stopped me from freaking out and thinking a marriage proposal was happening next week. Talk about a fast relationship. If this were a book, the reader would be getting whiplash by how fast this was moving. Wait.

"You need to talk to Lealla. She'll reveal more," he says. I'll let that go for now, so I ask him something else.

"Everything that's happening between us, is it going into a book? A book my friends, friends' parents, tons of people are going to read?"

"Lealla never puts anything in a book that those involved don't want in there. It's up to us to decide what we want or don't want in our story."

"That's if I even want my life written into a paranormal romance." I'm living a romance novel. What is going on? I need sleep. Lots and lots of sleep. And distance from the sexy guy next to me.

Rion strokes the back of my hand with his thumb. "I'm sorry. This is a lot to take in. You didn't have your whole life to get used to the idea of this world, like the rest of us did. I'm throwing it at you all at once."

"It's not your fault. I'm happy knowing this stuff. It's just... I can deal with you being a wolf. The mate thing is still screwing with me. And the idea of my life being in a book. I'm not sure how to feel about all of it." A book. It would be a fictional book and the average reader wouldn't know it's real, so there is that. If Lealla used our real names, then everyone would know it's me.

"We're going to take things one day at a time," he says

reassuringly. "You're too important to me to lose. I'll go at whatever pace you want."

"Thank you. I love the idea of everything magical being real, but I still have high school and graduation."

To think everything I read about is real puts a huge smile on my face. Leaning back with my head on the seat, I reflect on all that happened tonight. I managed to get myself a wolf boyfriend. A mate, if I'm ready to face that. And was told there's a whole other world out there. Maybe things aren't as bad as I thought. I can still have my high school life and just date Rion when not in school. Being a normal teenager isn't out of reach. Normal isn't the right word. Nothing about this is normal.

Rion pulls into the driveway twenty minutes before I'm due home. The lights are out, and I have no doubt both of my parents are passed out. They work hard and crash early. They may have given me a curfew, but if they were worried, they would have never let me leave the house. It's for show. I'm a good teenager after all.

Rion shuts off the car and turns to me. "Thank you for coming with me tonight. And thank you for accepting my wolf."

"As crazy as all of this is, I wouldn't change it for anything. I had fun tonight." That's the truth. It's very surreal.

"Really?"

"After I realized I wasn't losing my mind." I laugh.

Rion chuckles. "Let's see how you feel after having dinner with Lealla tomorrow night."

"What time should I be there?"

"I'll pick you up at five, if that's okay."

"I have my own car. I can drive." Just because it's old

and makes all kinds of rattling noises doesn't mean it won't get me from point A to B.

"Unless I'm physically unable to drive to your home, I will always pick you up. And even then, I'd ask Aries or one of the pack to. Your safety is something I take very seriously." One of the pack? I wonder who it would be. I could see Paige's face now if Cace, Carter, or Cash showed up. She would probably faint.

"I've managed to make it this far in life. I think an hour drive to Lealla's mansion is doable."

"There are paranormals out there that aren't all good, Ari. Some will want to harm you. Also, you now know of our world and are unmated. Other wolves will want to vie for your attention."

"Say what now?" Will wolves be circling, smelling my butt, trying to figure out if I'm unattached?

"There are a lot of unmated wolves who would love nothing more than to have you in their bed."

"Okay, let's clear something up right now. I have never been in any guy's bed, except for Bray's, and that was to strictly sleep." Rion growls low in this throat. "He was on the floor. He didn't sleep in the bed with me. Paige did. You can calm down."

"I don't like the idea of you sleeping in another male's bed."

"And I don't like the idea of wolves sniffing around where they don't belong." Seriously, am I going to wake up to unmated wolves at our front door, vying for my attention? I have to get back on the topic of my friends, though. "If you're going to accept me, you're going to have to accept my friends. I will not give them up so I can be part of your life."

"They can't know about me, Ari. Or the other members of the pack."

"And they won't. Your secret is safe with me. But they've been my friends for many years, and I won't get rid of them for you or anyone else."

ELEVEN

HE LAUGHS. CRAZY SHIFTER ACTUALLY LAUGHS. I'm on the verge of punching him. "I was right about you the first day I met you. You have a lot of bite. That will come in handy when dealing with a pack of wolves."

"Who says I want to deal with a pack? I have you and that's plenty of wolf for me right now. Oh, and by the way, I've decided to call you Rion and your wolf Orion. Helps me keep you two straight." I like the idea of him and his wolf called different things.

"You do know it's the same name, right?"

"One's a nickname. No need to be a jerk." He laughs. Again. Yup, I'm going to slug him.

"Calm down, little mouse. I love riling you up."

"Keep it up and see what happens." I cross my arms.

Rion pulls my hand away from my body and then reaches for the other. He shakes them gently. "Loosen up. No matter what you say or do, I don't think I could ever be angry at you. Picking a fight with me won't do any good. I'll still want to be with you."

"The week isn't over yet." You never know what I might do to screw things up. I haven't been single this long on purpose.

He chuckles. "Your attitude is one of my favorite features."

"That's good because it's not going anywhere." I have to admit it is fun arguing with him. Not arguing, per se. I'm the only one arguing. He's laughing at me, which is making me angrier. I'm essentially arguing with myself.

"Can I walk you to the door?"

I shrug. "Sure."

We both exit the car. Taking my hand in his, Rion walks with me to the front of my house. The outside light above the front door is on, as is the motion light over the garage. The rest of the house is dark.

"Your parents couldn't have been too worried about you if they've gone to bed."

"They could be up watching television."

"Wolves have exceptional hearing. If there were any noises in your house, I'd hear it, especially with the open windows."

I peer up at him. All of my anger receding. "Are you always so observant?"

"Where you're concerned? Yes. I told you I'd protect you." I could see how his protectiveness would come through as possessiveness. Nothing about this feels possessive, however. If anything, I feel like I'm the one driving everything. He isn't rushing me.

"What now?" I ask.

"What do you mean? We're having dinner tomorrow night with Lealla."

"No, I mean between us. What are we? And don't say mates. I'm not ready for that yet. We haven't mated or anything." My cheeks heat from the steamy scenes in Lealla's books as they rush to the forefront of my mind. The very adult, mating scenes. Considering I'm new to all of this, I have zero experience being with a guy. Oh, no. Will she want to write about my first time with Rion? In detail? I can't deal with that. I'm going to have to set some boundaries with her tomorrow.

He smiles that dazzling, dimpled smile of his. The one that touches me with his eyes and makes my knees weak. The one he's been hitting me with all night. I'm sure he knows the effect it has on me. "We can be boyfriend and girlfriend, unless that's moving too fast." He steps closer. There's barely two inches separating us. "I want you. I don't care about titles or what anyone else thinks. All I ask is that you give us a chance and don't date anyone else."

"I can do that. Boyfriend and girlfriend sounds good. It will also keep all the women off of you."

"Rest assured, there is no one out there who could come close to comparing to you." Yeah, right. I don't say that, of course.

"Good," I reply.

His eyes flash to green then return to blue a second later.

"I love when your eyes do that."

"I find I need to control myself a lot around you. There are many instincts trying to come to the forefront that I have to keep pushing back."

"Such as?" I ask, leaning closer so my hands are on his chest, our lips almost touching.

"I want to kiss you…all the time. I want to tell the world you're mine. My wolf wants to lie beside your bed to watch over you as you sleep. He wants the peace of mind of knowing you'll be safe. He wants..."

"What?" I ask in a breathy whisper.

"His mate."

He closes the distance between us and kisses me ever so lightly. My lips tingle at the contact. Standing on my tiptoes, I press closer, leaving no air between us. Sparks light my veins. I immediately part my lips to deepen our kiss. Rion doesn't hesitate. He takes what I'm offering as his arms come around my back to hold me to him.

It's when we kiss that I picture kissing only him for the rest of my life, and that scares me. I've never fallen in love. Never given my heart to another. I knew, once I did, I'd be opening myself up to heartbreak. From the books I read, to the girls I see in high school, I want nothing to do with mending back the pieces a guy can rip apart. But there's something about Rion that tells me I don't have to worry. That he would take whatever I give him and cherish it.

His hands remain at my back, not roaming over other parts of my body. For being nineteen, he's a gentleman. I'm close to climbing him like a tree. He's all hard planes, and my hands seem to have a mind of their own as they rove beneath his shirt. His body vibrates with a deep rumble as I explore every muscular ridge of his stomach, lightly raking my nails over his skin. It only makes me want to do it more.

Pulling away, he breaks our connection before I have a chance to explore his back. I also haven't missed the way he fills out a pair of jeans from behind.

He rests his forehead on mine. "You could tempt a saint with those lips of yours."

"I don't want to tempt anyone but you."

His eyes flash green as he growls again. I'm starting to love that sound.

"Can I see him again tomorrow? Your wolf?" I loved spending time with him in the woods.

"Of course." He lets out a long breath. "You need rest, and I don't want to be the reason you break curfew." He kisses me again—a quick peck on my lips. "I'll pick you up tomorrow for dinner. Until then, behave, little mouse."

I scoff. "I always behave."

"That was before you knew vampires and shifters were real. I don't want you searching for them."

I sweep my hand over my chest to my head in a salute. "Scout's honor."

"Were you a Girl Scout?"

"Never. I have no clue what I just did."

He laughs. "We're going to have so much fun together."

I smile up at him. "I hope."

We say good night then I go inside as quietly as possible. The Jag rumbles to life in the driveway. I glance out the front window until his taillights disappear from sight. Up in my room, I collapse on the bed with a dreamy smile on my face and lips that still tingle from Rion's kisses.

There's a knock on my bedroom door a few minutes after I close it. Mom is on the other side.

"How was your date?"

"Good. Rion was a perfect gentleman."

"He better stay that way." I laugh and then a thought

occurs to me. Rion said she was asleep.

"Were you up reading?" I ask.

That's the only thing I can think of that would give him that impression. Tablets don't make any sound when you flip the pages. And I know from experience how relaxed I get reading. That could account for him thinking she was asleep.

"I couldn't go to sleep until I knew you were home safe. I'll always worry about you." She gives me a small smile. "Night, Ari."

"Night, Mom."

Finally gathering my bearings, I change into my pajamas, and after reading one chapter, I drift off to sleep.

I'm running through a forest, unsure why. But I hear them—the sounds of paws traversing earth at a rapid speed. Growls and wolves panting aren't far behind me. They're closing in. No matter how fast I move, I can't outrun them. Up ahead is a break in the trees. Maybe there are people on the other side. Someone to help me. A place to seek shelter.

My mind drifts to Rion and how he told me not to wander. How I could be in danger. I didn't listen. I went into the woods on my own. Now I'm certain death is coming for me.

Stumbling into a clearing, I'm barely able to keep myself upright. Spinning, I realize I'm back in the same spot Rion brought me to when he revealed his wolf. The moon is full in the sky and is sooty in color. It's the ash moon. Again. Something life changing is about to happen. Or life ending.

Wolves enter the clearing and circle around me, making it impossible to escape. What do they want? I don't know who they are. None of them are Orion. I'd recognize his white-tipped ears anywhere.

The ring of wolves closes in, becoming tighter. This is all my fault. I'll never get to kiss Rion again. Never get to see my parents or Paige or Bray.

A man appears at my side, out of nowhere. The light of the moon highlights his brown locks, his eyes the color of the moon above. The wolves growl in unison upon seeing him.

"You about ready to leave?" he asks.

"Who are you?"

"Now's not the time for questions. We need to go before these wolves make a meal out of you. You have to trust me."

I nod because, really, what else am I supposed to do? There are angry wolves circling me. I'm out of options. The mystery man grabs me around the waist with one arm and snaps his fingers on his free hand.

The next thing I know, we're standing in my bedroom, bathed in darkness. I'd recognize my space anywhere. I glance around, disoriented, unsure if I'm awake or if this is all still a dream.

"You're very awake," he says before releasing me. He walks to my window to peer out into the trees behind my house.

"What just happened?"

He strides from the window, flips on a light, and turns to face me. It's then I take him in. Chiseled, clean-shaven jaw, black leather trench coat, black jeans, and black boots with the jeans haphazardly tucked into them. His hair appears as if he's run his fingers through it too many times. If this were a book, he'd be the typical bad boy.

"Typical?" He scoffs. "There isn't anything typical about me." What's going on? Is he inside my head?

I shake the thought away and focus on the problem at hand. This is the second time I have to ask this question.

"What just happened?"

"Well, you were dreaming, except it wasn't exactly a dream. More like a premonition. The difference is, you could have died. If I hadn't saved you, that is. Those wolves would have had fun with you." So many questions. One at a time.

"Who were they?"

"The Diaminsey Pack. It's the name of the pack who killed Orion's parents." No!

"Why are they after me?"

"They know you're the one."

"The one what?" I ask.

"The catalyst in the next pack war."

"Say what now?"

He laughs. Smug jerk. How can he possibly laugh at a time like this? "Easily," he answers. "You're too cute not to laugh at."

I scowl at him and cross my arms. He's obviously able to read my thoughts. Yesterday, I would have thought that was impossible, but after Rion shifted into a wolf, nothing is out of the realm of possibility. "Would you get out of my head?"

"Never. Listen, I'm going to give it to you straight, since apparently no one else has yet. You're the key to ending the pack war. Some think it's ended because everything's been quiet for a while. They're wrong. Your premonition tonight is proof of that. This is bigger than you and Orion. It's bigger than the wolves in Lealla's books. This pack war that's coming, it has the potential to change the entire paranormal world. If you can't prevent it from happening, maybe you can finally end this for good. Not only are the wolves involved but the vampires, fae, and everyone else, too. None of us want to see bloodshed. Okay, maybe we vampires do a little. I mean, it's blood after all. We live for it. Literally." That explains what he is. I finally meet a vampire, and I can't focus on it because of the bigger problem at hand.

"Could you get on with it?" He's starting to make me angry. He needs to stop rambling and get to the point.

"I saved your life. Stop giving me your attitude, princess."

"Again, stop reading my mind," I all but growl. "Also, I'm not a princess. Now keep going. I want the rest of the story!"

"Keep yelling and you're going to wake up dear ol' mom and dad." He's right. I need to keep my voice down. "Anyway," he draws out the word, "I can't help that I can read your mind. It's a vampire trait. Your thoughts flow freely to me, like the conversation we're having. If you don't want me to know what you're thinking, learn to block me. As for your nickname, it's a keeper. Plus, it has the added bonus of irritating you, which I take great joy in. And finally, you may want to sit down for what I'm about to say. Oh, and my name is Ford. Get used to me. It seems we're going to be spending a lot of time together."

TWELVE

FORD'S HEAD TURNS SHARPLY TOWARD THE window as a slow grin forms on his face. "You're boyfriend's here. This is going to be fun."

"What? Rion's here?" I rush to the window. Thanks to the light from the full moon, I see a big, black wolf standing directly behind my house with his fangs bared. "We have to go down there."

Ford closes the distance between us to quickly wrap his arm around me, and in a flash, we're standing in my backyard. I shove him away but stumble. Rion the human catches me. He makes sure I'm able to stand before placing his body in front of mine.

"What are you doing here?" he growls.

"It's good to see you, too," Ford replies. "It's been,

what? An hour since we last spoke?"

"Just because you and I are acquaintances doesn't mean I'll ever like you near my mate."

"Tsk tsk, young wolf. Remember who you're talking to. I saved her life tonight. I was beckoned into her dream state. Someone had to rescue her before the wolves shredded her to bits."

Rion spins to face me. "You were dreaming about wolves and they were about to harm you?" His hands roam over my face and body to ensure I'm not hurt.

"I did, but Ford saved me. He told me it was a premonition." Rion's teeth clench.

"You can thank me now, Orion," Ford says. "I was her dark knight in black leather." Rion quickly shifts into wolf form and bares his teeth at Ford with a snarl.

"Are we going to play a game of who can bite who first? If so, I'm completely on board. Princess, would you referee?"

"Both of you stop!" I snap at them. This is insane. There is a wolf and a vampire squaring off in my backyard. How did my life come to this?

Ford sticks out his bottom lip. "You're taking all the fun out of my evening. Let us fight, please."

"Just when I think nothing crazier can happen, you appear."

"I bring the fun. I can't help it that your boyfriend showed up and ruined our good time."

"Good time? You were about to tell me how I'm the catalyst in the next pack war." This has got to be one of the strangest conversations I've ever had.

That statement is enough to get Orion to shift back. "What are you talking about?" he asks Ford.

"Lealla hasn't told you? Interesting. Maybe she will at dinner."

"Would you stop reading my mind?" I say, seething.

"I wasn't reading yours, princess. Your boyfriend is saying enough for both of you." Ford scowls. "I guess it is back to reading yours."

Rion turns to me. "I need to teach you how to block him and other vampires out."

"That would be helpful."

At the same time, Ford and Rion spin toward the house.

"Mommy's up," Ford says. He walks over to me, but Rion steps in front of him. "If you don't move, her mother is going to know she's out of bed. I need to get her back upstairs, and last time I checked, you can't teleport. Now move before she discovers her only child is gone."

Rion hesitantly steps aside and growls low when Ford's arm comes around my waist. We're back in my room in a flash and I'm climbing into bed, throwing the covers over myself while Ford turns out the light. The door opens a split second later. My mom quietly walks over to my bed, pauses then leaves.

Once the door closes, Ford is back standing in my room. "That was fun," he whispers. "Can we do this again tomorrow? I'll bring a friend so your wolf has someone to play with while we talk."

"Why are you enjoying this?" I ask as I throw the covers off myself. It's then I realize I'm in nothing but a sleep shirt. One that barely covers my butt.

"And what a nice butt it is," Ford says while trying to peer at my backside in the dark. Great night vison must be a general paranormal trait. I quickly cover myself again.

"Sorry, princess. When you're immortal and have nothing but time on your hands, you have to find ways to entertain yourself. And I really love teasing you."

"How old are you exactly? A thousand?"

He flips on the light and rushes over to my dresser where the mirror is. He pulls at his cheeks and eyes then smiles. "You tried to pull one over on me. I don't look a day over twenty-five."

"I thought vampires couldn't see themselves in mirrors."

"I thought readers of paranormal romance would know better than to think every rule applies to all. Of course I can see myself. How do you think I stay so handsome?" He turns to give me a view of his profile and poses for me, with his hand on his hip. I just can't with this vampire.

"You didn't answer my question."

"I'm a hundred and eight, if you must know."

"You're young for a vampire."

"And you're nosy."

"How did you get your name?" Since he's standing here, I'm going to start peppering him with questions. It's not every day I get to meet a real vampire.

"More questions?" he sighs. "Fine, if you must know, my parents conceived me in a Ford Model T."

"Are they still alive?"

"They are, but you won't be if you keep asking me questions."

"Oooh, I'm real scared." I roll my eyes. "You didn't finish telling me about my role in the pack war."

"Yeah, about that. I'm not sure I will. I'm getting bored." He yawns dramatically. "And tired."

"Do you sleep in a coffin?"

He scrunches up his nose. "What? No. You've read too much and watched too much TV."

"I do not. I'm just getting caught up on my vampire facts."

There's a howl outside my window. Not caring about my current attire, I rush to the window, leaving my back to the vampire, and tug the curtain aside to find Orion pacing the width of my backyard. He freezes at the same time as Ford whispers, "Daddy's up. Time to bolt. I'll be seeing you, princess. Try not to have any more premonitions you need rescuing from." He snaps his fingers and he's gone.

Quickly, I flip off the light and dart into bed again. Hopefully, Orion ran into the woods to hide. With one eye, I glance at the alarm clock and see it's six in the morning. My dad is an early riser. He gets up at six, regardless what day of the week it is. I should try and get some sleep so I don't look like a zombie at dinner tonight with Lealla.

Today was fun. I woke up at noon when my mom decided I'd slept long enough, and laid around my room all day, utterly exhausted. I've done nothing. That is, until I finally decided to shower an hour ago. My mom asked me if I rolled around out in the woods, because I smelled like dirt and trees. I guess that happens when you run for your life from wolves and then get teleported around by a vampire. If I could die in my dream, then I can certainly bring smells with me. My feet were filthy when I looked at them. I was running barefoot through the woods, after all. I had to clean up two cuts on my feet. Even now, I'm hobbling around. But every time I see Mom or Dad, I try to walk like nothing is wrong so they won't question me. Who knew the life of a teenager could be so complicated?

I do the best I can to tame my hair, thankful for my flat iron. After messaging with Rion, I found out Lealla doesn't dress fancy and prefers to be casual. I suppose living with a pack of wolves will do that. Lealla has other homes, and in each one is a different pack. She has more than one shifter series. Foxes, bears, and jungle cats; each pack resides in a different house of hers. She brought all of them together and each pack likes to live together.

The more I learn about the packs, the wolves in particular, the more I accept this is my new reality. I have a wolf for a boyfriend, a vampire who apparently watches my dreams, and an entire pack of wolves living an hour from me. And let's not forget the pack war I was told about last night.

I'm downstairs waiting for Rion. My leg shakes as I try to rid myself of nervous energy. I want to get to Lealla's and find out what my role is in all of this.

"You look nice," my mom says as she sits beside me.

I glance down at my jeans and sleeveless blouse. I may have gone a little fancy with the blush-colored blouse, but I'll put money on the fact that there will be a lot of gorgeous women walking about that house tonight. My hair is pulled back on the sides and top away from my face, leaving the rest to fall straight down my back. I put on minimal makeup. Maybe no one will notice I got a little dolled up.

"Where are you off to tonight?" Mom asks. Dad is sitting in his chair, reading.

"Rion is taking me to Lealla's home for dinner." I decide not to lie to her about tonight. I'll omit what I need to but don't like the idea of constantly lying to my parents.

"The author of those books you read?"

"Yeah. Rion lives next door to her with his aunt and uncle."

"Have fun. The same curfew stands." I have to force myself not to roll my eyes. Most of the time I do it without thinking.

"You know I'm eighteen, right? I'm legally an adult."

"And as long as you go to high school, I get to give you a curfew."

"Fine."

The familiar rumble of the Jag is heard a moment before the doorbell rings. I'm the first to the door, waving goodbye as I push Rion toward the car. No need for pleasantries tonight. He's met both parents. Besides, I want to get to this dinner and find out everything Lealla knows about my role in the upcoming pack war. I haven't talked to Rion about it yet. Some things I'd like to learn about in person. This way I can gauge his reaction.

Paige texts me as soon as I sit down in Rion's car. We talked briefly today about my date last night. I had to leave most of the details out. I meant it when I said I wouldn't tell anyone, no matter how much I hate keeping things from my best friend.

Paige: Are you coming over tonight? I thought we could have a girls' night in since I didn't see you last night.

Me: Sorry, but I can't. I'm having dinner out with Rion.

Paige: Have fun! But don't forget about your best friend. I'll take a back seat to your relationship this weekend, but next weekend, one night is mine.

I smile.

Me: Deal.

I put my phone away and glance over at Rion, who still

hasn't left the driveway. His eyes are intent on me.

"Hi," I say. "That was Paige. I have to spend one night next weekend at her house. Girl time and all that."

He smiles that sexy, melt me in my seat smile. "Hi, little mouse. Spend as much time with your friend as you want, but know I'll be outside her house, in the shadows, keeping you protected."

"You don't have to do that. I've been sleeping at her house for years. I've been fine so far."

"*So far* being the keywords. Also, that was before you met me and before you had a premonition where you needed rescuing by a vampire." He has a point. I simply nod and put my seat belt on as Rion pulls out of the driveway, and we start the hour-long drive to Lealla's home.

My life has completely changed. I'm both excited and scared to learn what is going to happen next.

THIRTEEN

THE TRIP TO LEALLA'S SEEMS TO go by faster each time I come up here. Rion and I talked the entire drive but kept the conversation light. No speaking of impending doom, vampires, or anything of the sort. We talked about my high school, classes, and what Rion does to occupy his time during the day.

Aries is the resident handywolf around Lealla's local mansion. He repairs anything that needs it. Rion explained how every wolf in the pack has a job. Well, not the kids, but those eighteen and older. I asked what he did to help out and he said, "Sit around and look handsome." I laughed. He explained that for now he's a model and will be getting pictures taken soon for his book cover—our book cover. I dropped the conversation after that. Thinking of my life in a book makes my stomach churn with uneasiness.

Reaching the gates of the mansion, Rion hits a button in the car and the gates open. There's no creepy man waiting in the shadows. Or maybe there is, and I can't see him. Either way, I'm glad I don't lay eyes on him.

"Does the fence go around the whole property?" I ask.

"No. It's only across the front and more for show. The property is always patrolled by members of the pack. If someone is stupid enough to try to breach the house, they'd be met with a massive wall of wolves."

"I feel sorry for anyone stupid enough to try that." I can only imagine what kind of fury they'd find if they try to get into a home full of wolves, their mates, and children.

"If they're human, we redirect them with a stiff warning never to come again. If they're paranormal, they don't make it out alive."

I have so many questions. Like, how does a vampire fight a wolf? If the vampire keeps teleporting, the wolf is no match for him, right? What about the fae? They play tricks and are very cunning. Then there are mages, and yeah, so many questions.

Rion stops in front of the mansion. The same man from the other night is there to take his keys. The man doesn't open my door for me, though. Rion does. I remember reading how the males always take care of their females. No one else is allowed to unless the male is incapable of doing so. Then, other members of the pack fill the void as needed.

The inside of the house is just as I remembered it, absolutely gorgeous. Until a red wolf skids across the floor in front of us on his side. He snarls and quickly stands up, charging back the way he came. Growling and shouts are heard from my right. I'm frozen in place. What's going on?

Rion stays by my side, an arm protectively behind my back. Not in a way that means he's alarmed. He's not trying to push me out of the way or anything to keep me out of the melee. His arm is more like he's staking a claim on me. Telling others I'm his.

"What's happening?" I ask. I realize I'm asking this a lot lately.

"They're fighting again."

"Who?"

"Carter and Cash. They do this all the time. I think they were born too close together, so everything is a competition." I remember their stories in the series. Carter, Cash, and Cace are all blood brothers. Their father abandoned them when they were young, leaving their human mother to care for them. She got sick not long after he disappeared, leaving the boys on their own. Aries found them and brought them into his pack.

"You got blood on the floor!" Cace yells when he comes into the room. At this moment, I'm so glad I recognize him from the cover of his book. It doesn't leave me guessing as to who he is. I know his whole story.

Cace stops when he sees us and smiles. "Sorry about that. My brothers don't know how to behave, let alone welcome guests."

I stand still for a moment to marvel at Cace in all his shirtless glory. Muscles are bulging on his biceps as he bends to wipe the blood off the floor; his stomach flexing with each movement. Rion growls beside me, causing Cace's head to snap up and me to glance over at him.

Cace chuckles. "You'll need to control that a little better, brother. No one is after your mate." My cheeks redden with embarrassment. Nothing like being caught gawking at the hot man cleaning the floor. I think my whole body is about to go up in flames.

Cace nods toward me. "Nice to see you again, Ari. Excuse my brothers. Even mated, they know not what they do."

"I knew exactly what I was doing," Carter says as he enters the room. These men look so much better in person than on their covers. "Cash won't get off my back about patrol. I'm sick of it. You need to talk to him," he says to Cace.

"If the two of you can't get along, how are we to set an example for the other pack members who patrol with us? You're older, wiser. Stop behaving like a pup. Both of you!" he shouts over his shoulder as Cash enters, while wiping blood off his neck.

"Honestly, Carter, did you need to go for my neck?" Cash asks.

"You had your teeth sunk into my leg! That's going to take all night to heal. I'm going to have to shift multiple times." I notice blood seeping from Carter's calf.

Rion leans down to whisper in my ear. "This isn't the way I wanted to introduce you to the pack." Three heads swivel in our direction. They smile in unison as their eyes find me. Three shifters. All sexy. All shirtless. All smiling at me. If this is a dream, I never want to wake up.

Cace speaks first as he stands. "This is Ariane. She's Rion's mate. Ari, these are my blood brothers, Carter and Cash." They step forward, each taking a turn to shake my hand. For big, strong shifters, they are very gentle.

"I'm sorry about the scene we put on. Had we known we'd have a guest," Cash levels Rion with a glare, "we'd have been on better behavior."

Carter snorts. "No, we wouldn't have. We fight like this every day. You always do something to rile me up."

"Gentlemen, I think that's enough commotion for one day," Lealla says as she enters. "Our guest doesn't need to see any more fighting." Her chestnut hair is pulled back into a ponytail. She's wearing a pair of tight jeans that show off her slender legs and a black V-neck tank. Her feet are bare as she walks across the marble floor, toenails painted a light pink.

"It's okay. I don't mind," I reply.

She takes my hands in hers. "You're coming along quickly. Some of the other mates took quite a while to get used to being around a pack of wolves." The three brothers smile as they leave the room.

"Once I realized I wasn't going insane, I started going through everything in my head. It's like pieces of a puzzle slowly clicking into place. It doesn't happen all at once, but with the bigger picture in mind, it makes it easier to see."

"I'm happy to hear it. Come, let's eat." She releases my hands as Rion reaches for one.

I never thought I'd be the kind of girl who would want her boyfriend always touching her. But with Rion, it's subtle, not pushy. He seems to do it as much for his benefit as mine. Every time he touches my skin, those familiar jolts are there. They quiet to a hum much quicker now, as if my body is getting familiar with his.

Lealla leads us to a small dining room off the main entryway. There is a table and chairs for six in a rich cherrywood. Rion closes the door behind us. There is a matching hutch and ivory walls. The same marble floor from the entryway is throughout the room. No way is this where the entire pack eats. Maybe it's more for entertaining small groups.

Lealla sits at the head of the table with Rion on one side. I try to walk to the other side, but he pulls out the chair beside him.

"Your mate will always want you by his side, Ari. No matter the circumstances, you are safer with him than you are with anyone else."

"Is someone attacking us here?" I ask, joking. "I thought we were just having dinner."

"No," she grins. "It's instinctual."

Ford suddenly appears on the other side of the table. His jeans are tucked into black boots, and he's wearing the same leather trench he wore last night.

"What's for dinner?" he asks as he takes the seat opposite Rion and rubs his hands together. The room is silent. He glances up. "What? I was invited. Don't give me that look, princess. Consider me a second protector, if you will." He winks. Freaking vampire reading my mind, hearing the conversation we just had.

"Over my dead body," Rion growls and stands up. The chair he was seated in crashes to the marble floor behind him. Here we go. They're going to fight in this nice room. At least it won't be the first blood to be spilled tonight.

"But it could be the last," Ford replies while taking his cloth napkin from the table and placing it on his lap.

"It's never a dull moment," Lealla mutters. "Orion fix your chair and take your seat. Ari has enough to deal with without you two fighting. And Ford is right. You are both crucial to her life now."

"Can we rewind for a second?" I ask. "I need a manual or something."

Two women enter from a door across the room, each carrying a large tray filled with food: steaks, mashed potatoes, sauces, cooked vegetables, and salads. That's a lot of food for four people. Ford drops a large filet on his plate. Maybe not. I forgot who I'm dining with.

"You eat this and drink blood?" I ask.

"Yup. While blood gives us nourishment, I love the taste of food. Plus, it gives my body an extra boost of energy from the protein, which is always a positive."

"I really do need a manual," I mutter.

"You'll get it all straight in time," Lealla says kindly.

"And these are just the vampires and wolves."

Lealla laughs. "There is much to learn about the paranormal world. That's for sure."

"While I want to know everything, I'd like to get straight to the point on a few things. First, how much of my life will be in the book you're writing about Rion?"

Lealla puts her fork down to give me her full attention. "With every mated couple I've written, I've left it completely up to them. They are the ones who drive the plot and everything going on with the book. They are the ones who tell me what to, and not to, put in the book. I wouldn't put anything in the book they didn't want in there. Also, the book isn't written until they get their happily ever after. With each new story, there's a new problem—something that has to be solved. Something that continues from one book into the next. As an author, I need to keep the reader hooked and invested. I want them to look forward to the next book in the series. As much as these books—all my series—are my livelihood, they are my passion as well. But again, I wouldn't put anything in the books that those involved don't want in there. That's where my imagination comes into play, especially if the couple decides they don't want any of their real story told." At least I know that's an option.

"Okay, so after everything happens with Rion and me, then we sit down with you and retell our story?" This is all assuming Rion and I get our happily ever after. Who knows what's going to happen, or if we're still going to be together after all is said and done?

"Yes. You can tell me what to change, what to leave out, everything. I will fill in any gaps with fiction, and you'll have the final say over the book. You and Orion will both read it before I publish it."

"What about our names? If I'm to be part of this book, I wouldn't want my family or friends to know it's me in it. They know Rion is a model, so it wouldn't be too hard to say you used his real first name in the book. But me, they'll think it's odd that it's my name in there." Then again, maybe they wouldn't. Maybe others would think it's cool to have my name in the book. I think this might be one of those wait and decide when I need to things.

"We can certainly change your name. I can either use a middle name or a name you've always liked. As I said, you drive the story." So far so good. I like where she's going with this and that Rion and I control it. We have the last say. It's up to us what we want in it. And if we want a lot to stay between us, then she can fill it in with pure fiction. I have to wonder what happens if we don't have a dream ending. I push that thought aside, because if I'm honest with myself, I don't want this relationship to end.

"Is there a deadline?" I ask. "A date when we need to sit down and talk to you?"

"No. Your story concludes, at least in the book sense,

when you say so. You come to me when you're ready. Readers don't know whose book is next in this series. They only know there will be more. In the meantime, I have plenty of other books to write to keep them happy. It's one of the perks of having multiple series."

"And your other packs, they're okay with this? They come to you to tell their stories?"

She smiles warmly. "Yes. I've never pressured them, though. And like you and Orion, they are given the option to have as much of their real story included or none at all. I don't force any of them to tell me what happened, but they all come to me and want to, because in the end, they want readers to know their amazing love story. The love mates share is something wonderful and rare. If it can give others hope that the kind of love they read about actually exists, then those in my packs want to give it. You don't have to be of our world to find that kind of love. It happens every day to people all over the world."

FOURTEEN

WE EAT AND TALK MORE ABOUT how much or how little, if anything, is needed for the books. Lealla tells me her imagination is very good, and if need be, she can create a story from the inspiration of seeing us together. She said there's something magical about love, especially in the early stages.

Rion takes my hand in his. "I'm leaving it up to you, Ari. I'm happy telling the world how much I want to be with you and how we met. Any adventures we go on. But it's up to you whether or not we share it. I wouldn't want to agree to anything that would upset you. You come first." I nod and try not to blush as I go back to the meal before me.

After a few bites, I place my fork on the plate and face

Lealla again. "Tell me about the upcoming pack war. Ford said I'm important to it."

Lealla gives Ford a pointed look, then returns her gaze to me. "I wasn't going to tell you this yet. I wanted you to solidify your bond with Orion a little more first."

"I'm not ready to become anyone's mate yet, so I'm not sure how much solidifying there is to do."

"Every moment you spend with him, your trust and acceptance grows. That's what helps make your bond stronger. Not the actual act of mating with him and committing yourselves to one another. Though, that is the final piece of becoming his." And I'm back to blushing.

Ford leans forward. A wicked gleam in his eyes. "There are other options, princess. You could have me for a mate. You don't need a wolf."

Rion is back on his feet, but this time he shifts into a wolf and is rounding the table toward Ford as he snarls. Ford stands quickly. Instead of teleporting away from the wolf, he holds his ground, his fangs extending, ready to attack. If I weren't so worried about what was about to happen, I'd be fascinated watching Ford. There's a real vampire in front of me.

Orion doesn't hesitate, lunging for Ford. Now I'm going to have to get involved. I was perfectly content to remain on the sidelines. But them fighting changes things.

Standing, I rush to the other side of the table and throw my body weight into Orion, pushing him off balance. He stumbles and shakes his head. Those green eyes of his wolf finding mine.

"Don't," I state firmly. "I get it. You're jealous, but I'm here as a guest, and I'd like to learn as much as I can about my future—our future. So if you wouldn't mind, shift back and let's talk about things." I swing around to face Ford, who is chuckling at my back. "And you! Why must you provoke him? You know he's going to come at you. You're not new to this world like I am, and even I know better." I shake my head, walking back to my side of the table all the while mumbling, "Freaking wolves and vampires. I can't even have a nice dinner without them trying to tear into each other." Ford laughs.

Rion is back in human form and by my side in the blink of an eye. His hand grips mine; the familiar jolt of our connection rushing through my veins. When I'm fully turned toward him, he cups my face in his hands. His eyes are full of concern. "I'm sorry, Ari. I lost my temper. Where you're concerned, it seems I only have two modes—calm and rage." I'm lost in the sea of his eyes. He could probably say anything at this moment and I'd agree. How easily I get swept away in him.

"Hey, princess!" Ford yells from across the room. "Can we get back to the task at hand? I have places to go. People to annoy."

Reluctantly, I break the contact with Rion and turn toward Ford. "You're already accomplishing one of those, and you haven't even left this room."

"Feisty." He smiles. "I like it." Rion growls beside me.

"Ari is right," Lealla adds. "Can we please get back to our discussion? This fighting isn't helping anyone." She's not angry, at least not that I can tell. If anything, she's a bit amused.

We take our seats again. I hope this is the final time we have to stop the conversation. I'd like some answers.

"The pack war," I say, reminding Lealla where we left off.

"Right. Before I tell you what I know, please be aware that my visions aren't concrete. Normally, I only see as far as putting two mates on the same path to meet each other, along with a few other details. There are no glimpses into their futures, how many kids they'll have, if there's imminent danger, etcetera. But with you and Orion, it's different."

"You never told me," Rion speaks up.

She shakes her head. "I didn't want to upset you. Your feelings toward the Diaminsey Pack are strong, and rightfully so. What they did to your parents, it was horrible. At least Aries and Dante made things right."

"But they didn't," Rion replies as his fist slams down on the table, jostling the silverware and causing me to jump in my seat. "They may have killed the men who murdered my parents, but the pack, they didn't cast them out or punish them in any way for their crimes against other wolves. Their alpha and beta are the ones who need to pay. Everyone takes orders from them."

"Orion," Lealla says gently. "I know you want to get revenge. Believe me, I do. Aries has told you over the years that it wasn't the time, and he was right. Nothing you do will bring them back."

"They are still out there! I have a mate now. I must protect her! I don't want her living in this world, knowing paranormals like them are out there. Ones who have no regard for life and family."

I slouch down in my seat. Not at his hard tone, but at the fact that I don't want to be part of the reason he murders others. I understand his need to do so. He lost his parents. My world would fall apart without mine, but that doesn't mean more death is the answer. Then again, this is no longer my world I'm living in. This is pack life. The rules are different here.

"You running off and getting yourself killed won't do any good. Who will protect Ari then? You're not mated yet, Orion. Even now, she's fair game to any paranormal out there." Ford smiles at the same time as Rion growls. Lealla slaps her hand on the table. "Enough! I'm tired of yelling at you two. You're no longer children. Orion, from this point forward, your main focus needs to be Ariane. Nothing else matters but her. Every move you make, you better take her into consideration. If you don't, it won't just be your life on the line. Do you understand?" Rion nods. "Good. Now, let's get back to Ari's role in all of this." It's the first time I've heard her raise her voice. Now I see how she can be someone who looks out for all her packs. Someone who only has their best interests at heart. She's so strong and formidable.

I sit up tall again. "Thank you."

"You're welcome. Like I was saying, my visions aren't always far-reaching, but I have seen glimpses of the pack war. Although, what you saw in your dream, and what I see in my visions, are slightly different. Your dream shows a scene. One scene. Something you need your attention focused on and that of the pack; whereas, my visions can be of anything, not exclusively pack related. I've seen some boring stuff and some exciting." I nod, still confused, but what else is new?

Lealla continues, "In regards to the pack war, it's our Avynwood Pack versus the Diaminsey Pack. There has been bad blood between the packs for a long time. It also doesn't help that our pack is much newer than theirs. They've built theirs up over many, many years. We didn't have that luxury. Their pack is not stronger than ours, however. We may be on the newer side of working together as one cohesive unit, but we are a solid unit. Our wolves are tightly linked and the pack bond is strong. While they may let any good fighter in theirs, we don't. Our wolves need to get along and have a good heart. They must want to put more good into the world than bad. And they must, above all else, defend their family."

"That's all well and good, but I'd like to get to the point."

Lealla chuckles. "So impatient. You'll gain more of that as you get older. I have to wade through the fog that fills my mind at times to get to the pack war. Many paranormals are going to get hurt, some will die. At the heart of the battle, it's always you. You're the key to stopping the war."

"What if I don't want to be the key? What if I want to be an ordinary teenager, who goes to high school and does teenage stuff?"

"Careful what you say, princess," Ford warns. I wonder why but not for long.

"You'd go back?" Rion asks. "To knowing nothing about us—about me—if you could?" The hurt written all over his face sends a piercing pain right through my chest.

I reach out for him, but he pulls back. "No, that's not what I meant. You have to try and see this from my side. A week ago, I didn't know any of this existed. I thought shifters and vampires were all fiction. Now I'm having dinner with them. But that's not what's getting to me. I'm no one, Rion, absolutely no one. Yet somehow, I'm at the center of an upcoming war. That doesn't even make sense to me. Can't you understand how hard all of this is for me to handle? You've had your entire life to know what you are. I'm only me—Ariane Sanderly. An ordinary girl from middle of nowhere North Carolina. Not Ariane Sanderly, girl amongst wolves, who holds the weight of the future of two shifter packs on her shoulders."

"It's not only your burden to bear, Ari," Lealla says. "It's all of yours. No one expects you to shoulder this alone."

I stand and place my palms down on the table, leaning toward her. "I don't want to shoulder it at all! I'm eighteen!" How is this so hard to comprehend? Can't they see it from my side? Every word they say only adds to the weight on me.

"And you're growing up faster than most do at your age, but you can handle it. If you couldn't, then fate wouldn't have chosen you as a mate for Orion."

"Now we're back to that. Can we stay on point here? How am I to stop this pack war from happening, since there's no way for me to get out of it? How can I prevent it?" I glance at Rion, who is sitting with his head down, dejected. His feelings are hurt, and I'll apologize for that later. However, this is bigger than him and me. There are many lives in my hands, and I need to face these problems one at a time.

"I've tried so hard to see how we get to where we're heading. I can't. There's no clear path. No definitive way I see for it to be stopped." Lealla lets out a long breath. "Maybe I'm not meant to know. I wouldn't want to see the deaths of those I care about.

"It's not just your pack who will be at risk," Ford adds. "Other paranormals have spoken of a war. If it happens, you won't fight it alone."

"Nor will Aries want anyone else to get hurt in his

battle. It's not his way."

"He won't have a choice. We'll be there. Not the entire population, mind you. There are many who want to keep blood off their hands. Then there are those of us who feel that without our help, the Avynwood Pack might lose. And if you do, Diaminsey will become stronger. Their reign of terror is already spreading. They killed a male fae last week. He was part of a small family on the other side of the state. From what I've heard, they attacked him without any premeditation. And this is one instance. Imagine if the pack gets bigger or has smaller sects throughout the country. Their morals aren't intact. A lot of harm could be done."

"This is my fight—my pack's fight," Rion says harshly. "I don't want anyone else battling it for us."

"See past your little world, young wolf. There's a much bigger picture. Your pack is strong, but it's not enough. Theirs is larger, stronger. And they've been training for this for a long time. What have you been doing?"

FIFTEEN

NOT ONE WORD IS SPOKEN DURING the hour-long drive back to my house. We left after Rion and Ford got into it. Again. Dinner was forgotten. Lealla appeared completely exhausted by the time we left. Ford teleported away when I asked him to. If not, I feared they were going to physically fight.

Rion shuts the car off when we're in front of my house. Leaning his head back on the seat, he closes his eyes. I don't look anywhere but at him. He's only nineteen. One year older than me, yet his priorities are completely different. Mine are high school and getting good grades. Or they were before this. Now it seems I've been immersed in his world with his priorities.

So much information was given to me tonight. More

than I know what to do with or how to process. There's no way for me to prevent the pack war. The paranormal world is vast, and I only know a fraction of it. At this point, Lealla's books aren't going to tell me enough. I need to keep talking to Rion and Ford, to the other wolves, and any paranormal I meet.

I wish I didn't have the weight of this on my shoulders. The drive home put everything into perspective. There are a lot of things in our lives we wish we could change. Accidents that happened, deaths that might have been prevented, lies we told, friends we lost, but it's inevitable. Everything happens for a reason, and I'm not going to fight fate.

I saw it in my dream. I saw the wolves. Sure, I could shut it all out and pretend none of this is real. That I'm not sitting in the car with a cover model, who happens to be my fated shifter mate. Or I can do what I've done my whole life and face things head on. I'm not a coward. I stand up and deal with what's in front of me. And currently that's an upset wolf shifter.

"Would you talk to me?" I ask softly.

He meets my gaze. "I'm not sure what you'd like me to say."

"Anything. I hate this silence."

He sighs. "I won't force you into my world, Ari. If you want to go back to living your life the way it was before I came along, I won't stop you. But you will not toy with me. I want a decision made before you leave this car. Either I'll see you again or I won't. But what I will not do is let you string me along. I know what's between us. I feel it in my soul. It could be one-sided, though."

I reach for his hand, needing to feel our connection.

"When I'm with you, the rest of the world falls away. It's just us and the way you look at me. I've never had someone make me feel the way you do."

"How do I make you feel?"

"Cherished. Protected. Truly alive for the first time in my life." Every word I say is true. Before Rion, my life was boring, and I was merely going through the motions. I was never as happy as I am with him. That is, if you take away all this pack war stuff.

"And this is a bad thing?"

I shake my head. "No, absolutely not. But you had to know this wasn't going to be easy for me. It's hard enough finding out you're a wolf and that I'm your mate, but to add in this whole pack war thing, it's a lot for me to take in."

"You won't face any of it alone. Nor does anyone expect you to." He turns to gaze out the windshield. "I didn't know about the vision before tonight. Lealla didn't tell me. The first I heard was from Ford last night. It scares me to think of you in the middle of it. It makes me want to kill every single wolf in that pack so you won't feel an ounce of pain from them. I don't like your involvement in this any more than you do. Although, I've learned in my short life, I can't beat fate. I can't manipulate it to do as I ask. If I could, I would have my parents back with me. That wasn't my destiny, however. If it weren't for them dying, me going to live with Aries, and him being close to Lealla, I wouldn't have met you. It's twisted beyond belief, but it all led me to you."

"How can you be so sure about us? About me?"

"I already told you. It's in our touch."

"There has to be more than that. I can't base our relationship off a spark when we touch."

He faces me again, leaning close over the center console of the car. "What about when we kiss?" he whispers.

A shiver works its way up my spine as my lips part. "When you're this close, I can't think." All I can do is focus on his lips and the way his voice floats over my skin like a soft caress.

"Don't think, Ari. Just feel."

He closes the distance between us, capturing my lips with his. All those sparks are back; my entire being lights up on the inside at the rightness of us being together. Everything in me screams that Rion is mine, and no one could ever kiss me like he does.

His hand threads into my hair to gently grip the back of my head as we continue to kiss. It's as if he's the air I need to breathe. I choke back tears as my emotions pummel me.

Pulling back, I cover my mouth with my hand, trying to fight off the tears. "I'm sorry."

"What's wrong? Did I do something?"

"No, you're perfect. I'm sorry for saying what I did earlier. I was upset and lashing out." I feel awful for what I said. I was thinking about me and how everything impacts only me. Not how my words affected Rion. We're a team, he and I, and I need to start thinking of us as one.

"I don't blame you for being upset. I thought we were doing this together."

"We are, but you need to understand my side. I've never known this life before. The only people I've ever depended on are my parents, Paige, and Bray. To have a boyfriend, let alone someone who could be my mate—"

"Is your mate." I have to resist every urge in my body

to roll my eyes at his need to clarify that.

"Whatever. It's a lot. And to expect me to take it all in, and embrace it in a week's time, is a bit much to ask. Then to throw the whole pack war on me, I'm buckling under the pressure."

"Nothing you do will be alone. Besides," he smiles that smile that has me turning to goo, "you have enough bite in you for ten wolves."

"Let's see where that gets us when I'm running from wolves, if this pack war actually happens."

Rion turns serious. "You'll have the entire Avynwood Pack behind you, as well as others, from the sound of it."

"Like Ford?"

He growls. "We don't need to speak his name."

"You two are obviously friends. I don't want to come between that."

"Friends isn't the right term." I wonder what they really are. How long have they known each other? They obviously aren't new friends.

"No matter, I don't want to ruin your relationship with him."

"You will always come first, Ari."

I turn to hide my blush. I still can't grasp the enormity of the feelings he has for me or put into words what I feel for him. There is one thing I know for certain, I don't want to let him go. Good or bad. Pack war or not. I want Rion in my life.

"I should probably get inside."

"I'm going to park the Jag a few blocks away and be back to watch over your house. Since you had a premonition, I'm worried about something coming to fruition sooner than the pack war."

"I wish you were the one who could watch my dreams instead of Ford."

"So do I. If only wolves had that ability."

"Why do vampires?" I love getting these little tidbits of information.

"They can willingly transfer powers from one to the other. It's what makes them a strong race. Some keep the power to themselves and never share it. Those are the dangerous ones. They want to rule over everyone. But there are others who give their gifts freely to other paranormals to help them."

"Couldn't Ford share his dream walking ability with you?"

"Technically, he could try, but I'm not sure if it would work. Dream walking is a skill that takes time to hone. You have to be able to seek out the dreamer, know how to invade their dream. It's very complicated." Interesting. This is all going in the manual I'm mentally putting together about each paranormal race. I can't write any of it down for fear of someone finding it, but I have a pretty good memory. "Plus, I don't want that vampire's fangs anywhere near my skin." Do all wolves feel that way about vampires? Not wanting them to bite them, even if it means they could gain new powers? More questions for another day.

"Let's hope I don't have any more premonitions."

Rion brushes his lips over mine. "I'll be right outside all night if you need me."

"When will you sleep?" I ask breathily as the remnants of our connection from the kiss slowly fade.

"I'll sleep. Don't worry about me."

He kisses me again. This time, every part of my being wants to climb over the console and hold him against me. I want his warmth and his protection. I'm afraid… very afraid. I don't want this pack war to happen. I don't want anyone to get hurt. Why can't I just have this relationship with Rion and explore it? Have fun while getting to know each other? No, instead I have to worry about impending doom and how I'm smack dab in the middle of it. Me. Ordinary Ariane is somehow going to fight wolves. Uh huh. Sure.

Rion walks me to the door and kisses me once more. I can't seem to get enough of him. I also didn't know it was possible for a relationship to go from zero to a hundred so quickly. Maybe that's what happens when you date a wolf shifter who calls you his mate and determines there will never be anyone else for him.

Inside, I listen to the throatiness of his Jag as it drives down my street. Before I climb into bed, I take a peek out my bedroom window. There, in the dense trees behind my house, a pair of emerald green eyes stands out amongst the darkness. Those eyes will be watching over my house all night, keeping me safe. There's something very comforting about it. Now, if only I knew Ford would be there in my dreams to look after me. I'd love not to have another premonition. If I do, I hope he can rescue me from any threat. I'm not ready to die tonight.

I'm back in the clearing. Oh, no. This can't be good. This stupid clearing and the stupid moon above. This time it's a bright white. No ash moon. What does that even mean? Is the pack war going to take place on another ash moon? How many of those moons are there in a year? Or is the moon simply here to illuminate what's going to happen in my premonition? To give me a light to watch what's going to unfold?

Again, I have more questions than answers.

Glancing around, I scan the tree line surrounding me for any wolves. At first, I hear nothing, but then… Then there is a low growl. Slowly, four wolves step forward. Their heads low, ears back, and teeth bared. I don't stop to evaluate the situation. Instead, I take off in the opposite direction. Maybe if I run, it will give Ford time to find me in my dream. Not that I think I can outrun wolves, but you never know.

My feet are bare again. Sticks on the forest floor slice into them as I run. I don't stop. I can't stop. Not when there is a wolf so close behind me I can hear his breathing.

All of a sudden, a flash of black charges in from the side. A wolf races by me, rushing toward one of the wolves chasing me. I hear a loud yip and keep moving. Three wolves left. I wonder if that was Rion who took the wolf out. There's no time to stop and figure it out.

Another wolf closes in. This time, it gets a hold on the long shirt I'm wearing and tugs. I falter in my steps but am able to keep myself upright. Before I can spin around and try to free myself, a burning pain in my left thigh has me faltering again. I've been bitten.

SIXTEEN

I CAN'T BELIEVE *THIS WOLF BIT ME. It prowls around the front of me, staring at me with emerald eyes. It's dark, but not completely pitch-black. The trees above block out some of the moon. It's hard for me to make out any markings, but it's a grey wolf. A big one.*

"Why did you bite me?" I yell. "I've never done anything to you. You're attacking me while I sleep? How dare you!" I'm done running. Normal human or not, I'm not going to stand here and let some wolf kill me. Not without a fight. "That's it. It's on now!"

Arms like steel wrap around me from behind. Both of my arms are pinned to my side. I thrash around, but it's of no use.

"Calm down, princess," Ford whispers in my ear. "That's enough playing with the wolves for tonight." He snaps his fingers.

I'm transported back to my room. Ford releases me

and I spin on him.

"Why did you do that? You could have at least let me kick that wolf in the head or something." I'm seething. My chest rises and falls with each breath I take.

"With your wounded leg?"

"Oh, shut up."

"We can't keep meeting like this, princess. I knew something was off. I felt it. I quickly searched for you in your dream state, only to find you squaring off with one of the wolves of the Diaminsey Pack." He walks to the wall and flips on the light.

"He deserved for me to kick him! No one bites me and gets away with it."

Ford sighs. "You would have been dead had I not intervened. We can't have this happen again." He steps closer to me, our bodies almost touching.

"What are you doing?"

"Do you trust me?"

I roll my eyes. "This again? You saved my life for the second time a minute ago, so sure, I trust you."

Faster than I can track, my hair is brushed aside and teeth are sinking into my neck. My body goes instantly lax as Ford holds me up. His body is pressed to mine. His warmth enveloping me, quickly heating my skin. A sense of euphoria settles over me unlike I've ever felt. As quick as it happens, he releases me and I'm sitting on a towel on my bed. My head is foggy. My body tingles all over.

"What just happened?" I ask. Even my voice seems a million miles away, completely unattached to me.

"You can now teleport."

"I can what?" I yell and lurch to my feet. My body sways, still in a vampire-induced haze. Ford catches me before I fall to the floor and then I'm back on the bed again.

"You have to give it a few minutes for the effects to wear off. Any time a vampire bites someone, we give them a little something extra to help numb the pain and dull the senses. I tried to keep it as short as possible so you wouldn't get too much of it."

"Great. Now tell me again what power I have."

"You can teleport. I'm not always going to be able to get to you in time, Ariane. You'll need to be able to leave your dreams, or premonitions as they are, if I can't get to you." I don't miss his use of my name. He likes calling me princess. His tone was firm this time, nothing playful in it.

My eyes are finally able to focus on him. Everything in my room is clear again. "You're serious, aren't you?"

"Absolutely. I don't want your life in danger any more than you do."

"Awww, you like me." I laugh, loving that I can finally tease him back about something.

"You're crazy. I tolerate you."

"Uh huh, sure." I wink. This is fun, being on the giving end of this little game we play.

A howl pierces the night sky outside my house. "That would be your boyfriend. Can you stand? I need to take you to him before he storms the house and wakes up your parents."

"I'm surprised my yelling didn't do that."

"You and me both. Luckily, both of them are still sound asleep."

A thought occurs to me. "If I can teleport, that means I don't need you to get me to the backyard, right? I can do it myself." I line up my fingers to snap but Ford lunges at my hand, stilling me before I can do it.

"You will not be teleporting without me until you get the hang of it. You could end up in the Sahara and I wouldn't be able to find you. No snapping yet."

"Buzzkill."

"I'm starting to regret my decision to give you my power."

I smile wide. "I'm not. Look out world. Ariane Sanderly can teleport."

Ford gives me a hard glare. "You better listen to me."

"Whatever, Dad. Can you take me to Orion now? I don't want my parents waking up to a wolf and a vampire in the backyard."

"Wouldn't that be interesting?" He chuckles.

"Sure. Then, I really would need my new ability to ever leave the house again."

Ford grabs me gently around the waist and with a snap of his fingers, we're in the backyard, standing in front of a very angry wolf. He bares his teeth at Ford a second before shifting into a human. Rion's hand is around Ford's throat immediately.

"What did you do? I heard her yell!" he grinds out through clenched teeth.

"If you were listening to our conversation instead of raging out here like a rabid animal, you would have heard everything. She yelled because a wolf bit her."

Rion releases Ford and swivels to face me. "Where?"

I had almost forgotten I was bitten. I have to remember to thank Ford for putting a towel on my bed before I sat on it. The whole fact that I can teleport put my bleeding leg on the back burner. Turning, I show Rion my injury. Blood is running down my bare skin from my thigh.

Rion drops to the ground behind me and tears off his

shirt. He shreds it into a long strip then wraps it tightly around my leg. I'm swept up into his arms before I can bat an eye.

"I need to get her to Desmond. Do you have someone who can fill in?" he asks Ford. Fill in? What's he talking about?

"One second." Ford snaps his fingers and disappears. He's back before I can ask Rion where he went. Ford brought a thin blonde back with him.

"This is Kiara. She's going to change to make herself look like you, princess, and take your place in bed, in case your parents come knocking before you're back."

"Say what now?"

Kiara laughs. "Ariane, it's nice to meet you. I promise I'll only speak to them if necessary. This is so you can get your leg mended." How fast did Ford talk for her to get all that information? He wasn't even gone a minute. In the darkness I have a hard time making her out, except for her hair and slender frame.

"Thank you, I guess. I'm not sure why I can't go to the hospital and get stitches there."

"You've been bitten by a wolf, Ari," Rion states. "How would you explain that?"

"Dog bite?"

"That's no small bite on your leg. No one would believe a dog did that."

"Uhhh... I could tell them it was an enormous dog who had all its shots."

"And when they want to call your parents?"

I smile. "I'm eighteen."

"This is stupid," Ford states. "You're going to the pack's doctor and that's all there is to it. Kiara will cover for you. I'll clean up any blood in your room. I'd offer to teleport you, but your mate wouldn't like that." Rion growls at him.

"Since when do I take orders from you?" I ask.

"Since you and I have a lot of work to do."

Rion's eyes narrow. "What's going on that I don't know?" Ford's right. If Rion were paying attention to us talking, he would have known all this already, thanks to that super strong wolf hearing of his.

I pat his chest. "I'll fill you in when we're inside the car."

Kiara steps forward and takes my hand in hers. Something passes through us and then she's me. Literally my replica. My mouth hangs agape as I take in as much of her as I can under the moonlight.

"How do I look?" she asks while twirling around.

"I really need to brush my hair," I mumble.

I can't believe this is what I currently look like. Rion is holding me. My face is inches from his. I'm not sure this could get more embarrassing. Oh, wait, it can. I have no pants on and he's holding my bare legs in his arms. Yup, it's worse. You'd think I'd learn to put pants on before I sleep. That's going to change after tonight.

Ford and Kiara teleport into my bedroom as Rion carries me through the woods to keep us hidden until we get to his Jag. We break through the trees, and the next thing I know, I'm gently placed on the seat. We're speeding down the road in the middle of the night as he places a call to Aries through the car.

"Orion, what's wrong?" he answers through the car's speakers.

"Ari's been bitten. I need you to wake Desmond. Tell

him I'm bringing her in."

"Will do, but Rion? A wolf bit her?"

"Yes, one of the Diaminsey did in her dream." Aries starts to say something, but Rion cuts him off. "I'll fill you in when we get there."

"See you in a bit."

Rion ends the call. "You're going to be okay, Ari."

"I figured as much. I haven't passed out yet or anything, and I'm not foaming at the mouth. It's just a bite." I'm not concerned. It doesn't even really hurt, which is odd. Shouldn't it hurt or burn or something? Maybe the little bit of vampire juice Ford gave me numbed it.

"It's not just a bite," Rion states harshly. "A wolf bit you. It's not something to joke about."

"I'm not! I know a wolf bit me! I was there! I would have handled him, too, if Ford hadn't shown up."

"What do you mean?"

"I was ready to kick his mangy butt. Ford teleported me away."

Rion turns briefly to me. "Never again, Ari. Don't ever try to confront one of them."

I cross my arms. "I will if I have to. They were chasing me. It wasn't the other way around. And I was alone. There was no way I was outrunning them."

"I understand that."

"No, I don't think you do. I had to run for my life through the woods. Again. I had to do what I needed to so I could defend myself. Although, now I have something else I can use."

"What do you mean?"

"I can teleport," I say with a wide smile. I'm pretty proud of my new skill. Not a skill yet. I still have to learn how to use it.

Rion's mouth hangs open for a moment then slams closed before opening again. "That vampire!" He smacks his hand hard on the steering wheel. I'm surprised he didn't break it right off the steering column.

"I'd think you'd be happy knowing I'll be able to take care of myself. I won't need Ford to visit my dreams."

"He bit you, Ariane! That vampire had his fangs in you!"

"I know. I was there." One of us has to stay level-headed. I should have known he'd react this way. A part of me thought he'd be happy I now have a way to get out of a bad situation. I won't have to depend on anyone to rescue me.

Rion hits the gas hard, accelerating the car to well over a hundred miles an hour. At least we're still on the highway. "Did he drink your blood, too?"

My hand instinctively flies to my neck where Ford's teeth sunk in. Thankfully, I don't feel any mark. "What? No! I wouldn't let that vampire suck on my neck."

"You let him bite you!"

"Not the same thing, Rion. One, I didn't know what he was doing until he did it. Two, it was for three seconds then it was over. He only shared his power with me. He wasn't getting his fill on my blood."

"So you didn't have any effects from his fangs being in you?"

"I didn't say that."

"I'm going to kill him," he growls.

I squirm in my seat, ignoring the pure hatred pouring off of Rion for Ford. The seat! I'm sitting on Rion's gorgeous leather seat and probably bleeding all over it.

Once I’m stitched up, I’ll try to clean it. This is so embarrassing. Rion’s car is gorgeous, and I'm sure I’m bleeding on the leather. Even with his shirt around my leg, blood has to be seeping through. Maybe if I shift to lean on my good leg, I’ll be able to keep my bloody one off the leather.

“Ari, please stop moving. The more you do, the more blood you'll lose. We don't have a blood bank like hospitals do. Wolves repeatedly shift to heal. Our bodies rapidly regenerate what is lost.”

“I’ll clean the car after I’m patched up.”

“You will not. I don’t care about the car. I care about you.” How could he not care about this car? It’s a work of art and worth more than some homes.

“What happens if I need blood?” I ask, trying to get my mind off of me ruining the Jag’s interior.

“You'll get mine.” Interesting. I wonder...

“Will I turn into a wolf if I get your blood?”

“No. You'll get nothing but blood.” Hey, it was worth a shot to ask. This goes in my mental paranormal manual as well.

I squirm again. My leg is starting to throb in pain. So much for the vampire juice numbing it. I hope we're almost there. I haven't been paying attention to the scenery, unless you count what's inside the car. I've been fixated on Rion's profile. It's like he's carved from stone. He's so perfect. And here I sit completely flawed. A mess, based on the look of Kiara as me. I have no idea what Rion sees in me.

“Sometimes I wonder how much of Lealla's series you retained,” he states, breaking through my thoughts.

“Hey!” I yell, grateful for something to get my mind off my insecurities. “Those books are long. I don't remember every word I read. Plus, it's not like she only has the one series. I'd have to have a photographic memory to retain all of that. And let's not forget all the other paranormal romance books out there. How am I supposed to know if any of those are real?"

"They aren't. Just stick to Lealla's."

"I will… While thinking about my shifter boyfriend the whole time." I give up on keeping the seat blood free and move to try to find a position that's not making the pain worse. It's ratcheting up with every mile we drive.

When we finally reach Lealla's mansion, there's a tall, ruggedly handsome man standing out front, waiting for us. Rion's headlights hit him just right, and I know instantly it's Desmond. I'm not going to pretend I don't find him attractive. Every one of the men on those book covers is gorgeous. Desmond, the pack's doctor, is no exception.

SEVENTEEN

DESMOND IS ONE OF THOSE PEOPLE who looks intimidating to the point I bet he'd make grown men wet their pants if they ever crossed him. Dark brown hair, full beard, and the size of a linebacker. He's beyond attractive.

He approaches the car as it comes to a stop and opens my door. Leaning down, he smiles warmly. "Ariane, I'm Desmond. I'm going to look at your wound and fix you up. Okay?"

I nod. He's still intimidating, even with his smile. Gorgeous but intimidating. I'm frozen in the seat. My legs won't work. Desmond is not a small man.

Rion shoulders him out of the way so that he can lift me from the car. My arms immediately go around his neck. Not out of fear of him dropping me, but for the comfort of the connection we share. I need it, especially with the way my leg sears in pain.

With every step he takes through the mansion, my nerves get worse. What if I need surgery? What if there is more damage than a simple bite? Maybe I should have gone to the hospital.

I'm brought into a bright room off the long corridor to the left of the entranceway. I remember going this way when we came for the party. All thcsc doors were closed. Now I know what's behind one of them.

There's a hospital bed covered in clean linens against the center of the far wall. Carts fully loaded with supplies are there if needed. Rion places me gently on the bed and rolls me so I'm lying on my good side with the back of my injured leg exposed.

"I'm going to cut the cloth, Ari. I have to look at the damage to your leg."

I wince as the cold scissors meet my skin. The pieces of the shirt fall away as does the pressure it was putting on my leg. Pain courses through me to the point that I squeeze my eyes shut and my hands ball into fists.

"The bite is pretty deep. I'm going to numb you so I can clean it and stitch you back together. Then I'm going to inject you with a serum I created, which will accelerate the healing. The last thing I want is for you to go home and have to explain to your parents why you have stitches across the back of your thigh."

"Does that mean I'll be able to heal fast forever?" I ask, trying to keep my mind off the pain. How amazing would it be, though? I'd have another superpower.

Desmond chuckles. "No, unfortunately not. It wears off as it works through your system. I have it here specifically for the human mates in our pack. If I use it in conjunction with an intravenous antibiotic, it rapidly heals any infection or wound."

I rest my head on the pillow. Rion comes around the bed and crouches down in front of me. "I'm sorry I couldn't protect you. I'll make sure this doesn't happen again."

"Orion," Desmond warns.

"Don't," he replies sharply. "One of them injured my mate. I'm not going to sit by and let them get away with it."

The door to the room opens and closes with a soft click. Lifting my head, I find Aries. He leans against the door, a formidable presence blocking anyone from leaving. In this case, my guess is Rion, who growls at his uncle.

"You may be my nephew, but I'm still the pack leader. You'll stay here with your mate." Aries must have known Rion would want to go after the other pack. This was only a premonition, though. They weren't really there. I'm too focused on the pain to say anything.

"I don't want you leaving to seek vengeance," Aries continues. "We're a pack, and we handle things as one."

Rion stands as Desmond injects me with a numbing agent. It burns pretty bad. I suck in a breath as it sears into my skin. Rion is back down before me, his hand holding mine as he whispers words of comfort. As quick as the pain appeared, it's gone, and my leg slowly starts to lose feeling around the wound.

Metal clangs behind me as Desmond tells me what he's doing before he does it. Rion remains a constant presence in front of me, though I suspect his mind is running through how he's going to find the one who hurt me. If there's one thing I remember with clarity about Lealla's series, wolves are very protective of their mates. No, we aren't officially mated, but Rion will want to get revenge on my behalf.

I'd rather he didn't. While I don't doubt his strength,

it's his experience that worries me. He's still young. Some of the others are hundreds of years old. With those years comes a world of knowledge and skills Rion doesn't possess yet. I can only hope Aries can talk some sense into him and keeps him from running into a situation he might not be able to fight his way out of. An entire pack could be waiting for him. And he's only one wolf.

"Interesting," Desmond mutters bchind mc.

"What?" Aries asks.

"The wolf who bit her lost one of his canines."

"Wow," I murmur. "Those leg lifts I do must be working. I have legs of steel." No one laughs. Here I am trying to make light of the situation, and it's not working.

"The wolf who bit her must have recently gotten into a fight to loosen that tooth. It wouldn't normally break off in the flesh," Aries states.

Rion stands. "It'll be easy to spot who bit Ari with a tooth missing."

"You won't find out. You're not going after them." I decide to keep quiet and let them have their conversation. Me inserting myself into it won't do any good.

"You're not going to tell me what to do. My mate was hurt!"

"I'll tell you exactly what to do. Remember your place. I'm your alpha."

"No, my dad was my alpha. No one will ever take his place." His hand finds mine again as he turns his back to Aries. In his eyes I see so much pain at the loss of his parents. It might have happened years ago, but he still carries that anger and hurt with him. The fact that I've been bitten by one of the same pack who killed his parents is brewing more hatred for that pack in Rion.

I always thought wolves heeded every command of

their alpha, but things seem different between Rion and Aries. There's respect, I've seen it. It's mutual. But Rion doesn't view Aries as anything other than family. From what I've read, wolves don't go against their alphas, ever. And right now, Rion's mind is probably racing with what he's going to do once I'm healed.

I can't blame him. If I had the strength he does, and the ability to shift into a predator, I'd be doing the same thing. I'm furious one of them bit me, but I'm human and defenseless. Well, except for my new ability to teleport.

There's going to be a learning curve, I'm sure. I might have to wear gloves so I don't accidentally teleport myself out of class one day. Or if I'm sitting at the dinner table and snap my fingers without thinking, disappearing in front of my parents' eyes. That wouldn't be good. I wonder if there's a way to prevent it if I snap and don't mean to.

"All done," Desmond says. That was fast. "I'm going to hook you up to an IV so I can give you antibiotics. Once that's done, I'll inject you with the healing accelerator. You should be ready to return home in a couple of hours. I need to make sure you're completely healed before you leave so I can remove the stitches."

"Couldn't you have done all this without the stitches?"

"No. While the accelerant works well, it won't mend a gaping wound. I need your skin back together for it to work. Also, this will minimize scarring. I'm hoping you won't have any scarring whatsoever, but that part isn't a sure bet. Sometimes, if the wound has been open too long, a minimal scar will remain."

No one in the room speaks as he gets the IV ready in my hand and the antibiotic slowly drips into my body. I would give just about anything right now for Ford to show up and break the tension. He'd probably rile the wolves up.

At least I wouldn't be bored out of my mind.

Aries and Rion spend the entire time staring each other down. Desmond stays on the other side of my bed to monitor the IV and the incision. I also think he's staying in here in case a fight breaks out.

Minutes tick by. Achingly slow minutes. The antibiotic finishes dripping into me, so Desmond removes the tube connecting me to the bag of medicine, but he leaves the port in and prepares to administer the accelerant.

"Your heart is going to race, and you're going to feel like you could run a marathon, but you can't get out of bed. You have to stay where you are. Don't be alarmed when we hold you down. It's for your own safety while the medication works to heal your body. It will burn through you fast. Probably in under five minutes. Your skin will mend and your heart will go back to a normal rhythm. Okay?" I nod, not at all looking forward to being held down. Although, there could be worse places to be than being pinned to a bed by hot wolf shifters.

"Orion, Aries, I want you two on either side of the bed. Each of you need to hold down one of her arms and one of her legs." They come up on either side of me. "Ari, I'm going to roll you to your back. Your leg might hurt a little when it touches the bed, but I promise in a few seconds, you won't feel the pain."

"Okay."

I'm not ready for this. How could I be? Shifters will be holding me to a bed after one from another pack bit me. This is all insane.

Desmond gently grasps the side of the thigh where the injury is and injects me with the accelerant. At first, I feel nothing. Then, it feels like a thousand horses are running through my body. My heart speeds up to the point that I swear it's going to pound out of my chest. My eyes widen, and it's as if I'm seeing everything with new eyes. There's a new clarity. I look at Rion and take in every little thing about him. The way his eyebrows are drawn together in concern. The little flecks of silver in his eyes that I've never noticed before. The tiny scar at his hairline, which almost blends perfectly with his skin.

His pulse, I feel it where he's holding my leg to the bed. His heart is beating in tandem with mine. Both racing, adrenaline coursing through us as our eyes meet again. I try to sit up, but I'm no match for those holding me to the bed.

"Let me up!" I yell. "I have to move. I have to run. I can't lie here any longer!" I've never felt anything like this in my life. Like, if I don't get out of this bed and burn off this energy, I'm going to self-combust. It's not a desire, it's a necessity. I bet I could run a marathon and not tire out. I'm like a lit fuse with no chance of ever exploding. It's all contained in me, flowing through my body never to be released.

"Her heart is beating too fast," Desmond says hurriedly. Though he sounds far away, his voice is slightly muffled.

"What did you do?" Rion asks with urgency in his tone. He's closer, his hands still on me.

"I didn't do anything but give her the same drug as I do to all the other mates when they need it."

"Ari, can you hear me?" Rion asks, panic lacing each word. He moves the hand holding my arm and smoothes my hair back from my face.

"Yes," I pant out, unable to slow my breathing. I'm not sure how he's so calm when I still feel his pulse.

"This should wear off in another minute," Desmond says. "Orion, is there anything you can do to calm her?

Something to distract her?"

Rion bends down, his face in front of mine. Instinctively, I lick my lips, my sole focus on his mouth. Oh, how I want to taste him again. To have him kiss me and get lost in his touch.

His lips press to mine as if he heard my silent plea. That's when I notice the normal electricity we have between us is absent. It wasn't there when he was holding me down either. Then again, my body is already high on the medication Desmond gave me. I try to lift my arms, but it's no use. Rion's hand is back to holding me down and Aries still has a solid grip on me. I want to touch Rion. I want to run my hands through his silky hair and pull him closer to me. I want him more than I've wanted anything in my entire life.

"Please," I whimper against his lips.

He releases the arm he's holding down, but Aries doesn't let up. I thread my fingers into Rion's hair to keep his lips pressed to mine.

"It's working," I vaguely hear Desmond say.

I'm not sure what he's talking about. I don't feel any different with Rion's lips on mine than I did before I was kissed. There's still the distinct feeling of tons of pent-up energy in me. Maybe it's my focus that's changed. It's Rion's lips and his taste that pull me away from the energy. The way he moans into my mouth. Oh how I wish Desmond and Aries would leave so I could be alone with my boyfriend.

EIGHTEEN

"ALL RIGHT, ORION, SHE'S GOOD. I need to check her wound," Desmond says.

Rion's lips stay on mine as our tongues continue to dance with one another. His sandalwood scent wrapping around me.

"Rion!" Aries yells. It's enough to snap me out my haze and release the grip I have on Rion. He pulls back, those mesmerizing eyes of emerald green on me, and growls deep in this throat.

Aries' hands lift from my leg and arm. "Calm down. We're good. Ari's okay now. Des needs to check her over." Rion doesn't move. His hands are planted on either side of my chest as he hovers over me. Somehow, he still has his feet on the floor.

Sliding over on the bed, I push myself closer to Aries and Desmond and then pat the bed next to me. It's Rion's turn to calm down, and I'm going to help him do so any way I can. He hesitates for a moment but then realizes I'm inviting him to lie beside me. His strong body climbs onto the bed, his eyes still only on mine. I roll to my side so I can face him while giving Desmond access to the back of my thigh.

"Good job, Ari. Keep it up," Desmond whispers. I can feel the slight tugging of my skin. He must be removing the stitches.

The effects of the drug are wearing off quickly. Where I was ready to run before and burn off this energy, I feel like a deflated balloon now. Tired—exhausted—wanting to do nothing other than rest my head on Rion's chest and go to sleep for many hours.

"You healed perfectly, Ari," Desmond says. "Not even a scar." He stands, hooking me back up to the IV. "I'm going to give you some fluids now. It might make you a little cold as it starts to go into your bloodstream. I'll get some blankets."

He returns a minute later with two white blankets and tries to drape them over me, but Rion sits up and takes them. He carefully puts them on me.

"Orion, Aries and I are going to leave you two alone for a bit. Ari needs to rest though. Ari, we'll be right outside if you need anything."

"Thank you," I whisper but don't take my eyes off Rion. His wolf is still front and center, demanding his turn to look over me.

The lights dim, and the door to the room clicks closed. Rion's green eyes still shine brightly. Gently, I run my hand with the IV in it through his hair and down so I can cup his cheek. He takes my hand in his and presses it against his chest. Our hearts still beat in tandem.

"I'm okay," I say quietly. "I'm healed. Good as new."

He releases my hand to run his over my hip and down the back of my thigh. He's making sure I'm healed. While he's doing it out of concern, he's lighting a fire in me which no guy has ever lit before. He slowly runs his fingers over my leg, caressing me as his eyes change from green to crystal blue. I breathe a sigh of relief. I was able to appease his wolf, show him I'm all right.

"Are you okay?" I ask. The last thing I want is him running from the room to go after Desmond or Aries—or worse yet—the wolf who bit me.

"I am now that I know you're healed."

"Are you still planning on going after the wolf who attacked me?"

"You're my mate, Ariane," he says quietly, with none of the anger he had earlier. "I won't sit by while he, whoever he is, gets away with attacking you."

"But it was in a premonition."

"That may be, but his bite was very real. We have the tooth to prove it. "

"Well, maybe he didn't lose it in real life. Maybe a future version did." We could really use Ford right now to explain this to us.

And just like that, he appears. I don't even jump this time when I see him. Rion's hand grips my hip tighter, but I hold his eyes, silently trying to tell him not to start anything.

"Can you read my mind?" I ask Ford.

"No," I can hear the smile in his voice. "I wanted to

check on you. Oh, and also tell you that Kiara is a convincing version of you. Your dad is up, but she's pretending to be asleep."

"Please thank her for me. I'm healed but exhausted. I'll be home soon."

"You're going to need me to take you."

"That I am."

Rion breaks our eye contact and sits up. "Can I ask you a question?"

"If you want to play a round of who can bite who first, we better take it outside. I don't want to get yelled at by Lealla."

"No, it's about Ari. Her premonitions, to be exact. How real are they?"

"Ari was bit in her dream state and showed up here with blood running down her leg. I'd say that's pretty real."

"I've gathered that much," Rion says dryly. "A tooth was found in her wound. Would the wolf who bit her be missing a tooth right now, if I found him?"

"Interesting question." He taps his cleanly shaven chin as he thinks about it. "I'm going to go with no and here's why. That wolf doesn't know anything about the dream he was in of Ari's. He wasn't there nor was he dreaming the same dream. For instance, Ari, has Rion been in any of your dreams?"

"I think he was there last night. A black wolf took out one of the wolves who was chasing me."

"I did?" he asks, shocked.

"Yeah, at least I think it was you. I'm not sure who else is a black wolf that would come so quickly to my defense." Though, it's not like I know the color of every other wolf in Avynwood Pack either. "You came in from the sidelines and slammed into him. Of course, a bunch of others were still chasing me, but that was one less I had to worry about."

"Rion, did you sleep at all while you were guarding her house?" Ford inquires.

"No, I was alert the whole time."

"Then my theory is proven. That wolf still has his tooth. While Ari returned with it in her thigh, and a very real wound, she is the only one with a memory of it. And me of course, but I didn't see her get bit. I came in, grabbed her, and got out of there."

"That reminds me," Rion murmurs and gets out of bed. He slowly rounds the bottom where my feet are to get closer to Ford. His voice drops into a thick, menacing snarl. "Did you bite Ariane earlier?"

"Yes. She needs to be able to protect herself in the premonitions, in case I can't get to her fast enough. You should be a happy wolf." He pats Rion on the shoulder and my whole body tenses. "She has a new way to help her survive."

Rion's arm whips out, and in an instant, he has Ford against the wall by the throat, a good foot from the ground. "Don't you ever sink your teeth into her again. If I hear you drank from her, I will end your life. You won't be able to teleport far enough away where I can't get to you."

The door to the room flies open, almost hitting Rion in the back. Aries and Desmond are about to pull Ford and Rion apart. I clear my throat and both heads swing to me while Rion continues to hold Ford against the wall. Shaking my head, I tell them silently not to intervene. Ford and Rion need to work this out between them or it's never going to stop. Aries nods and closes the door after they leave.

"You know," Ford chokes out in a raspy voice. "You

can't kill me this way. I'm the undead, remember? Unless you're pocketing a silver stake, this does nothing. I'll heal from anything else in a matter of seconds."

"We're in a mansion full of wolves. How much do you want to bet there are at least twelve pure silver stakes in this house? I can have one in my hand in seconds. All I have to do is ask."

"Furthermore," Ford continues, as if Rion didn't say anything. Bringing his foot up, he plants it on Rion's abdomen then shoves him away. "I'm stronger than you. And one snap of my fingers will have me teleporting both of us to the top of a mountain, where I will leave you to freeze to death."

For the love of… I jump off the bed a little too fast, gripping the IV pole, and sway on my feet. Rion is by my side, holding me up. "I'm okay. Just a little tired." I grip his shoulders to steady myself as the room slowly stops spinning. "As I was about to say, you two need to knock it off. Did you ever think that if you worked together, you'd both be helping me? All you're doing now is fighting with each other, and no one in this room is the enemy. The other pack is. Can we get on the same page, please? Yes, Ford bit me, but in doing so, he gave me the power to teleport. That's not a bad deal." Ford gets all cocky and smiles wide. "As for you," I say pointing to him, "next time you think about biting me, maybe ask first before gifting me with one of your abilities."

"That I can do."

"Fantastic. Can you please tell Kiara I'll be there in a few hours? I need to sleep. I'd rather do it here, without having to worry about my mom coming in and thinking I'm sick or something. Tell Kiara if that happens, just to mumble to Mom something about staying up late reading. That's a common occurrence with me. She'll buy it and let her sleep a while longer."

"Deal, but I'm going to pick you up after school tomorrow. We have practicing to do. And no snapping at all until then." I hope I don't need to snap for some reason. What if there is a situation that requires snapping? Ford snorts with a laugh. "What kind of situation requires snapping?" he asks, reading my thoughts.

"You never know. And get out of my head!"

"Not going to happen." He winks and teleports away.

"Bed," I mumble to Rion. He gently helps me back to the hospital bed and crawls in beside me. I quirk an eyebrow at him.

"You let me lie here before."

"Yes, because if I didn't, I was afraid you were going to shift and attack Desmond or Aries." He moves to stand, but at the last second, I grip his shirt and pull him back down. "I changed my mind. I don't want to be in here by myself."

"As long as there is air in my lungs, you will never be alone." If I weren't so exhausted, I'd let out a breathy sigh at how sweet he is. But I am tired and need sleep. I'm also grateful he's not talking to me about what just happened with Ford.

A chill works its way up my spine and down my arms, causing goosebumps to break out. Rion reaches toward the foot of the bed and pulls up the blankets that were covering me before Ford popped in.

"You should sleep, too," I say while yawning. "We're in a mansion surrounded by wolves. No one is going to attack us here."

"I'll agree to sleep if you agree to stop talking so you can rest, too."

"Works for me."

My eyes flutter closed. Rion's hand finds mine and our connection flares to life once again. When it calms to a low hum, I finally float off to sleep.

Voices drift to me, rousing me from a deep sleep. "What's going on?" I ask sleepily.

"Ford's outside the door. We need to get you home. Your mom has been in your room twice, and Kiara isn't sure how much longer she can stall her," Desmond states.

That wakes me up fast. Sitting up, I'm grateful the room doesn't spin this time. I toss the blankets aside and again curse myself for not putting on pants. My shirt is covered in blood from where I touched my leg and smeared it on the shirt, or from when Rion held me after wrapping his shirt around my leg. Desmond hands me a shirt that looks similar, but not exact to the one I'm wearing. It's an oversized unisex shirt. It'll work.

I quirk an eyebrow at Desmond and Rion. Both turn around so I can change without their eyes on me. Quickly, I slip out of my ruined shirt and into the one Desmond handed me. It smells of the woods and crisp mountain air.

"All right, I'm good."

Both men turn back around. Rion moves to stand before me. I give him a quick kiss. Any more than that and I'd be lost in him. There's no time for that. I need to get home.

"Come visit me tonight after eleven," I say. "I'll sneak out to see you quick before I go to sleep."

"Sounds good, little mouse."

Ford opens the door to the room, obviously not caring if he's wanted or not. "Let's put a move on it, princess." I roll my eyes.

Rion clenches his jaw, but I don't have time to reassure him that I'll be fine. Ford is by my side and teleporting me back home before I even have a chance to thank Desmond.

NINETEEN

WHO KNEW ONE DAY I'D LOOK forward to going to school? Sure, I get tons of looks now that people have seen Rion pick me up in his super expensive car. There is something nice about normal, though. My weekend was anything but.

After Ford brought me home from the mansion, I was still exhausted. At least I showed my face at breakfast then crawled into bed for a few hours. Later that night, I met Rion outside for a little bit, but I was still tired and crashed not long after coming inside.

Paige picked me up this morning, immediately asking for the details of every moment I spent with Rion. There was no way that was happening. I did tell her we had dinner with Lealla, though. I had to give her something. Sure, she was upset about not being invited, although she calmed a bit when I said Lealla is his neighbor and they're close. I didn't bring up all of the other wolves I met. Unfortunately, I didn't get to meet any more of the mates during my time at the mansion. Not all the mates are shifters, though. Some are human.

I'd love to be able to talk to Paige about all of this. It would be a relief to get it off my chest and get someone else's perspective. Someone that isn't immersed in the world of paranormals.

At the end of the school day, I gather my belongings and head for the front of the school. Guys have been asking me out since Rion showed up. Like I'd dump Rion for any of them. Fools. I've lost count how many I've turned down. It's getting ridiculous. No one was interested in me until they saw someone as gorgeous as him show up. They think they're missing out on something amazing with me. Ha! If they only knew. They'd pee themselves and go running to Mommy at half the stuff I now know.

There's a deep pit of dread in my stomach. Ford will no doubt be outside the school. While I'm excited about exploring my new power, the rumors that are going to fly at seeing him with me will be insane. I'll probably be called a slut for having two men after me. Back to being picked on, I guess.

I open the front door and walk smack into a mob of girls. There can only be one reason why. I have to shove through them to get to the front of the crowd. Ford is sitting on the hood of a grey Mercedes SUV, which I can only imagine cost more than every car in the parking lot. Girls are drooling all over him and his SUV.

"Princess!" he calls out when he sees me. He lifts his

stylish sunglasses to reveal grey eyes, which match the paint on his vehicle. He's wearing his black leather trench, even though it's warm enough today that no coat is needed. His boot laces aren't done all the way up and his jeans are bunched at the top of them. His hair has this sexy, messy thing going on. Oh, he's attractive, that's for sure. But not as attractive as my wolf.

Hopping down from the hood, he stalks toward me like the predator he is. "Are you ready to have some fun?" he asks, smiling. Wicked vampire. He knows what he's doing. All the girls around us let out a breathy sigh in unison. I wonder what they think when they see me with these guys. I'm nothing special in my faded black T-shirt and jeans.

I'm about to answer Ford when a familiar black Jag pulls up in front of the Mercedes. Rion is out of the car and immediately walking toward me. This should be fun.

"Have you come to join us?" Ford asks.

"If you thought you were going to do anything with Ari today without me, you're wrong. Nice try on the flat tire, though. Maybe next time you'll remember we have an in-house mechanic, who can patch stuff like that up rather quickly."

Ford puts his hand to his chest in mock astonishment. "I'm appalled you think I would do such a thing." I quirk an eyebrow at him, causing him to drop the façade. "Okay, fine, I admit it, but I don't regret it." He leans in close so only we can hear him. "This attention I'm getting isn't so bad."

I roll my eyes. "Can we please go?" All the people surrounding us are making me uncomfortable. I don't miss the whispers about a fight possibly breaking out. If they only knew what would happen if it did. None of them would ever be the same.

Rion's arm wraps around my waist. "Ari will be with me."

"Fine by me," Ford replies. "We're going to her house. She needs a familiar place to practice."

Ford spins on his heel and faces at least a dozen admiring girls. I'm more than ready to get away from this circus. Rion's hand finds mine and our connection flares to life. We walk to his car where he opens the door for me.

"Hi," he says, with his crystal blue eyes holding mine.

"Hi," I whisper back.

He dips his head to brush his lips against mine. As quickly as they're on me, they're gone. What I wouldn't give to have extended that kiss. Then I remember where I am, and the fact that I don't want to give the mean people of my high school more ammunition about me. It's bad enough Ford will be talked about all day tomorrow. How I not only have one hot man but two.

I'm glad I'll be graduating soon. Had this been any other year, I would have begged my mom to homeschool me. Maybe tomorrow Cace, Cash, and Carter will show up and make the entire school think I'm getting it on with a whole group of men.

After two hours of practicing teleportation, I'm exhausted. It's also far easier than I imagined it would be. Ford said it gets trickier when I've never been to the place I'm going, but jumping from one spot to another place I've previously visited is simple. All I have to do is visualize my destination and snap. Nothing to it.

He did have me teleport to places I've never been to so he could see if I could do it. Of course, he held on to me every time, in case wherever I landed wasn't good and he had to get us out of there fast.

There has to be a strong desire to find a location you've never seen before. For instance, Ford's house. I've never been there and have no clue what it looks like, but the nosy part of me wanted to see if he lived in some palatial estate or a dark house in the middle of nowhere. To my surprise, it's a three-story, oceanfront home in Duck, North Carolina. I doubt anyone in the Outer Banks realizes there's a vampire living amongst them. Who would have thought it would be the location he'd choose to live? A vampire. On the beach. It's a good thing he can be out in the sun without worrying about burning up. That's another myth. Vampires can easily be out in the sun with no ill effects.

While I've never been to Ford's house, I have been to the Outer Banks countless times. It wasn't hard to imagine the scenery, but his specific house was difficult. I had to mix what I knew of the area with what Ford told me about the home. I still say it's sheer luck I ended up in his kitchen.

I'm also fortunate no one saw us as I was teleporting all over the place. He had me picture places I've never been that were most likely empty, like his house. Or deep in a national park.

All in all, I had a fun afternoon learning my new power—my only power. Well, except for Rion being miserable. I hate seeing him unhappy. Every time Ford and I disappeared, he growled. Or when Ford held my waist. Or told me to teleport to his home on the beach. I think Rion growled pretty much the entire time. There were countless times his eyes flashed green. I had to keep reminding him it was for the greater good. If I can master it, then I can escape my premonitions while I sleep. No more wolf bites. That calmed him a little, though not enough.

Ford and Rion both left twenty minutes before my mom got home. I have no doubt Rion ran back to my house in wolf form to watch over me.

Paige texts me as we're sitting down to dinner. I get the stern look from my dad, reminding me no phones at the table. I'm sure she heard about Ford showing up at school today and the almost fight between him and Rion. If only they knew we weren't close to a fight. At least Ford wasn't egging Rion on too bad this time.

I eat fast and go up to my room, saying I have more homework to do, when in fact, I want to read Paige's text.

Paige: Who's this?

She attaches a picture of me standing between Ford and Rion, who is at my back. Of course someone from school took a picture and posted it on social media.

Me: That's Ford. He's a friend of Rion's.

Paige: Two things. One, I'm not liking this whole other life you have outside of me. We need to fix that. Two, to make it up to me, you're going to introduce me to Ford tomorrow. I'm going to drive you home after school. Not your boyfriend or your new boy toy. Your best friend. I want details, and I want to meet Ford. I'm feeling neglected over here.

Me: Fine by me.

There's no way I can get out of it. Paige is very persistent when she wants to be. I'll have to find Ford tonight and ask him to come to the house tomorrow. If I can't appease Paige, she won't drop it. Then, there is no chance of me being able to practice teleporting more. I can't do any of that with her here.

Paige: I'm glad you agreed. I was prepared to use persuasive tactics.

Me: I'm sure you were.

Paige: Bray is coming, too. He's been asking about you and was none too happy to hear you left school with two guys today.

Me: Since when did he become so protective of me?

Paige: Ever since he and every other guy at school finally realized how hot my best friend is.

Me: Oh, please.

Paige: I only speak the truth, my friend.

Me: I don't believe you. Bray has never had a thing for me.

Paige: Whatever. He's our best friend and he cares about you as much as I do. Tomorrow. Me, you, Bray, and this hot Ford guy. We'll all meet so we can stop worrying about you.

Me: You aren't worrying.

Paige: Worrying, jealous, same thing.

I laugh and toss the phone onto my bed. It's time to dig in to my homework. I've got a mountain of it and got nothing done this afternoon, thanks to all the teleporting. If Ford doesn't pop by tonight, I'll pay him an unexpected visit. I'll leave a note on the counter or something. Now that I've been in his house, I can visit him whenever I want. Time to drive him as crazy as he drives me with all of his popping up unexpectedly business.

TWENTY

FORD IS IN MY DRIVEWAY, WAITING for us, when Paige pulls up the next day after school. She turns to me. "How many friends do you have that are exceptionally wealthy?"

I laugh. "This question coming from you is funny."

"You don't see me driving around in a car that costs well over a hundred grand."

I level her with a glare. "You would if your parents would give you one." Money hasn't been a concern for Paige and her family for a long time.

"That's so not the point," she says and flips her hair over her shoulder. She's out of the car before I can respond.

We walk up to Ford, who is standing next to his Mercedes AMG G 65 SUV with a little yellow sticky note in his hand. He holds it up in front of my face. "I can't believe you left me a note."

I smile. "I don't have your phone number. I couldn't exactly text you."

He reaches into my bag without asking and plucks out my phone. After gesturing for me to unlock it, he quickly types in his contact information. It's then I take him in. He's wearing the same thing he always does. His closet must be rack after rack of the same T-shirt and jeans.

"Don't like me paying you surprise visits?" I grin. I was in and out of his house in seconds. Luckily, he wasn't downstairs when I got there. I smacked that little yellow sticky note on the front of his microwave and left.

"Don't make me regret—" he pauses, finally noticing Paige standing next to me, "being your friend," he finishes. I have to hold back a laugh. He turns his attention to Paige. "And who might you be?" he asks in an overly friendly, *hey, I just noticed your hot friend*, kind of way.

"Paige, Ari's best friend," she says and offers her hand, which he gladly takes and presses a kiss to the back of it. She tries hard not to blush, but I know her. Her lips are parted, and she's breathing a little harder than normal. She's definitely affected by him and his good looks.

"Do you have a last name?" he asks.

"Yes, but you haven't earned more information about me yet."

"Feisty. I like it."

"Don't," I interject.

He faces me. "What?" The last thing I need is for Ford to get his hands on Paige and screw her over. I'd have to deal with the aftermath, not him. Since he seems to be a permanent fixture in my life, at least for the time being, I can't have anything bad happen between my friends. Did I just call Ford my friend? He smiles. I level him with a glare. He needs to stop reading my mind.

"The wheels are turning, princess. Care to fill us in?" Freaking vampire and his need to make me miserable.

I'm about to open my mouth when another car pulls up. Saved by the Jag. And then another car—an older Volkswagen Passat. Brayden. He overslept this morning and drove himself to school instead of riding with Paige and me.

Rion greets me with a quick kiss and a knee-weakening smile. Bray steps up next to us.

"Did you see what your girlfriend left me?" Ford asks Rion as he holds up the sticky note. I'm going to kill him.

"Are you serious right now?" I ask incredulously. "You're being childish." He sticks out his tongue. "I give up."

Rion winds his arms around my waist to bring me in close. Those eyes of his feel like they're staring into my soul. He brushes my hair aside to whisper, "No visiting a vampire's house without me, little mouse." His breath tickles, causing a thousand goosebumps to break out over my skin. Before pulling back, he places a kiss just below my ear. My knees finally say screw it and I go lax in Rion's arms. It's a good thing he's holding me up.

Brayden clears his throat behind us, officially snapping me back to reality. "Care to introduce us?"

"Ari doesn't need to," Ford replies before I can. "I'm Ford, a friend of Ariane's and Orion's." He shakes Bray's hand.

"I'm assuming you live close by, if she was able to leave you a note." Bray states. Uhhh...

Ford is quicker on his feet. "She left it on the window

of my SUV yesterday. She must have seen me at the coffee place in town."

Quickly, I add, "I ran out last night to grab something at the grocery store and saw his SUV parked along the street. I stopped and left him a note, since you said you wanted to meet him." Paige nods and I'm grateful I made that up so fast.

Somehow, and I'm not exactly sure how, Rion and Ford play well with one another for the next half hour. We stand in the driveway and talk. Paige grills them both, and they handle each question with lies that easily roll off their tongues. That's not to say there was no truth with what they said. They sprinkled a little in here and there—but for the most part—lies.

I don't invite anyone inside. I have a feeling if I do, Ford will never leave. I swear he feeds off of irritating Rion. I kick both of them out of my driveway long before my parents are due home. I want to spend time with Paige and Bray.

Paige throws herself down on the couch. "I'm going to need you to get me a date with Ford."

The jealous side of Brayden appears on cue. "You can't be serious?"

She ignores him. "Please, Ari. There's something so sexy about him. He's not like the guys our age." I snort but quickly cover it up by going to the kitchen to rummage for something to eat. If Paige only knew how old he really is. Or what he really is for that matter. I grab a couple of things and go back to the living room.

Placing two bags of chips on the coffee table with a few bottles of water, I turn to Paige. "I'm not going to ask him out for you."

"Why?" She pouts. Then it's like a light bulb goes off in her head. Her eyes widen; she smiles. "It's because you want him for yourself."

I bark out a laugh. "You've seen Rion. Why on earth would I want Ford?" Not that Ford isn't attractive. He truly is. But he's not Rion.

"I'm not sure what's going on with you, Ari, but you have both of them wrapped around your finger. The whole time we were out there, they each stood on either side of you, like they were guarding you. From what, I don't know." Were they doing that? Rion does stand like that, always. But Ford? Paige taps her finger on her chin as she watches me. "What am I missing? There's something you're not telling us."

I sit next to her on the couch. "Nothing. I'm dating Rion. Ford is a friend. That's it." I take a sip of water.

"Go out with me, Paige," Bray states. The water in my mouth sprays out across the living room. Did he just ask what I think he did? I couldn't have heard him right. He glares at me.

"Good one," Paige says with a light laugh.

"I'm serious."

She focuses on him. "Bray, we've been over this. We're friends, that's all. I'm sorry that I don't see you any other way." At least she softened her tone for the apology. I do think she's genuine. She's never seen Bray as more, and I doubt she ever will.

He stands. "I've gotta go. Homework. Dinner."

"Brayden, stay," I tell him.

"Sorry, Ari. I only came by because I wanted to make sure you're all right. I can see you are. I doubt anyone would screw with you while you have those two by your side. I miss us all hanging out, but I get it. I'll see you in school tomorrow."

Paige doesn't utter a word until the door shuts behind him. "What am I supposed to do?" She frowns.

"He's liked you for a long time."

"I see that now, but I don't feel the same. And I can't force myself. I'm trying to be honest with him."

"I know. Give him time." There's not much more for me to say. Bray has always loved Paige. At least she sees it and is trying to cut him off before he gets his hopes up. I'm surprised he finally asked her out. Maybe with us graduating soon, and college around the corner, he felt like he had nothing to lose.

Paige stays for dinner, which makes my parents happy. They don't mind me spending time with Rion, but I notice their relief at me hanging out with Paige.

Darkness has settled over our small town by the time I walk her out. My parents are already in bed. Paige and I stayed up a while talking. I wonder if Orion is out here somewhere, shrouded by the trees.

Thankfully, there is a light over the garage that comes on when it detects motion, lighting our way. We walk around Paige's car and stop in our tracks. There's a massive, pure white wolf sitting beside her driver's side door. Paige backs up and opens her mouth to scream, but I quickly clamp my hand over her lips. I don't want to alert my parents to something going on out here.

The wolf isn't growling or snarling. Its ears are up but not forward. No teeth are showing. If anything, it looks calm but curious. I motion with my head to the back of the house where it's darker. Out front, there are lights and nosy neighbors. I don't want to have to explain to anyone why there is a wolf sitting in my driveway or have them ask my parents if we got a new dog. I'm so not good at lying on demand.

The wolf pads around us to stride ahead. I'm not sure if I'm walking into a trap, but I keep my arm around Paige. I whisper in her ear to be quiet and to trust me. If anything happens, I'm teleporting us out of here. However, I need to be holding her in some way to bring her with me. At least I'm not defenseless anymore.

The wolf walks to the edge of the trees in my backyard, while Paige and I stay close to the house. Her body trembles against my side.

I focus on the wolf. "If you expect me to speak to you, I'm going to need you to shift."

Paige turns to me. "What are you talking about, Ari?"

"I told you to trust me," I whisper.

This wolf is going to shift in front of us, and Paige is going to lose it like I did when I first saw Rion change. I have no clue how I'm going to calm her down enough to figure out what this wolf wants.

The wolf transforms before us in the blink of an eye. What once was snowy white fur is now a guy who appears to be around our age with dark hair and dark eyes. It's hard to tell the exact color.

He steps forward. With the moon still bright, I notice he's wearing a white T-shirt under a waist length, dark leather jacket. What is it with these paranormals and leather? He takes another step toward us.

"Don't come any closer," I warn.

Paige goes limp in my arm. I can't hold her up. She slides to the grass at my feet. So much for having to explain shifters to her at the moment. Fainting was not what I expected, however.

"Who are you?" I ask as I crouch down by Paige. I need to keep a hand on her just in case I need to teleport.

"My name is Wake."

"Wake isn't a name. It's what you do in the morning."

He chuckles. "I can see why Orion likes you."

"You know him?"

"Knew is more accurate." So this is someone who used to be friends with him. Rion hasn't mentioned his name to me before. In fact, I haven't heard it in any of Lealla's books, which leads me to believe Wake isn't one of the Avynwood Pack.

"Why are you here?"

He steps closer. "I've come to warn you."

"One more step and I'm out of here."

He cocks his head to the side. "So, it's true then. You've acquired powers."

"Listen, Snooze, I don't know who you are or why you're here, but rest assured, I can be gone and back with a whole lot of hurt in under five seconds." Which reminds me… Where is Orion?

Paige stirs. I help her sit up and gently rub her back before moving my hand to her shoulder. Peering up, she looks from me to Wake and back again. My focus returns to Wake now that I know Paige is okay.

"I'm a watcher, Ariane."

"A what?"

"As you've probably figured out, I'm not a part of Orion's pack. I'm in Diaminsey. I'm one of their dream watchers. I have premonitions in my sleep and have to stay observant so I can report what I see back to my alpha." He's in the pack that's chasing me when I sleep. The pack who killed Rion's parents. I have to stay calm. Wake hasn't tried to harm me…yet. He's the same as me, though. He dreams as I do.

"I'm not sure what any of that has to do with me. Whatever you're selling, take it somewhere else."

"They're coming, Ariane—the whole pack—and they're after you."

My eyes narrow. "Why should I believe you?"

"Because if my alpha knew I was here, he'd slit my throat." He has a point. I doubt the alpha of his pack would be happy about him warning me. Then again, this could be a game he's playing under the direction of his alpha. I'm not sure what to believe.

"When are they coming?"

"I don't know. They're preparing for a war. Training night and day. They won't come until they know they have every angle covered. Every paranormal they can get on their side. And you in a vulnerable state." I have no clue why the shifters are so focused on me. I'm supposed to be the catalyst, but why? How? Each day I get some of my questions answered only to have new ones.

"I'm no threat to them."

"You're a game changer."

"I'm an eighteen-year-old girl in high school." This is ridiculous. I'm one person. How can I be a threat to an entire pack?

"You're a human with powers."

"And? You're a human who shifts into a wolf. I fail to see your point."

"You have a friend who's a vampire and a mate who's a wolf. You're already part of a pack. Every paranormal who meets you is helpless to your charms."

TWENTY-ONE

"I HAVE NO CHARMS. I'M BORING. I like to read. There is nothing fun or exciting about me."

"You have premonitions when you sleep."

I release Paige and stumble back, landing on my butt. She's stayed quiet throughout our conversation. I can only imagine what she's going to say when we're alone. "How did you...? I haven't told anyone."

"We share premonitions." Here we go. It's like talking to Rion and only getting partial information.

Standing, I brush grass off of myself. "Huh?" What's going on here? I swear every day and night something else is thrown at me, making me question the world as I know it.

"You're a dream watcher, too. Every pack has at least

one—a person who can do as we do."

"The Avynwood Pack isn't new. They probably already have a watcher or whatever it is you call it."

He shakes his head. "They were without one. Lealla tries her best with her abilities, but they aren't the same as ours."

"So I'm the watcher for the Avynwood Pack, yet I'm not part of the pack? I'm a human. I don't know how many times I have to say this to everyone. I'm no one special." How is it I'm the only one who sees how dull and boring I am? I fly well under the radar. That is, until I met Lealla.

"You have a shifter mate, Ariane. You're part of the pack, whether you think so or not."

"Every day my life gets more and more confusing," I mutter. Ford appears at my side, causing me to jump. "Do you always have to land right next to me?" I yell. "There's an entire yard here and you pop in practically touching me."

He ignores my question. "Princess," he greets as his eyes focus on Wake. "You didn't invite me to the party? I'm a little hurt. Wake, I haven't seen you in years. I heard you found a new pack." I don't miss the bite in his tone.

"Ford," Wake nods.

"Say what you came to say fast. Orion is hot on your scent."

"Ariane," Wake begins. "I'm in the premonitions with you but not in the same area. Run toward me. I'll howl next time I'm in one. Follow my call. I want you to pull me out of the premonition with you. Bring me to Ford's house. It will give us more time to talk."

My eyes narrow. "Why should I trust you?" I don't know him at all, and he's asking me to take him to Ford's house? My life is like a bizarre movie that keeps me guessing up until the very end. I'm that confused person sitting in the back row of the theater, wondering if it will ever make sense.

"Ask Ford." His head whips to the side. "I've gotta go." He shifts back into a white wolf and runs into the night. Seconds later, Orion tears past us at a fast clip, right on Wake's trail.

"Let's get Paige and you inside," Ford says. "You can try to teleport all of us. It will be another lesson for you."

"Seriously? You want me to learn now?"

"No better time than the present."

Nothing like a nighttime lesson in teleportation. My parents could walk out here at any moment and see me standing in the yard with Paige all wide-eyed, like she's seen a ghost, and some random guy next to her. That won't look suspicious at all.

Ford wraps an arm around Paige's waist and places his other hand in mine. With him holding Paige, and me holding on to him, I can teleport them both. Visualizing my bedroom, I snap my fingers and we're standing in my room in under a second.

Walking to the bed, Ford gently helps Paige sit. She still hasn't spoken a word, which is very unlike her.

I have to focus on Ford at the moment and what happened outside. "What was all of that? What's going on?" I hiss. I want to yell at Ford but can't. The last thing I need is to wake my parents.

"We only have a few minutes before your boyfriend is back, calling for you. What I'm going to tell you, it's something he should say, but I fear he won't and you need to know. Wake and you are dream watchers."

"Thanks, I knew that."

"Most packs have a watcher who has premonitions and lets the alpha know if danger is coming. Or if someone will be hurt. Or if they're getting a new member. It's not always horrible, end of the world stuff. The Avynwood Pack used to have one—Wake. He's Aries and Cassandra's son." I gasp. Their son? I had no idea. It wasn't in any book. No mention of him at all. I would have remembered that name. And Rion never mentioned him.

"Why isn't he still in the pack?"

"Because he and Sevan both pursued the same mate. They both felt the mate connection with her. None of this made the book, by the way." I remember Sevan's book. It was the last one released and really good. I loved him and Dalia together.

Ford continues, "In the end, her connection with Sevan was the true one. She didn't have sparks, or whatever you mates feel when you touch one another, with Wake. But he wouldn't stop. He insisted she was his mate. It wasn't good. Even under Aries' command, Wake wouldn't quit. He became violent with the other males. Lashed out at Aries and Orion. No one could reason with him. The whole pack was in a flux. Wolves thrive on the bond with their pack and mates. When one is disrupting the whole unit…" he shakes his head. "As the alpha, Aries has to make tough calls. The pack is his responsibility. When it came down to it, he knew Sevan and Dalia were mates. Aries had no choice but to remove Wake from the pack. It was best for the pack. Wake was angry. He wanted to get back at Aries for taking Sevan's side. So Wake did the one thing he knew would anger his father above anything else—he joined the Diaminsey Pack."

"Holy..."

"Yeah, so you can imagine how Orion felt picking up Wake's scent near you. It's not good. He'll see Wake as coming after his mate."

"He wasn't. He was only talking to me. I think he wanted to help."

"I know, but Orion won't see it that way. Wake wasn't angry just now. He seems to have calmed quite a bit since leaving the pack years ago. He appears more level-headed. I doubt he and Orion will ever be close again, though. Before everything happened with Sevan and Dalia, they were more than cousins. They grew up together and were best friends. Orion and Aries received a lot of hate from Wake when everything was going down. It wasn't good, nor do I think it's something they'll easily be able to put in the past." This is a lot to take in. It gives me a glimpse into Rion's past I wasn't aware of.

"People change, Ford. They grow up, mature. There might be a way to salvage their relationship if Wake has changed."

"People maybe, but these are wolves, Ari. They act on pure instinct. Yes, they're human, too, but they are their wolves. They are one and the same. Once Dalia and Sevan were officially mated, Wake should have let it go. But he didn't. Had Aries not been his father, I'm sure Sevan and Wake would have fought to the death." I can't believe all I'm hearing. I'm living in a wolf version of a soap opera.

"Did Wake feel the spark with Dalia?" I ask.

"He said he did, but she didn't reciprocate. You can't force someone to be your mate. Both have to go into it willingly and accept the other." Makes sense. No one should be forced into a relationship they don't want.

I pace around the room, letting everything I've learned

tonight sink in. Wake came to warn me. He wants to help. Should I do as he said? The next time I have a premonition, follow his call and go to him?

"Do you trust him?" I ask Ford.

"I have no reason not to. Sure, he was kicked out of the Avynwood Pack. However, I'm not a wolf. He never did anything to me. Yes, he hurt my friends, but he felt the mate connection with Dalia. I can't fault him for fighting for whom he thought was his."

"You have a point," I say while tapping my finger against my chin.

"Of course I do." He grins.

"You're really cocky, you know that?"

"It's part of my charm."

"Do I take him to your house next time I have a premonition?"

He shrugs. "I can't tell you what to do, princess. You have to go with your gut. But I'll make sure to be home every night, just in case. You can teleport. I don't have to dream walk to make sure you're okay. You've been to my home. It will be an easy jump for you to make. If you want more answers, then maybe talking to him is a good idea."

"He could be setting me up."

"At my house? In the presence of a vampire who has age and skill over him? If he were going to hurt you, he would have done it tonight. You need to remember that you have a power he doesn't. That allows you to teleport anywhere. Even if he tries to trick you, drop him in the Avynwood mansion. That'll teach him." Wouldn't that be interesting? Wake isn't only asking me to trust him. He's trusting me in return. I could teleport him anywhere in the world. I could drop him in front of Rion or the entire pack.

"I think you thrive on drama," I say.

"I do. When you're as old as me, you have to do something to keep yourself busy."

"You're not that old. You haven't even been around for a millennium yet."

"Says the girl who has only been walking this earth for eighteen years." I roll my eyes.

"Okay, I'll give Wake a shot. If he screws me over, I'll let Rion have him."

He nods. "Don't tell Orion about your plan. His history with Wake will cloud his judgment, and rightfully so. Orion doesn't think rationally when you're around."

I chuckle. "You're telling me."

"What we know for certain is that you're at the center of this pack war. How or why, I'm not sure. Take any advice you can get and maybe, just maybe, Wake has good intentions where you're concerned. If he does, you could get insider information that could help give us the edge."

"You'll have my back in case something goes wrong?" I need a fail-safe. Someone who I know will look out for me. Since I can't count on Rion with this, I hope Ford will be there. I won't stand a chance against Wake on my own if he tries to harm me.

"I might tease you, Ari, but I will always look out for you."

Stepping forward, I tuck my arms under Ford's trench and hug him. It's not something I thought about doing, but a gesture to show him how much I appreciate all he's done for me. He might annoy me to no end; however, he's been here for me when I needed him.

Ford returns the gesture. Up close, he smells like leather and the salty ocean air. Peering down at me, he says,

"You know, if you weren't Orion's mate, maybe we could have..." He waggles his eyebrows.

I shove him back. "You had to ruin a perfectly good moment, didn't you?"

Paige chuckles behind me. I completely forgot she was there. I was off in my own little paranormal world. Ford and I turn to her.

"I'm not sure how to process what I've seen and heard tonight," she says quietly. "I should be panicking. I should faint again. What I thought was fake is real. You," she points to me, "can teleport? When did that happen? And you," she directs to Ford. "What are you?"

I step in her line of sight. "There's so much I need to tell you."

She stands. "Ya think?" Rubbing her temples, her eyes hold mine. "I'm not dreaming, right? This is all real? There are wolf shifters? You can teleport?" The only thing to do is tell her the truth. She knows too much at this point. There's no going back.

"No, you're not dreaming. Yes, this is real. Wake is a wolf shifter. Ford is a vampire. The fact that I can teleport is very new. And what we read about in Lealla's books are true. Well, for the most part. And you can't tell anyone what you saw, will see, or what I tell you."

She keeps rubbing her head. "I don't know what to say."

Ford steps up beside me, parts his lips, and lets his fangs descend. Subtle.

"I don't... Are those...? You're a vampire?" Ford nods. "I thought you were hot!"

His fangs retract. "I still am. I'm the immortal kind of hot that can make every one of your desires come true."

"Ewww!" I yell. "Could you not?"

Ford slaps his hand over my mouth. "Quiet, princess. You just disturbed Mommy."

Panic settles over me. "Oh, no."

Quickly, I shove Paige into bed and jump in beside her. Ford switches the light off before making himself scarce. I have no idea where he went. Paige pulls the blanket up over us a second before the door opens. Fake snores come from Paige.

I turn and blink a few times. "Mom?" I say in my best sleepy voice.

"Go back to bed. I thought I heard something. I didn't know Paige was staying over."

"Last minute decision. I knew you wouldn't mind." I fake a yawn.

"Not at all. Go back to sleep." She quietly tiptoes out of the room and gently shuts the door.

A solid minute later, Paige throws the blanket off us. "You have some explaining to do."

TWENTY-TWO

PAIGE AND I BARELY MADE IT TO school on time. We were up talking most of the night. She took it better than I did when Rion first shifted in front of me. Except for the fainting part. Maybe it was because she knew I wouldn't lie to her. Plus, it wasn't like me to make stuff up. Whatever the case may be, she's now in the know, and I have someone I can confide in about all things paranormal.

By the time our final class of the day is over, Paige and I are nothing more than walking zombies. Huh, I wonder if they're real, too. I'll have to ask Rion. If they are, that's a whole other ball game. Zombies are no joke.

Rion is waiting outside the school next to his Jag when I exit the building. Paige doesn't go to her car. Instead, she's right by my side, walking up to my wolf.

"So," she says quietly when she stops in front of him with her hand on her hip. "You're a wolf."

He looks good—really good—but there's more. He's tired, too. It's in the way he stands. The average person might not notice it, but I do. I never saw him again last night after he ran past me, so I'm not sure what happened with him and Wake or if he ever caught up to him.

"Good afternoon, Paige," he greets with a forced smile.

"Yeah, yeah, no need for pleasantries." She steps closer. "I'm warning you. I don't care who or what you are. You hurt my best friend and I will rain hell down on you as you've never seen before."

He laughs a humorless laugh. "Hell?" He straightens to his full height, his gaze turning serious. "You have no idea what I've been through or what I will go through for Ari. I would die for her. So, before you lecture me on taking care of her, remember who your audience is. She's my mate."

Paige doesn't bat an eye at his tone. "It's good to see you're not just a pretty boy who thinks the world owes you everything." She pats his chest. "You'll be good for Ari. You better remember she was my best friend first, though. I refuse to be pushed aside because you're demanding all of her attention."

"Just know that where she goes, I follow. You won't see me or hear me, but I won't leave her unprotected, especially after what happened last night."

A crowd starts to gather around us. Not that it's surprising anymore. It seems whenever Rion or Ford show up, everyone from the school comes out to either drool over them or hate on them. Thankfully, every word Rion and Paige say to one another is kept low so no one outside the three of us can hear it.

Paige doesn't speak another word to him. She spins on her heel and faces me. "Ari, I'm coming by tonight for dinner again and staying over. We have more talking to do." Her tone is hard, but she winks before leaving. I'm guessing now that I've covered all aspects of shifters and other paranormals, she wants the kind of dirt only a best friend can give. Like how great of a kisser Rion is, or if he has any single wolf friends.

Once she's gone, Rion takes my hands in his, igniting our connection. He dips his head down to kiss me. I think it's going to be a quick brush of the lips, since we're standing outside the school for all to see, but it's not. He pushes his body closer, his hands find my hips to hold me in place as his tongue goes in search of mine.

Sparks fly in earnest as my body melts into his. Everything about him makes me fall harder for him daily. It's nothing I'd admit to yet. I've barely been able to come to terms with it myself. But I can't deny the way every part of me comes alive in his presence.

I fist his shirt, not wanting to let him go, even though his lips are pulling away.

He rests his forehead against mine. "I've missed you."

"I missed you, too." Not being able to see him last night bothered me more than it should have. All night while I was talking to Paige, I kept hoping I'd hear his howl calling me to the back of my house. As the hours ticked by, my worry increased. There was no point in voicing it to Paige. If I did, she probably would have suggested we leave and look for him. She's always up for an adventure.

"Will you come home with me for a bit?" he asks. "I know the drive isn't short, but I want to show you my room at Aries' house. This way you can teleport there if you ever need to." I nod.

Rion opens the door to his car for me. Once we're both inside, we start the trip to his home.

Nothing is said by either of us until we hit the highway. I can't take the quiet anymore. My curiosity is getting the better of me.

"What happened with Wake last night?"

"Why don't you tell me what he said to you?" So we're back to answering a question with another question. I don't think so.

"That's not how this is going to work today. I ask a question, you answer. Then, and only then, can you do the same. You're going first."

He smiles a truly genuine smile, which makes me feel lighter that he's relaxed a little since I came out of the school. "I chased him for a while until I finally caught up to him. Wake's fast, but I've spent years running with him, so I know his moves when he turns, which is what he does when he feels trapped. I was close to the Diaminsey Pack border when I finally reached him." I have so many questions. Screw the rules I just put in place.

"How far away is their pack from here?"

"About four hours west."

"Isn't that near the Avynwood Forest?"

"They are close to one another."

"Why isn't your pack located there? Where they got their name from?" I'm jumping subjects, but my mind is racing with questions. I'll come back to Wake.

"Have you heard about the forest and the tales that come from it?"

"Yes." It's well known to anyone in the state about

what happened in the Avynwood Forest. Charles Avyn was the name of the man who lived in a cabin in the forest. It was only him. His family owned the forest's land going back many, many years. He was the last surviving member of his family.

One night, a bear attacked and killed him. He was found the next day by someone hiking through the area. It was common to have people passing through the land. I heard he never minded others there, so long as they respected the animals who roamed it, the trees, and the vegetation. Ever since then, the forest is said to be haunted by his ghost. Many people have gone into those woods and come out with stories of how they were chased through its dense foliage by a spirit. I'm not sure how much truth there is to it or if it's just people who want to say they saw something.

Locals used to call it the Avyn Woods while Charles was still alive, but he gave it the official name of the Avynwood Forest. I remember someone telling me he made the sign that still sits at the border of the land with the forest's name on it.

"Charles was Lealla's husband."

"No!" I shout. "I never heard Charles was married."

"No one outside of the paranormals did. Before she started publishing, she was married to him. Their lives were very private. Even his burial was only attended to by her and a priest. He was buried behind the cabin they once shared."

"Did a bear really kill him?"

"Yes, but it wasn't an ordinary bear. It was a shifter who attacked him. She didn't know it at the time. She was asleep when it happened. Their home was heated with a fireplace and the flames had gone out late one night. Charles presumably woke up to a cold house and went outside to get more firewood when he was killed. When Lealla rose the next morning, she was freezing. Charles wasn't in bed and the front door was open. She found his remains behind the cabin. There wasn't much of him left."

My hand flies to cover my mouth as I gasp. Poor Lealla. I can't even imagine. My heart breaks for her loss. To lose someone in such a vicious way is terrible.

Rion continues, "She didn't know anything of shifters then. A wolf, who appeared at her door one day not long after Charles died and changed into a man, told her. That was her introduction into our world. The man was very kind to her. He was a lone wolf, who'd been running through the forest when he heard the bear. He ran toward the sound, but Charles was already gone. He attacked the bear, driving him off after shredding his shoulder and hind leg."

"That's awful. Why would someone want to hurt Charles? Did he do something to provoke the attack?"

"A week before his death, a bear was spotted near their cabin. Charles and Lealla always left the animals alone, but this bear, it threw its body at their door. It smashed one of the home's windows, intent on getting inside. Lealla never found out why. To protect his wife, Charles shot the bear dead. That bear who killed Charles was the brother of the bear Charles shot. He was exacting revenge for his death."

"Wow. Who was the wolf?" I ask.

"You don't know? There's only one it could be. Although, nothing of this was stated in his book. Then again, why would it? Lealla's personal life with Charles was always kept private."

I sit and think for a moment, going through the story

Rion just told me. The answer hits me. He's right. There's only one it could be.

"Aries."

He nods. "That's how he and Lealla met. She was alone and understandably very upset about losing her husband. Aries was a lone wolf at the time. The two quickly formed a friendship."

"Is the cabin still there today?"

"It is. Lealla moved out shortly after she met Aries. Charles built the cabin from his own two hands and she couldn't bear to tear it down. It held too many memories. Charles had a lot of money but lived a simple life. He had sold off some inventions he created and had a small fortune stocked away. Lealla used it to build the mansion. She wanted to provide a safe haven for wolves, who didn't have anywhere to go. It was the first of her shifter homes."

"Wow. She took a tragedy and turned it into something amazing. I give her a lot of credit. I probably would have wanted to kill every shifter I saw if they took away the love of my life."

"Lealla is a gentle soul. While she was very upset over the loss of her husband, she didn't want the bear who took his life to be killed. She found out years later, when she met another group of bear shifters, the bear who killed Charles moved far west with his family. They wanted to get away from the land where they lost one of theirs."

"And Lealla has a clan of bears in one of her homes, doesn't she?"

"Yes. She loves them like family. Like the wolves, foxes, and big cats. Charles always loved the wildlife in the forest. He only killed that bear out of self-defense and protection of his wife. He wouldn't have hurt it otherwise.

Lealla continues his legacy of love for all creatures with the homes she provides them and the stories she tells."

"Fascinating. I really do learn something new every day. It's amazing to me how deep this shifter world goes with her." Lealla is truly a wonderful woman. She's been through so much yet found a way to give back.

"The love she has for us is in her very being. We're like children to her. All family. She and Charles never had a child of their own." After hearing all of this, I have no doubt Lealla would have made an amazing mother.

"Do shifters still reside in the forest?"

"A clan of bears does, but no one else. Lealla uses the land as a neutral ground for paranormals. If they're seeking refuge or looking for a place to sleep while passing through, they go to the Avynwood Forest. They can rest easy knowing no one will hurt them."

"Do the bears watch over it to keep everyone in line who visits?"

"Yes, they keep the peace."

So Lealla named the wolf pack after her husband and the forest. I figured it came from there. But what about… "The forest is haunted, though. Right?" I ask.

Rion chuckles. "It's not haunted. When the fae visit the land, they like to have a little fun with any tourists who might be there." As the tales of the forest being haunted grew, more and more ventured there so they could search for the spirit.

"Does the public know there are bears and other creatures in the woods?" I haven't heard any stories of wild animals bothering humans.

"Some have seen them. If a tourist gets off the trail, or gets dangerously close to a shifter, one of the bears will shift into human form and pose as a forest ranger to get them to leave safely. Not once since the bears started running things for Lealla has there been an issue, and we all hope there never will be. Charles would have wanted a peaceful forest."

TWENTY-THREE

I BET RION HOPES I FORGOT about asking him about Wake. Nope, not even close. I still need to know what happened there, especially with how close he got to the other pack's border.

"Tell me what happened with Wake," I remind him. Of course, this comes out of my mouth a second before we pull up to his house.

"Inside," he states. "I promise I'll tell you. I just want to get out of the car. I'm tired of driving."

His exhaustion was evident at the school. I haven't stopped to think about the toll watching over me night after night—while I sleep—has taken on him. I could also offer to teleport him every day, but what if something happens to me, and he's home waiting for me to get him? I'm sure he's thought the same thing. Rion likes to be in control. He wouldn't want to wait. He'd want to be there in case I needed him.

"You didn't have to pick me up today," I tell him. "I could have gotten a ride home with Paige."

"I was already there." He scrubs a hand over his face. "I've been nearby all day. After what happened, I don't want to take any chances with your safety."

"Wake didn't hurt me, Rion. He was only there to talk. Besides, Ford showed up. If I needed help, he was there."

"He wasn't there the whole time, though, was he?" Rion can't be around me night and day. He'd never sleep. Nor would I expect him to be. I have a new ability. I'm not as helpless as I was before.

"No, but I can teleport now. I could have gotten Paige and me out of there fast, if I had to."

"And take her where? Inside your house? You wouldn't be safe there." I feel like I'm being tested.

"I could have taken us to Ford's house. That's far enough away. I don't think many know where he lives."

"And leave your parents unguarded? Someone could have gone for them, too. While you were out back talking with Wake, someone could have entered your home." Cold dread pours over me. He's right. They could have. Hold on. Is he trying to make me paranoid?

"No one else was there. Wake was alone."

"You're still naïve, Ari. You have a lot to learn about my world." He opens the door and gets out of the Jag before I have a chance to reply.

I don't wait for him to come to my side. I'm out of the car a second after him. "Don't talk to me as if I'm so much younger than you. You're only a year older."

He rounds the car and is in front of me, his crystal blue eyes staring me down. "I may only be a year older, but I have a world of knowledge behind every one of those years. I know Wake as well as I know my uncle and everyone else in this pack. He's not your friend," he says harshly. Turning, he walks toward his home. Over his shoulder he adds, "He knows where Ford lives, by the way. He used to be friends with him."

"Are you seriously walking away from me right now?" I stomp after him. Can't he stand here and have a conversation with me?

"I am, because you're acting like a child."

I freeze in my tracks. "Take me home."

He spins to face me. "I will not. I want you to see where I sleep so you can come here for protection if you need it."

I widen my stance, firmly planting my feet. "I'm not going." Okay, so this is a little childish, but I'm not going to let him talk down to me. Arrogant wolf. It serves him right to have someone stand up to him and tell him no. If he thinks I'm going to have a relationship with him and bow to his every command, then he's very wrong. Mutual respect is the only way I'm going to be in this with him. Right now, he's trying to strong-arm me, and I won't have any part of it.

"If this is going to work between us, then you're going to need to respect me," I say. "Our relationship has to be fifty-fifty. I won't have you thinking I'll do whatever you want, whenever you say."

"Fifty-fifty?" he yells as he stalks toward me. "Don't you see how much pull you have where I'm concerned? This relationship is ninety-ten at best." He's lost his mind.

“You're insane! You're barking orders at me and telling me who I can and cannot speak to.”

“One person, Ari! One! Person! Do you know what he did to this pack? To his own father? To me?”

I nod. “Ford told me.”

“Then how can you stand here and be okay with talking to him?” Everything he’s saying only angers me further. I’m surprised I’m not shaking.

“Because he's the only other watcher I know! That's what I am, Rion! Yet no one bothered to fill me in on what that entailed. How me having premonitions has a name. How I'm the only one in the Avynwood Pack with that ability. And while we're at it, when did I become a member of your pack? I'm human! I'm not mated to you!”

“Do you want to officially be mated to me, Ari? Are you ready for that?” I don't reply. He’s aware I’m not. “I thought so.” He makes a fist and thumps it on his chest, over his heart. “I am! I'm that committed to you! This isn’t a game for me. You’re my life! But I'm giving you the chance to feel for me what I do for you.” Some of my anger falls away. He is giving me breathing room in that instance. He’s not pushing me to fully commit to him outside of us being boyfriend and girlfriend.

“I told you I feel something for you. I'm not denying that.”

“Do you love me?” he asks. “Does your heart beat solely for me?”

“I-I've never told any guy I've loved them.” I’ve also never been in a relationship before. Neither has he, for that matter.

What I'm not saying is that every day I'm with him, I fall deeper and deeper into this. Is it love? I think so but have never been in it before; it's hard for me to know for sure. What I don't want to do is utter those three words until I'm absolutely certain I am in love with him. There's also this tiny part of me, which screams: this is moving too fast! I shove that part away. This isn't a human-human relationship I'm in. This is a human-paranormal one, and after all the books I've read, I understand that none of this goes along with conventional standards.

He closes the distance between us; his body only a breath away from mine. Leaning down, he peers directly at me. The emerald green eyes of his wolf front and center when he speaks. "I've been falling for you since the moment we met. No, you don't do as I ask. You don't bend to my will, and that only makes me want you more. My wolf and I don't desire a weak mate. We want someone strong who will challenge us. But we also need to protect you. I love you, Ariane, with every part of my being."

Tears prick my eyes. I try to blink them back, but it's of no use. One escapes, trickling down my cheek. The barrage of emotions I'm feeling has a lump forming in my throat. "How can you know for sure? It's been less than two weeks since we met."

"Because I'm a shifter. Everything in me runs on pure instinct, and that instinct pulls me to you like a moth to a flame. You're my soul mate—my one true love. I would do anything to prove how deep my love for you runs. I would drop to my knees and show the world I'm submissive to you. My wolf would lie at your feet, in front of the entire pack, if that's what it would take to prove how I will always yield to you."

I open my mouth, but no words form. What could I possibly say that would communicate how I feel? I understand everything he's telling me, but I can't get those words past my lips. Instead, I stand on tiptoes and press a kiss to his lips. Rion tilts his head as I part my lips, inviting him in. The kiss deepens as I try to convey my emotions through it, hoping a tiny bit of what runs through me flows to him.

Then I'm jolted—rocked where I stand. It's as if there's an earthquake, but as I break away from him and look around, nothing has changed. It's only Rion and me. And he's wearing the same shocked expression I am.

"What just happened?" I glance to the ground, trying to make sense of things. I'm standing on the same smooth, dirt drive I was before. The cabin is still there. The car is fine. No one came running out saying they felt it, too.

My eyes settle back on Rion as he rubs the center of his chest. "We connected," he says softly in awe. "I heard you in my mind."

"Say what now?"

"Think of something and let me see if I can hear you."

"This is crazy. You know that, right?" What am I saying? Every day since I've met him has been this way. Why should today be any different?

I think for a moment. This is going to be embarrassing to admit, but I have nothing to lose and everything to gain. Focusing on Rion, I think of something and try to send it to him, even though I have no clue what I'm doing. *"There have been a few days since we met, when I've counted the minutes until I saw you. It felt like I couldn't breathe until you were standing in front of me again."*

His response is to kiss me again. It's sweet and brief. He pulls back wearing a huge smile. His voice enters my mind as clear as if he were saying the words aloud. *"I love you, Ariane. I love you so very much."*

"Whoa. How can we…? Why did we?"

"We're truly mates. Not that I had any doubt. You must have given a part of yourself over to me." He pauses for a moment. "You believe my love for you is real. That this between us is genuine."

"I don't doubt your love, Rion. It's only hard for me to believe that this is all happening. This is my life now. I have a shifter for a boyfriend and a vampire for a friend. Know another wolf who gets premonitions like I do." I pause. "Wait! We need to talk about Wake."

I wonder if what I think automatically goes to Rion or if I have to intentionally send it. *"Rion? Can you hear me?"* He smiles and nods. I think about the way his lips felt against mine. How my heart opened up and part of my very being became one with him. I didn't surrender it all. Maybe I will someday. I'm not there…yet.

"Did you hear anything after I asked you if you could hear me?"

"No," he replies.

"Okay, so I have to intentionally send you a message. You can't hear my thoughts. I can't hear yours."

"Correct. I don't hear anything unless you specifically send it." Good to know. It's not like Ford. He hears everything I think. There's an open stream of my thoughts that flows right to him.

"Back to Wake," I state, needing to finish this conversation.

"I'll tell you what happened, but you need to see my room first. I want you to know where I sleep so you can find me." If going to see his room means I get more information, I'm in.

"Hey, I wonder how far apart we can be and still communicate."

"I'm not sure. We can try tomorrow when you're at school."

I smile. "Sounds like a plan."

We go inside the cabin. Cassandra and Aries aren't home, so we have the house to ourselves. On the upper level, we pass two bedrooms and a bathroom before reaching Rion's room.

It's spacious, with a large sliding door and its own small deck. There's a king-size bed, a long dresser, and two nightstands, all in sleek, black wood. The walls are a slate blue. An adjoining bathroom and walk-in closet complete the area. No clothes are scattered about. Everything is tidy, including the closet. The door stands open, giving me a glimpse into how Rion keeps things. For some reason, I imagined clothes thrown everywhere, an unmade bed, and blinds haphazardly closed.

"I think half of the upstairs at my house could fit in this one room," I observe.

He shrugs. "It's home. For now."

"What do you mean for now?"

"Once our book is done, I don't know that I want to stay here. Maybe in the area, but not in this house with my uncle. The pack has a lot of land. I could build a home on it to have my own space, away from everyone else. Most of the pack love being in tight quarters, but I don't. The only one I never minded sharing with was Wake." The pain in his voice causes my chest to tighten. It's not anger but hurt.

"Have you tried mending things with him?"

"No. He was trying to talk to me last night, but a broken jaw got in his way of forming words." I knew something must have happened. It would have been too easy to have a conversation. No, Rion had to get all shifter tough and fight.

"What happened?"

"I chased him to their boundaries. Not once did he try to attack me as we ran."

"Maybe that's because he doesn't want to fight you. He's older now. Maybe he's changed."

"Of course he's changed. He's part of a rival pack. He could have gone anywhere, but he went to them." Rion sits on the edge of the bed, putting his head down in his hands.

"Maybe because at the time he knew that would hurt the most. He was in pain. He lost the woman he thought was his mate. Can you imagine that? Think about it, knowing and feeling what you do now. If that were you and there was another shifter after me, saying I was their mate, wouldn't you put up a fight?"

His head snaps up and he growls. "I'd kill them."

"Wake didn't kill Sevan. He lashed out, running off pure emotion. Instead of passing judgment, maybe try putting yourself in his shoes."

His eyes flash green briefly before returning to blue. "I'd still kill whoever challenged me for you."

TWENTY-FOUR

"DID YOU KILL WAKE LAST NIGHT?" I have to know.

"No, but I could have. I caught him. My wolf tore into him. When Wake shifted, so he could start the healing process, I tore into him as a man. Every time he shifted to try and heal, I went at him again and again in whatever form he was in, as his equal. My wolf never bit his human, and I never struck his wolf as a human."

"Why did you let him live?" I'm grateful he didn't kill him. Wake is the only one like me I know. There's information he can give me.

"Because he told me he was trying to help you. I'm not sure I believe him, but if he wanted to hurt you, he had his chance. He also asked me to punch him so hard I knocked him out." Rion smirks.

"Why would he do that?"

"Because we were at the border of his pack's territory. If they found him conscious, they would've wondered why he didn't bring in the wolf who hurt him. They're going to ask him who did it, and he'll say me. There's no point in hiding it. Also, they'd expect it from our pack."

"But won't this bring their pack to yours? They'll want to fight you." Now I'm panicking. With the whole pack war thing lingering over us, this will only add to their hatred of the Avynwood Pack.

He shrugs. "If there's one thing you get out of this conversation, little mouse, it's that we always protect our mates. My pack will have my back. I couldn't let Wake get away with approaching you when he knows what you mean to me."

"You still shouldn't have attacked him like that." I hate to think of Rion tearing into Wake for trying to help me. He didn't come to my house with malicious intent. But Rion was acting on his shifter instinct.

Peering up at me, he says, "You asked me to see it from his perspective. Now I'm asking you to do the same for me. I have a history with him. He's a wolf who went after someone else's mate in the pack. He fought, made enemies, and joined a rival pack. Of all the packs out there, he went to Diaminsey, knowing how we'd react.

"How should I have taken it when I caught his scent near your house? I was late showing up to watch over you. Aries and I got into an argument. Cassandra had to intervene. Then, when I finally get to you, I smell a wolf whose scent I will never forget. A wolf who's known for trying to take another's mate. How would you feel if a female wolf was after me? Trying to persuade me to be hers?" He's trying to rationalize his response, and he's facing the wrong audience for that. I'm not a shifter. I don't see things like he does, even though I'm trying to.

"One, that's not what Wake was doing. Two, I can't compete with another wolf, or any other paranormal, for that matter. There's no competition there."

"No?" he asks, standing, keeping an arm's length between us. "No one, except you, has this connection with me. No one has given me a part of themselves as you did today. And I have never loved anyone as I do you." A blush quickly rises over my cheeks. I duck my head to try and hide it, but Rion doesn't let me. He steps forward and lifts my head with his finger until my eyes meet his. "Never hide from me, Ariane. You forget that you reside in my heart. It will only ever beat for you."

"It's not your feelings I'm trying to come to terms with. It's the intensity of them and the speed in which this happened." To know he cares about me so much, and would risk everything to keep me safe, is a lot to take in.

"Time doesn't matter to me. My life expectancy is a thousand years. Whether I met you weeks ago, or three hundred years from now, my feelings would be the same. The intensity would be as it is at this moment. And this," he says as he takes my hand in his. "This energy coursing between us when we touch, it would be there then as well. Fate put us together for a reason, Ari."

I let out a breathy sigh and wonder how many times in one day Rion can make me melt for him. He's a dream come true. A guy who only wants me and doesn't have eyes for anyone else. In turn, no one could make me feel like he does. This deep connection we share, and how we can speak to each other in our minds, it's amazing. More than I could ever have wished for.

Then something he said comes back to me. "Why were you arguing with Aries?"

He smiles. "Should I add investigator to your list of traits?"

"You must have forgotten that I remember everything you say, even when you try to bury it with sweet words that make me swoon."

"I make you swoon, huh?"

His hand meets the small of my back to pull me close as he dips his head to kiss below my ear. My body trembles at his touch. His other hand finds the bare skin of my stomach, where my shirt has ridden up. He skates his fingers along my skin as his lips work their way over to mine. A moan quickly rises in my throat while his hand skims higher. Electricity courses through me at every stroke of his fingers.

He pulls back and leaves me wanting more. But I don't forget what I asked him.

"Nice try," I mutter.

He barks out a laugh. "Fine, you win. I was talking to Aries about building my own house on the property, once our book is out. He tried to forbid it, told me he's my alpha, and I should listen to him. He said I should be living in the house with the other wolves."

"Why don't you obey him like the others do?"

"Maybe it's because Aries tries to be a father to me. Yes, he raised me, but he can never take the place of the dad I lost. I respect him as the pack's alpha, but I won't bend to his will. I've always done what I wanted, not listened to anyone. Aries instilled a lot of great traits in me, but I also watched him lead from an early age. He was always the alpha. I respect him, but I challenge him, and he doesn't like it.

"What I will never do, however, is challenge him in front of others. The pack dynamic is too strong. I don't want to weaken it by showing them I don't do everything Aries asks. We butt heads a lot. Cassandra usually pulls him away from the situation before it gets heated. Sometimes, I think he tries to push me too hard. Maybe it's because his son isn't here for him to look after. I'm not sure."

Rion is old enough that if this were a human relationship he had with Aries, he'd probably move out of the house and live on his own. But this is a pack and packs always stick together. Aries is trying to maintain order.

"Does he know about what happened with you and Wake?"

He nods. "I came home briefly and told him. I didn't have much choice, though. Wake's blood was on my clothes. I'm still tired. At first, he didn't fight, but then he got some good shots in. I had to shift a few times to fully heal."

"Was Aries mad you fought him?"

"No, he understood my reasoning and said I was justified in my attack."

"One day I'll understand all of this." I'm not sure when. I'm honestly not sure how I'll ever be able to sleep again at this point. Not because I won't be tired. But because my head will constantly be spinning with the massive amounts of information given to me.

Rion chuckles and lies down on the bed. "I think you know more than you realize. You're absorbing everything we're throwing at you. It's a lot to take in."

I sit on the bed beside him, peering down at his

gorgeous face. This guy appears to be carved from stone. That's how gorgeous he is.

"Why are you looking at me that way?" he asks.

With my mind, I send him a message using our new way of communication. *"Because you're the most handsome guy I've ever seen. There are times when it's hard to believe you chose me."*

He sits up and cups my cheek in his palm. "It's I who cannot believe you chose me."

His lips press to mine and the second we touch, fireworks go off inside me. With them, so much love and hope. Rion is everything I could ever wish for and he wants me. He loves me.

A throat clears behind us, causing me to jump. I turn and Ford is leaning against the sliding glass door, but on the inside, facing us.

"Good afternoon, lovebirds," he says with a smile.

Rion growls. "What do you want?"

"Oh, well, I thought you should know that Travis is aware you hurt Wake. He wasn't surprised, but this is more ammo he has against your pack."

"Travis?" I ask.

"The Diaminsey alpha," Ford replies.

Rion stands. "I knew he'd find out. Wake surely told him. I knocked him out cold before I left. My scent would have been all over him."

"It was. He lied, though."

"How so?"

"He said your mate came on to him. That he was helpless to her advances. That when you found out, you went for his throat." Ford smirks like he approves of the lie.

"It's decent."

I turn, leveling Rion with a hard glare. "How are you okay with him saying that?"

"He has a pack, little mouse. If he returns beat up, they're going to want to know what happened and why. This makes him look better and doesn't look like I'm merely attacking for no reason. We know they're coming for us. The pack war is getting closer every day. But these fights, we've been at each other for many years. My fighting with Wake won't seem like anything out of the ordinary, especially given our history."

Mulling it over, I say, "That makes sense, I guess." I look at Ford. "How did you find this out?"

"Kiara and Travis spend time together, if you know what I mean." He waggles his eyebrows.

"And she went behind his back to tell you this?" I ask incredulously. I can't believe she would do that. Not that I know her well. But she was so sweet and kind. Her doing this doesn't match up.

"She isn't loyal to him. He's nothing more than a toy for her. She overhears things, tells me along with some of the other vampires. I relay information back to Aries or Orion."

"Wouldn't Travis suspect her of doing such a thing?"

"He probably does, but he's a single alpha male and doesn't always have the purest thoughts."

I put my hand up before he gets any further. "I get it." So, Kiara is essentially a spy. Interesting. Wait one second. "Does that mean she goes back to him and tells him information she gains from you and the Avynwood Pack? How she stayed in my bed overnight? How I was bitten by one of his pack?"

"No," he shakes his head. "She's met many members

of the Avynwood Pack. When the time comes for war, she'll be on our side."

"So, you're on Rion's side, too, right?" He said so at dinner with Lealla. I want to make sure, however.

He smiles wickedly. "I'm on any side you are."

"Me? Why me?" I wish people would start leaving me out of the equation. I hate my role in this. Everything is resting on me to stop the war, that's been going on for far too long, and I have no idea how.

"Because I have a feeling you're going to be more powerful than any of us realize. You're feisty, princess. You have a tenacity that many lack. Paranormals will want to follow you."

"Here we go again," I mumble.

"What?" Rion asks, completely confused.

"Wake said something similar. How people are helpless to my charms or whatever."

"He always was a smart wolf," Ford adds with a grin. Rion tenses at the comment, but I place my hand on his arm to silently tell him not to start. Ford and Rion don't need to fight again.

I glance over at the nightstand and see the time. Jumping up, I say, "I've gotta go. My parents will be home soon." Rion stands as well.

"You're forgetting something, princess," Ford states. "You don't need Orion to drive you home. You can snap your fingers and be there in a second flat."

A slow grin spreads across my face. "You're right. This power will come in handy, for sure."

"It's good having powers." Ford winks. I need to remember this power of mine doesn't only come in handy when I'm facing down impending doom. I can use it for everyday stuff, too. Like getting home fast.

"How come you never offered to give Rion any of your powers?" I ask. "I'm sure teleportation would work well for him."

"We wolves don't run from our problems, Ari," Rion states firmly. "I charge into battle, not flee from it." I roll my eyes. I get it. He's strong and a fighter but come on. It would have to be a bonus to have more powers. Less isn't more in this case.

Glancing over, I find Ford making a face. His lip is curled up like he ate something gross. "What's with you?"

"I'm not biting him."

"You bit me."

"Ah, but you're a woman who is very—"

In a flash, Rion is across the room with his hand wrapped around Ford's throat, pressing him to the sliding door. "If I were you, I wouldn't finish that sentence," he warns through clenched teeth.

Ford brings up his arm, slamming it down over Rion's, effectively removing his grasp from Ford's throat. As soon as he's released, Ford swings at Rion, landing a solid uppercut to his jaw. My mouth hangs agape. Did Ford really just punch Rion? I can't break this up. I'm nowhere near strong enough.

"Listen, wolf. You and I may go back a while, but I'm getting sick of you putting your hands on me every time I say something about Ariane. Enough. I'm just teasing. You need to get a grip. I have no interest in your mate. Loosen up."

Rion shifts into a wolf and widens his legs as he lowers his head in a fierce growl. Oh, for the love of…

With a quick snap of my fingers, I place myself

between Ford and Orion. My back to the vampire. "Would you two stop? This is ridiculous. You're friends. Friends tease and joke around. Orion, shift back. We have enough problems without you two fighting."

Ford's hand finds my hip as he pulls me back to his chest. "Listen to your mate, wolf."

I elbow Ford in the ribs, causing him to release me. He laughs. Orion shifts back into a human and immediately puts his arms around me, pulling me away from Ford.

With his mind, Rion says, *"You're right. I need to gain better control over my wolf when you're around. He doesn't like it when another person, or vampire as it is, speaks about you that way."*

I peer up into his eyes. *"I think that's a trait both you and your wolf share."*

TWENTY-FIVE

ONE SECOND, I WAS IN RION'S room, the next in mine. I'm getting used to this teleporting thing. There are so many possibilities. I could go to Paris or Italy. Australia or Ireland. I'd have to get guidance from Ford, since I don't want to end up in the middle of somewhere I shouldn't be. How cool to be able to travel anywhere in the world and not have to spend hours on a plane to do so.

I text Paige, letting her know I'm home. She wants to come over again tonight so we can talk. I'm sure she still has a lot of questions.

Five minutes later, she's up the stairs and in my room.

"Were you waiting down the street for me to text you?" I ask.

"No. I figured you'd be home soon, so I was headed

this way when I got your message." She drops onto my bed. "What happened this afternoon? Did I miss anything?"

"Rion told me he loves me."

Her eyes widen. "Get out!" She stands and rushes over to me, engulfing me in a quick hug. "How did he say it? Was he all brooding and hot, or was he sweet and gave you flowers or something?"

"We were arguing, and he came out and told me. Then we kissed and something happened. We're connected now." I tap the side of my head. "I can talk to him telepathically."

"Interesting. So, can he hear your thoughts?"

"No. I have to deliberately send him a message."

"This could be fun. Ask him where he is."

"You're not serious."

"I am. I want to know what he's doing. Also, I think it's great you can talk to him this way. I wish I could hear the conversation."

"One sec." I send a silent message to Rion, stating Paige wants to know where he is and what he's doing. He sends one back. "He said he's in the mansion talking with Cace about security. He'll be headed our way after he eats." He doesn't call it the mansion. That's all me.

I told him that he doesn't need to be at my house every time I am; that he should take some time to himself or do things with the pack. I love that he's protective, but he needs to do other things as well. One day I'll understand this shifter mate business.

"Cace... He was very hot when we saw him at the signing," she says.

"Oh, yeah. And his brothers..." I fan myself. "Red wolves, who are so different in personality, but all gorgeous."

"I need another invitation to the mansion. So much hotness in one place. I could get lost in there for weeks."

I cock an eyebrow. "They have mates, Paige."

"I'm sure some of them are single. Not every wolf in the pack is mated. You never know, one of them might be my mate." She winks. Paige can never be left in that house unsupervised. She'd cause all kinds of mayhem.

I'm back in the clearing, but the wolves don't appear. I'm alone. Then I hear the snarling and snapping of jaws. I take off in the opposite direction, my bare feet carrying me as fast as they can through the dense forest. A wolf howls, and I know this is my chance to find Wake. There are answers I need, and he's the key to what the other pack knows.

Making a sharp right, I dart toward his howl. He and I are the only ones in this dream who know what's going on. The others are merely part of the premonition and will have no recollection of any of this. Wake howls again, this time a lot closer. He must be running toward me as well. Then I see him, a blur of white fur rushing toward me. He stops fast when he reaches my side, his wolf's green eyes assessing me, scrutinizing me.

My breath is coming in fast pants. "You must be Wake's wolf," I get out through short bursts of breath. I need to talk to him. He has to be willing to go with me. No way am I going to try to grip a wolf by the scruff to teleport him when he doesn't want to go. I could lose a hand that way. "I'm Ariane, Orion's mate. Wake said we could leave next time we're in the dream together." Nothing happens. I don't have time for this. The others are closing in on us. Their footsteps are getting louder. "Wake, please come out so your wolf stops looking like he's going to jump at me at any moment!"

Wake's brown eyes flash through a second before he shifts to a human. His hair is mussed, he's wearing nothing but a pair of black sleep shorts. And holy muscles. Every hard ridge of him is on display for me. It's like the trees parted where we stand so the moon could shine down and showcase the magnificence that is Wake.

"Ari, we have to go," he says while shaking my shoulder. How long was I staring at him? I might be falling fast for Rion, but I'm not blind. Wake is incredibly handsome.

"Oh, right. Give me your hand," I state, finally getting my act together.

He reaches out for me and I do the same. The second our skin touches, a group of five wolves charges us from all angles. I snap my fingers quickly to get us out of here.

We appear inside Ford's home in the Outer Banks. It's still dark outside. I have no idea what time it is or how long I was asleep. Tall windows are in front of us. If it weren't still nighttime, we'd have a view of a tall sand dune, covered in grass and other vegetation, and the ocean past it. The way his home is situated, the dune protects the house from the sea in case of storms. You can't see the beach on the other side of it, only water. But it's there: a gorgeous beach where families spend time enjoying the beauty of the area. From a higher vantage point, you'd be able to see more.

"Boo!" Ford yells behind us, making me jump high in the air and causing my heart to pound in my chest. Wake has a different reaction. He immediately shifts into a wolf.

"Why would you scare a wolf shifter?" I ask, throwing my hands up in the air. "Honestly, sometimes I wonder about you."

"You should wonder about me every day, princess." He winks then turns his attention to Wake. "Good evening, fine sir, and welcome to the Verascue home in magnificent Duck, North Carolina." Ford bows for show. "If you wouldn't mind shifting back into a human, I don't like fur on my floors or furniture. Go on, back to a human now."

Wake growls at him but ultimately returns to his muscled glory.

"Why, Ari," Ford observes, "this does add a lovely twist to your little situation, doesn't it?"

"Get out of my head!" I keep forgetting to have Rion teach me how to put a block up so Ford can't read my mind.

"What's going on?" Wake asks, clearly confused by our conversation.

"It seems our Ari likes the way—"

I get in Ford's personal space. "If you finish that sentence I'm going to remove a certain part of your body you won't want to part with."

"You're no fun," he pouts.

"Can we get down to business and talk? We're here for a reason." Freaking vampire. He's always got something to say.

"You mean not so Wake can walk around and model for us?"

"Ford, I didn't know you thought of me that way," Wake responds with a grin as he bats his eyelashes.

"Could you two be serious?" I ask. As if Ford's penchant for joking isn't bad enough, Wake seems to enjoy doing it as well. Lovely. I focus back on the matter at hand. "My mom could enter my room at any second and see me missing. It's one thing for me to be in a dream state, but quite another to be at the beach with a vampire and a wolf." Paige. I forgot about her. She's going to flip if she wakes and I'm gone. "One second," I say and snap my fingers to go back home.

The light on my desk is on, and Paige is leaning her

back against the wall where my bed is tucked into a little alcove in my room. I love how it's set up. With walls surrounding three sides of the bed, it's like a massive window seat, minus the window. I always feel so cozy in there.

"Were you going to tell me you split?" she asks. "I woke up because you were thrashing around in your sleep and then poof, you were gone."

"I had another premonition, and I found Wake there, so we left to go to Ford's house where I could talk to him."

"Wake, huh?" She stands and pulls her hair into a high ponytail. "Let's go."

"I'm not taking you with me."

"Oh, yes you are. I'm not staying here alone while you get to have a midnight rendezvous with two smoking hot men. Nuh uh. Teleport me away, bestie."

She steps up to me and entwines her fingers with mine. Looking at us together right now, we're complete opposites. Even in the middle of the night, she's stunning, whereas I appear to have crawled out of a cave. She has on a tight tank, no bra, and boy shorts, while I'm wearing an oversized T-shirt and yoga pants. At least I remembered to put pants on before bed this time. I have to stay comfortable if I'm going to run through the woods every night. My feet! I glance down and notice I'm bleeding on the hardwood in my room.

"Shoot!" I walk on my heels to my dresser, where I pull out some gauze and bandages I stashed here after my first jaunt in the wilderness. Then I hobble to the bathroom to wash my feet quick before I bandage them up.

Paige is waiting for me when I emerge. "You really should start wearing sneakers to bed. Your feet are all torn up."

"I know. But really, who wants to wear sneakers to bed?"

"The girl who runs through the woods while she's asleep. I bet you move faster with sneakers on, too."

"Probably," I mumble. I wipe up the blood on the floor and take Paige's hand in mine. We're about to leave when Kiara appears.

"Don't mind me," she says while yawning. "Just filling in for you." She takes my hand in hers and something passes between us. Her body transforms in a flash to be my twin.

"What was that? Ari, there are two of you," Paige says, looking back and forth between us.

"Sorry. Paige, this is Kiara. Kiara, Paige."

"Nice to meet you," Kiara says as she climbs into my bed. "It's a good thing you've got a comfortable bed, Ari." Her eyes flutter closed.

"If my mom comes in, tell her Paige is in the bathroom not feeling well." Kiara doesn't reply but gives me a thumbs-up. I quickly turn the light on in the bathroom and shut the door. Then I flip the light off on my desk.

"Let's get this show on the road," I say to Paige. With her hand in mine again, we teleport to Ford's house.

"What took you so long?" he asks. "I'm bored over here. Wake is tired and not very entertaining. Nothing I say is irritating him."

"Poor baby," I reply to him. You'd think I took away his toy.

"You did. You left."

"Get out of my head, vampire! I'm not your toy!" I yell. At least here I can raise my voice all I want and not have to worry about waking my parents up. "He can read your thoughts, Paige. Keep things locked down the best you can." I don't know what I'm talking about. If I did, I'd be able to block his spying butt.

"Paige, your mind might be more interesting than Ari's." He smirks.

"I have nothing to hide, sexy. Feel free to take a spin inside my brain." Her eyes are on Wake as Ford trains his on her.

"You dirty minx," Ford states. "I like you."

"I knew you would." She winks. For the love of…

"Can we please get on with this?" I ask.

I take a seat on the couch and look out the front windows into the darkness. Wake sits down beside me. "You should be wearing shoes to bed," he notes as he takes in my bandaged feet.

"I've figured that much out. Thanks."

"Ari, I'm not the enemy." I give him a hard glare. "Okay, so my pack is, but I don't want to be part of fighting beside them. I've learned a lot since I've joined the Diaminsey Pack, and part of that is they don't show mercy, ever. They know it was Rion who hurt me and left me knocked out. They knew it was over you. They're more enticed than ever to capture you."

"Hold on. They want to capture me?"

He nods. "They think if they can sway you to their side, you'll make a powerful ally."

"I have an Avynwood mate."

"Not yet you don't. Until you two are fully mated, you're free game for any wolf out there." This again? I still have the vision in my head of wolves circling me, each trying to pee on me to claim me as theirs.

TWENTY-SIX

"I'M EIGHTEEN! WHAT IS WITH you wolves? I'm too young for this."

Wake takes my hand in his, turning it so my palm faces up. I let him, curious to see what he's going to do. He traces his finger over the inside of my left wrist. "Once the two of you are mated, you'll have a tattoo here. It's the final step in the mating process." Each mate in Lealla's series gets a tattoo when they're finally a joined pair. But it's not a tattoo artist that puts it there. It's pure magic.

"The print of the mate," I mutter.

Wake nods. "It'll be Orion's paw print on the inside of your wrist. It marks you as taken to any wolf around. Not only that, but your scent changes. Yours and Orion's will join as one to our sensitive noses. Females will know he's taken, as will males." Does that mean I'll have his sandalwood smell on me all the time? The thought of it causes me to shiver in a good way. I love how he smells.

"And the males get their mate's paw print, if they're a shifter, on their chest over their heart," I say. "If their mate isn't a shifter, it's their name." I remember this from the books. It's a good thing Rion got on me about reading them again. All the information does come in handy.

"Yes, exactly."

"So until then, I'm fair game to every male out there?" He nods. "Rion told me the same, but I just thought it was him being overprotective."

"He is overprotective. Every mate is. That's their job, though. It's ingrained in them. Their one true role is to be there for their mate at all times. To protect them and keep them safe. To ensure they're fed and never want for anything. The job in the pack, any outside careers, it's all secondary to their mate and children. They will always come first." Each word Wake speaks is done so in a somber tone. He lost someone he thought was his. Every day he must think of her.

"He does," Ford says quietly.

"What?" Paige inquires.

"I was talking to Ari." I turn to find Ford behind me and Paige standing next to him.

"Do you two have a thing going on?" she asks, motioning between Ford and me. "I thought she has a mate. Are you into her, too?" Why, oh why, can't Paige stay quiet?

"I don't have any romantic feelings toward Ariane. We have a connection. She's becoming one of my best friends." Something about Ford's words warms me inside. I like having him in my life. It's been a short amount of time, but the longer I spend with him, the more I like him. Even if he does drive me up a wall with all his joking and teasing. There's more to him than that, though. It's a matter of him opening himself up to our friendship now.

I wonder how many actual close friends he has. He's known Rion and the pack for a while, but I haven't heard him talk about other friends except for Kiara. They seem close, however.

Paige doesn't miss a beat. "She already has a best friend. Move on, vampire."

I bust out laughing. "I can have more than one, Paige. What about Bray?"

She waves me off. "He doesn't count." I laugh again. Paige has always tried to keep me to herself, saying Bray is a backup bestie in case she's not around.

In my head, I formulate a message to send to Ford—a deliberate one. Not one where's he spying on my thoughts.

"I don't spy."

I've never done this with anyone but Rion, so I hope it works. *"I'm sighing in my head. I hope you can hear that."* He chuckles, letting me know he can hear me. *"Anyway, I wanted to say I like the idea of being your best friend. I've never had a vampire for a friend. The only other guy friend I have is Brayden, and I swear he's only there because of Paige. If you're going to be my friend, Ford, I need to know we can talk and keep things between us. Like tonight. I don't want Rion to know I was here. I also would love to be able to talk to you and ask you questions, without you being a jerk and picking on me or constantly making jokes."*

His eyes meet mine, all humor gone. "I'd like that."

"Have you two been talking?" Paige asks.

"Yup," I reply. "Just working some things out between us."

"Uh huh." She is always so skeptical of people. I'm sure she'll ask me when we get back home what we were saying.

"Ariane?" Wake brings my attention back to him. "Whatever happens, I'm doing this for Orion, the whole pack, and you, of course. I've had a lot of time to think. I didn't handle things as I should have. This is my way of proving I'm not as horrible as they think I am. I was caught in what I thought was love. Now, I'm not sure what to think about my feelings back then." He stares out the window as the sun starts to light the ocean. I wonder if there's someone new in his life.

"I tried to talk to Rion about you," I tell him honestly. "I told him he needed to see your side."

"How did that go?"

"Meh."

He laughs. "I miss him. He was much more than my cousin. We did everything together."

"Maybe you two can patch things up."

"That's wishful thinking."

"You never know."

"True." I watch him as his eyes stay trained out the window in front of us. It couldn't have been easy leaving his family behind. No matter how angry someone is, family will always be a part of you.

"Is there anything else you wanted to tell me? I should get back. I have school tomorrow." No time for reading. I do need to keep reading the series, though. In my free time. When I'm not being chased in my dreams or getting visited by wolves or vampires.

"No fae yet. Or mages," Ford chimes in.

"One paranormal race at a time," I reply. "There's only

so much I can wrap my head around at once."

Wake and I stand from the couch. He walks to Ford. "I need a lift home. Into my room in Diaminsey, if possible." Ford's lucky, he can easily peer inside Wake's head to find out what his room looks like. Then it's simple for him to teleport there. Vampire gifts.

"Fine, but next time, the one who brings you here can take you home." Ford gives me a pointed look.

"You'd seriously want me to teleport to a place I've never been, where there is a pack of wolves that wants me to join their little club of darkness so that I can go against Rion and everyone else?"

"Good point. Let's go. You first, princess. I'm going to follow you to your room to make sure you get there safely, then take Wake home."

I smile. Ford isn't so bad after all. He returns my smile, but it's wicked and full of mischief. I roll my eyes before grabbing Paige's hand.

With one snap, we're back in my room, standing in front of my duplicate, and my mom.

"Ari?" Mom stammers. "Why are there...? Who is...? What's going on?" Oh, no. How do I handle this? My mom is seeing two of me. Two of her only daughter!

Ford and Wake pop up beside us. A slow smile appears on Ford's face. "Well, this certainly made things interesting."

Kiara steps forward and instantly changes back into her normal, gorgeous self. She then steps up to my mom and places her finger on Mom's temple for a moment. "Everyone out who shouldn't be here," she says quickly. "Ari, I erased the last two minutes of her memory."

Ford, Wake, and Kiara all teleport away. I tug on Paige,

pulling her into my bed. I have no idea what Mom remembers last, but I'm going to play it off that I was asleep.

"Ari?" my mom whispers. Her eyes on Paige and me in bed.

I fake yawn and blink a few times. Paige pretends to be soundly asleep beside me. "What time is it?"

She shakes her head as if she's trying to clear it. Peering at my alarm clock, she says, "You slept through your alarm. If you and Paige don't get up, you're going to be late for school."

"Thanks," I mumble and close my eyes again, exhaustion settling over me. Too bad I can't go to sleep. I hadn't realized we were at Ford's that long.

Mom leaves the room, closing the door behind her.

Paige sits up. "That was crazy. Your poor mom. Do you think her memory of that is really gone?"

"I hope so. She'd probably think she was losing her mind if she remembered that, and I don't want to explain to my mother how my new boyfriend is a wolf, and I've also got a bestie who is a vampire."

"I'm you're bestie. Ford is nothing more than a fill-in within the paranormal world when I'm not around."

I smile. "Whatever you say."

"I like that vampire less today than I did yesterday," she pouts.

"No one is going to take me from you. Come on. Mom's right. We have to get moving."

Putting my feet on the floor, I wince from the pain all that running did last night. I have to remember to put sneakers on when I sleep. It's not that I want to, but this pain every time I have a premonition isn't going to cut it. Hopefully, my mom never notices, or I'll have to lie about wearing them to bed.

This whole immersion into the paranormal world has upended my life. Not that I'd change it for anything. I actually sort of love it. Everything I thought was fiction isn't. And now I'm a part of it. Every day, I'm adding to the history that is the Avynwood Pack. I'm going to be in one of the books. Well, as much as I want to be, anyway.

Paige showers first, since she takes longer to get ready. Luckily, we keep clothes at each other's houses in case we decide on an impromptu sleepover. I don't have to do anything other than shower, brush my teeth, and throw on clothes. It doesn't matter if my hair is wet or if I look like I haven't slept in weeks. I seriously don't care. I'm exhausted.

When we finally descend the stairs, the house is quiet, both of my parents having left for work already. Outside, there is a familiar black Jag waiting with a very sexy Rion leaning against it. His jeans are slung low on his hips. His black T-shirt has ridden up a little, showing off a sliver of taut skin. Yeah, my boyfriend is hot. And yet, I'm standing here looking awful. Wet hair pulled back into a ponytail. Jeans and a navy blue T-shirt, which were the first things I grabbed. I really should put more effort into how I look. At least, when I'm not completely sleep deprived.

"Someone's waiting for you, and he's looking mighty fine," Paige whispers in my ear. She smacks my butt before getting into her car.

Stopping in front of Rion, I push on my tiptoes to give him a quick kiss. "Good morning. What do I owe the honor of having you drive me to school?" This is the first time he's done it.

He smiles. "I wanted to check on you. Make sure you're okay. I tried to talk to you last night. I texted you; sent you a message." He taps on his head. "You didn't respond to anything." I haven't checked my phone since yesterday.

Luckily, the lie rolls off my tongue. "I'm sorry. Paige and I spent the night in then crashed early. I haven't been getting much sleep lately." It does make my stomach sour keeping the truth from him. If he knew who I saw last night… It's better this way. For now, at least.

"Me neither."

"You don't have to watch over me at school today. I'll be fine. I'm in a building full of teachers and students. I doubt anyone is going to bother me there."

"I won't leave you unprotected, but I am going home to sleep. I'm no good to you if I can't keep my eyes open. Cace is coming up to your school. He'll drive you home after school and be outside all day should you need him."

"In wolf or human form?" I have to ask.

"In wolf, for most of it. He'll park his SUV down the road then shift. Our hearing and eyesight is much better in wolf form." I nod.

Rion opens the passenger side door for me. Walking around him, I move wrong and wince from the pain in my feet. I tried to find the most comfortable pair of sneakers I own this morning, but it wasn't enough cushion to help with all the pain.

"Are you okay?" he asks.

"Yeah, just hurt my foot walking up the stairs last night. No biggie." If he knows I went into the woods in my dream again, he'll ask if I saw Wake and I can't reveal I did.

"Ari, don't lie to me."

"Fine, I was running through the woods and cut my feet. I washed and bandaged them. They're just a little sore. That's all."

His jaw clenches. "They were chasing you again, weren't they?"

"Yes, but I got away and safely teleported home." Not a complete lie. I eventually did end up at home.

"Is that why Ford and Kiara were in your room last night?" Oh, no. I forgot about his crazy wolf hearing. He would have heard their voices. But not Wake; he didn't say a word.

"Yes." I drop my gaze, unable to look him in the eyes. "I'm sorry for not telling you."

"You should have. I gave you every opportunity."

"Why didn't you come right out and say something then?"

"Because I wanted to see if you'd lie to me."

TWENTY-SEVEN

THANKFULLY, THE DRIVE TO SCHOOL is short. Any more silence and I would have screamed. There was nothing more for me to say. Yes, I lied, but I did it for a good reason. If he knew I was deliberately with Wake, he'd be livid. But I'm my own person with my own power. I'm also the one caught in this never-ending loop of premonitions. What's frustrating is that I've seen nothing of importance. I'm always being chased, the scenery blurring past me.

Rion needs to start understanding I can take care of myself. But I'm unsure how to make this right with him. He gets out of the car and opens my door for me. Of course, there is a group of girls who stop and practically drool seeing my boyfriend. I stare them down, causing them to shuffle away. Be gone, trollops. He's mine, and he isn't going to leave me for you.

Taking my hand in his, Rion pulls my attention back to him. He holds our hands up, staring at our palms touching and the invisible connection we share. It's there, flowing through my body in a low hum. "I don't like it when you lie to me, Ari."

"I didn't want to worry you. I could have this dream every night for all I know. It was handled, however. I was able to teleport out of it."

"Tell me next time when I ask. Please."

"Okay."

"And please come by Lealla's and have Des look at your feet after school. Cace can bring you."

"It's a few cuts. I'll be fine."

"I don't like seeing you in pain."

Without thinking, I reach up with my free hand and run my fingers through his hair. He leans into my touch. "And I don't like seeing you so tired. Please go home and rest. Cace is out here somewhere. I'll be in school learning boring stuff all day. You need sleep."

"I know." He kisses me as the bell rings loudly. Lovely, I'm late. "I love you, Ariane. Have a good day." Instead of giving him a verbal reply, I kiss him and pour my emotions into it. One day, I'll be able to tell him how I feel.

I take a seat in third period English when one of the guys in my class comes running in before the bell rings. "There are wolves on the baseball field!" Oh, no. This can't be good.

I grab my bag and run from the room, while everyone

else sits slack-jawed for a second. Maybe if I can beat most of them out there, I can find out what's going on.

The bell rings, alerting everyone to be in their classes. My hurried steps ring out in the silent hallway as I run from one end of the school to the other. Pushing open the door, I don't stop running until I reach the baseball field, where I find a small group of students and two massive wolves. This is just fantastic. The students are stunned speechless, and luckily, none of them have their phones out recording this yet.

"Go inside!" I yell. "Get everyone to safety!" They don't move. You've got to be kidding me.

Ford strolls around from the side of the bleachers like nothing is going on. He steps up to the students and taps each one on the temple, causing a glazed look on their faces, then he's by my side in a flash. "You grab Cace, I'll get our other visitor. Bring them to the clearing by Lealla's." I nod and run toward the fight without thinking about my safety.

The wolves are snarling at each other, teeth bared, as a wolf I don't know starts to lean back as if he's about to pounce. Ford teleports to its side and grabs a fistful of fur. The wolf is startled and swings around on him. Then they're both gone. I run over to Cace and grab him by the scruff. He growls at me, not liking my rough handling of him, but his wolf must recognize me, because Cace doesn't hurt me. The damage he and this other wolf did isn't good. No way can Ford wipe everyone's memory.

I teleport to the clearing where Rion first revealed himself to me and where my nightly dreams bring me. Ford and the mystery wolf are on the other side.

Cace shakes my hand free and puts himself in front of me. The red fur of his wolf standing out in contrast to all the greenery around us. Ford still has a grip on the grey wolf. It snaps at him then tries to lunge toward me. Ford grips him tight and bares his fangs in warning.

"You're not getting near her," he hisses.

"Who is that?" I ask.

"Javen. He's the beta in the Diaminsey pack. Shift," Ford commands, in a tone I've never heard. Javen does. I'm not sure how Ford got him to do it, but I'm glad he did.

Standing before us is a tall man with lean muscle and nothing on but a pair of basketball shorts. His hair is blond and neatly combed back. He looks no older than thirty. But his smile is menacing.

Cace follows suit and shifts, appearing in a pair of jeans and a grey long-sleeve shirt. "What were you doing at the school?" he asks Javen, venom dripping from his voice. "Why were you near Ari?"

"Don't speak to me as if you have claim over her. She doesn't belong to your pack," Javen replies.

"She certainly does. Her mate is one of ours."

"Yet, I don't see a tattoo on her, nor does she smell mated. She isn't; therefore, she has no allegiance to any pack."

"Why did you come?"

"To talk to her." That's enough of this.

Moving around Cace, I start to approach Javen. Cace grips my arm as I pass by to hold me back, but I give him a hard glare and shake him free. He releases me, though he stays by my side. I don't stop walking until I'm standing in front of Javen. Ford steps away from him, flanking my other side.

I cross my arms. "What do you want?"

"The rumors are true. You do have quite an attitude

for someone so young who can't shift."

Rolling my eyes, I ask, "Seriously? Is this why you came? To find out if I'm tough?"

"Tough?" he cocks his head. Okay, that was the wrong word. I'm winging it here. "I'm not sure about that, but you're intriguing."

"Get on with it."

"Travis would like to invite you to our pack's home tonight for dinner at six. We've all vowed not to harm you. You can even bring that wolf of yours and your vampire, if it makes you feel comfortable."

"You've lost your mind!" I reply. "I'm not coming to your den of evilness. You can find another girl to invite."

"But we have." A chill creeps its way over my skin as a feeling of foreboding settles over me.

"Who did you invite?"

"I wouldn't use the word invite. But your friend Paige is visiting us. She kept insisting we shouldn't bring you by, but Travis would like to meet you in person. We're making a dinner party of it." My body turns cold. What am I supposed to do? I can't leave Paige in their clutches.

"Ford, can you teleport in and out of their place and grab Paige?" He shakes his head. *"Get Kiara!"* He shakes his head again. *"You can leave me. Cace is here."*

"I know you two are talking," Javen observes.

"Your point?" I ask.

"Kiara won't help you. We have her, too. She won't be going anywhere. We're not as stupid as you think we are."

"I never thought you were stupid. I don't even know you, but you taking my best friend doesn't exactly make me all warm and fuzzy inside."

"Dinner tonight at six. Ford knows the way, but then

again, you can teleport, too, now can't you?" I narrow my eyes. "And before you try to pop into our home and grab your friends, there's a ward up. No teleporting in or out. Having a mage for an ally is definitely helpful."

"Ford…" I prompt with my mind.

"Mages can create different types of wards. The ward he's speaking of does exist."

"How do I know I can trust you?" I ask. "You say you won't hurt me, but you still could."

He straightens. "A wolf would never promise something and go back on it. When our alpha says you'll be safe, you will be. If anyone tries to harm you, they will be dealt with swiftly. You have his word and mine."

"I'm bringing Ford and Rion."

"And me," Cace adds.

"Fine," Javen replies. "That's it, though. No alpha and no beta."

"I also want your word that Paige and Kiara won't be harmed either." As much as I want him to vow to not harm Rion, Ford, and Cace, I know I'll never get it. They're paranormals, and they'll be in the Diaminsey Pack house. Rival wolves. There's no way they will agree to that. So I bite my tongue. I'm not stupid. I can only push Javen so far.

"You have it. I'm sure you've been told a lot about us, but we aren't savages. We're a pack like any other."

"Except part of your pack killed Rion's parents."

"And they were dealt with."

"Yeah, by our alpha," Cace replies. "Ari might be new to this world, but I'm not. Don't you dare try to pull anything in her presence, or you'll regret it. I'll make sure you suffer a long, painful death."

"As will I," Ford adds.

He rolls his eyes. "I get it. Ari is important to your pack. Though, the vampire being so committed to her is interesting."

"Is it?" Ford asks, cocking his head. "Why's that?"

"You don't fool me, Ford Verascue. We know you're friends with Orion and others in the pack, but you've never put your neck on the line for anyone."

"Let's talk more about necks," he says as his fangs descend again. "I can hear the blood coursing through your veins, wolf. One wrong move tonight, and I will drain your body before any of your brothers can come to your rescue."

"Very interesting."

"All right, that's enough of this," I interject. "You go your way," I tell Javen, "and we'll go ours. I'll see you tonight for dinner."

Javen shifts into a wolf and is off running through the forest. I spin and face Ford and Cace. "That was fun. Can we not do it again?"

"We need to get to the mansion," Cace states, a muscle ticking in his jaw.

"Yes, and someone needs to do damage control at the school," I state. "The fact that wolves were seen fighting on the baseball field won't go over well."

"We know all the wildlife officials in a wide radius. They're shifters posing as ordinary humans. They'll be able to say they'll scour the area and make sure the wolves are gone. Put on a nice show of it, too. This isn't the first time we've been caught fighting in public. The team we have in place is good at making everyone feel safe. I'll call them back at the house. Can you teleport us?"

Nodding, I take Cace's hand in mine and face Ford. We both teleport at the same time, appearing in the entryway of the mansion, suddenly surrounded by the rest of the pack, including Aries and Rion.

"Ari!" Rion shouts and rushes forward. He engulfs me in his arms, lifting me from the floor. "Are you okay?" he asks when he puts me down. He glances from my head to my toes, then carefully over my face.

"I'm fine. Honest."

"What happened?" Aries asks. "The alarm sounded, but you appeared before we could get out there. One of our wolves caught Javen's scent."

Cace steps forward. "He went to Ari's school today. He and I got into it. Well, our wolves did."

"In front of students," I add. "On the baseball field."

Aries drags a hand down his face. "You couldn't have kept it hidden? You had to make yourselves known?"

"It wasn't intentional," Cace defends. "We started fighting in the woods but somehow made our way onto the field."

"And while they were fighting, Paige was taken from school property," Ford interjects. "My guess is Javen was merely the distraction so that they could grab Paige. Once they had her, Javen could deliver his message."

"How did you know they were fighting?" I ask Ford.

"Your thoughts were very loud. I'm used to getting those kinds of messages at night when you're sleeping. Apparently, now I'm getting them while you're awake, too. Like the other night with Wake and today. When you're upset, angry, or scared, I can hear you and come find you. We share a connection, princess. One you should be thankful for."

"I am. I wouldn't have been able to teleport both wolves out of there." Oh, no. The cameras.

Ford focuses on Cace. "Can one of your brothers hack into the school's security system and erase the entire incident from the feed? It'll help if there are no videos of them fighting on property. It'll be the kids' word against the video. Plus, we don't need anyone knowing Ari can teleport."

Cace nods. "Cash!"

"On it," he replies and leaves the room. I hadn't even noticed who all was here, just that there were a lot of guys.

"Now that we have that taken care of, tell us what Javen wanted," Aries states.

TWENTY-EIGHT

WE SPEND THE NEXT FIFTEEN MINUTES filling Aries in. No one is happy about tonight's dinner, but they can't think of another way to get Paige and Kiara out of there safely. Even if the Avynwood Pack stormed the Diaminsey, Paige and Kiara could be killed. We're going to have to play nice, and that means us going there for dinner. Lucky me.

Rion is fuming. He doesn't want me anywhere near them, but there's nothing else to be done. In all honesty, I'm not afraid. Not even a little bit. What I am is worried about my friend. That's my sole purpose in going there. To get her and Kiara free. Neither deserves to be mixed up in this.

My phone buzzes in my pocket. Removing it, I see my mom texted me.

Mom: Did you leave school early?

I completely forgot she'd be alerted if I didn't show up in my classes. Time to lie.

Me: Yes, I wasn't feeling well. I asked Paige if she could drive me. We went to her house since it's closer to the school.

Mom: You have to tell the school when you leave. They called me asking where you were; saying you and Paige didn't show up for your next class.

Me: I thought I was going to throw up. I'll probably stay here tonight. I don't want to move at the moment. I'll be home tomorrow after school.

I'm not sure if she'll buy it. She's a nurse. She always insists on taking care of me. The one thing in my favor is that she's at work still. Also, the fact that both of Paige's parents are currently traveling for business. No one would know if I'm at her home or not. I do have to get her car to her house, though.

"On it," Ford states and teleports away. He's turning out to be someone I can seriously count on. As much as I hate him hearing my thoughts, it does come in handy at times.

Mom: Are you sure you're okay? I can come pick you up after work.

Oh, no. She can't do that. I won't be there. I'll be hours away having dinner with wolves.

Me: I'll text you if I feel worse, but honestly, I'm already feeling better.

It helps that this isn't the first time I've been sick at Paige's. It's common practice for us to stay at each other's homes even when not feeling well.

Mom: Okay. Get some rest. If you need me, I'll come right over.

Me: Thanks, Mom.

"Okay, I have my alibi in place. Mom thinks I'm at Paige's house and Paige's parents are out of town, so both of us are covered," I tell Rion.

Ford pops back into the room minutes later. "Her car is at her house. Everything looks good. You might want to erase me teleporting into the parking lot and then to her car, though. I had to dodge police as well. I can't remember who on the force is a shifter and who isn't. They were there investigating the wolf sighting. From what I heard, however, only one teenager saw it and no one believes the story. You'll have to cover yourself back at school tomorrow, Ari. They're going to wonder why you ran out at the same time."

Cace leaves to tell Cash to take care of the video of Ford teleporting. I'll use the same lie I told my mom for school tomorrow.

"I can't believe our only option is to let you walk into their home tonight," Aries says, with his head in his hands where he sits on the couch. We migrated into a large sitting room so we could sit down.

"If you storm their home, they'll kill Paige," Ford states grimly.

"I know. I just wish we had another way." He glances up at Ford. "Are you sure you can't teleport in there?"

He nods. "I tried. I'm blocked. Javen must have been telling the truth."

"I don't want you going," Rion says to me.

I turn to where he sits beside me. "It doesn't matter what you want. My friend is in danger, and I'm not going to sit here and do nothing about it."

"You're human, Ari. You could get killed."

"They gave their word."

He barks out a laugh. "And you believe them? You know nothing about them."

"They aren't going to hurt her," Ford interjects. "I read Javen's mind when he thought I was only talking to Ari. They have no ill will with her. They merely want to talk but knew the only way she would was if she had no choice. They don't want to hurt her."

"Or he learned how to project what he wanted you to hear in his mind," Aries interjects.

Ford shrugs. "Anything's possible. It's a wolf's word, however. That's a pretty strong assurance."

"You're right. We don't give our word for just anything. We do it when we mean it."

Rion stands abruptly. "I can't believe all of you. You're fine with my mate walking in there? To handle things she only recently learned about? She doesn't know anything about our pack politics or the way things work between rival packs. And let's not forget that we're on the brink of war."

"Maybe Ari can help calm the rift between our packs," Aries says. "Maybe she can stop the war before it happens."

Here we go. I don't know what kind of voodoo these wolves think I have.

"Hold on," I state. "I'm going in there to listen to whatever little talk they want to give me, then I'm going to get Paige and Kiara, and leave as fast as possible. I'm not going in there to negotiate or anything else. I'm not part of your pack or any pack. My friend was taken, and I need to get her back. Kiara, who has done favors for me, is being held. She needs to be freed. I get that you're looking at the bigger picture, but that stuff needs to be handled between

Aries and Travis. I'm no one in this battle. Everyone keeps telling me I play a huge part, but I have yet to see it. I honestly just want my friends back."

"I know, Ari. And we'll get them back. You're taking two strong wolves and a vampire with you. I'm only thinking ahead," Aries says. "My guess is Travis has an ulterior motive by getting you there. He's not going to want to have a small conversation. He wants something from you."

"He wants her to join their pack," Ford states. All heads swivel toward him. "That's what I read in Javen's mind."

I breathe a sigh of relief and send a silent thank you to Ford. The last thing I want is for Rion to find out about our conversation with Wake.

My stomach growls in hunger. Rion turns my way. That's not embarrassing at all. I can't help it that I missed lunch. I need food and a nap. This day has been crazy, and I barely slept last night.

Rion takes my hand in his, lifting me from the couch. "Come on. Let's get you something to eat."

I turn toward Ford and say in my head, *"I want to talk to you after I eat. Meet us in Rion's room in a bit. I'm going to suggest he take me there to rest. I have a favor to ask."* He nods subtly.

Rion leads me through the house to the kitchen, where two women are cleaning dishes and preparing food for dinner. My phone vibrates again. This time it's Brayden. I tell him the same thing I told my mom. He says he wants to come by later to check on me. I text back that it's not necessary and I'll see him in school tomorrow. That I'm in no shape to see anyone else. Fortunately, he acquiesces. I should have thought to text him earlier. No one else will care about me not being in school. Sometimes it's good to only have a few friends.

After filling my stomach, exhaustion hits me full force. I ask Rion to take me to his house so I can lie down. I don't tell him Ford will be paying us a visit.

Five minutes after we get there, Ford appears. Rion and I are sitting on the edge of his bed. "What's up, princess?"

"Why are you here?" Rion asks. This time it's not done in a growl or an irritated snarl; it's a simple, tired tone.

"Ari asked me to come."

"Okay," I start. "I'm going to ask Ford something and, Rion, you can't stop me. No matter what I ask or say, it's my decision and you need to respect that."

"I don't like where this is going," he says.

"I do," Ford replies and rubs his hands together.

Here goes nothing. I face Ford. "I want you to give me more of your power."

Ford lights up like a Christmas tree, while Rion looks like he's about to internally combust.

"Have you lost your mind?" Rion yells. "You want Ford to bite you again? Wasn't it enough the first time?" His face gets redder with every word. I'm surprised steam isn't rising from his ears.

"Hear me out. I'm walking into a pack of wolves tonight. I have zero defense, outside of being able to teleport. What if I can't get out of there fast enough? What if they do try to kill me?"

"If they get close enough to try and kill you, that means Cace, Ford, and I are all dead. The chance of that happening is slim to none."

"I know, but it can't hurt to have another power no one there knows of. And let's be honest. The deeper I get into this paranormal world, the more my life seems to be in danger. More powers would be a good thing." My only defense is to teleport. I used to have no problem being a simple human. That was until I was immersed in this paranormal world where I'm a catalyst and a dream watcher.

"What kind of power were you thinking?" Ford asks.

"Is it possible to be invincible?"

He laughs. "You can become immortal, but I'd need to change you to a vampire for that. What do you say?" He waggles his eyebrows. "Join us. Become one of the undead."

"No!" Rion shouts. "Absolutely not!"

"While I don't share Rion's hatred of me becoming a vampire, I'm not sure that's for me."

"What about the ability to heal instantly? If someone were to cut you, you'd heal. Bite, heal; anything shy of decapitating you, you'd heal," Ford suggests.

"Wouldn't that make me immortal? I'd heal from anything."

"You'd still age normally. You wouldn't have to worry about cancer or other illnesses, however. That is, until you mate with Rion. Then you'll gain his gift of a long life."

"Say what now?"

"When a human mates with a shifter, there is a transfer of power, so to speak. You'll get to live as long as Orion if you can keep your head attached."

"Now I remember. I read something about it in Lealla's series."

"You need sleep, Ari," Rion cuts in. "You should rest

then decide something like this."

"I'm tired, sure, but my mind isn't going to change just because I took a nap."

"Let's do this," I tell Ford. Not that I'm looking forward to him biting me again, even if it was an amazing euphoric experience. But this could help me have an edge over Travis and his pack.

"Okay, but there's a catch," Ford says. I quirk an eyebrow. "I can't give you that power. Well, technically I could, but it might be a weaker version of it. That power was given to me by my mother. I inherited it. It's not like teleporting. This is your life we're talking about. My mom is much older and stronger than me."

"How old?" I have to know now.

"Four thousand."

"Years?" I ask in a high-pitched voice. Ford nods. "That's insane!" Wow. I'm going to meet a four thousand-year-old vampire. "One day, I'm going to ask you to write all this down for me. My head is going to explode with information overload."

He chuckles. "Do you want me to ask her?" I nod. "Okay, give me a few. I have to find her. My parents tend to travel around a lot." He snaps, disappearing out of sight.

Rion shakes his head. "I can't believe you're doing this, Ari. You're choosing to let a vampire bite you for the second time."

I shrug. "It's not like she's going to drink my blood. She's only passing on one of her powers. Think about it. I might be dead if I couldn't teleport. Wolves chase me in my dreams. You have no idea what that's like. I can't outrun them, Rion. They aren't there to play fetch." He gives me a pointed look. "Okay, bad dog joke. Sorry. You get my point, though. I have to keep myself safe when you can't. And truth be told, I don't like relying on other people to always be around, watching me, protecting me, putting themselves in harm's way, just so I'm okay. Why do that when I can gain the power to do it myself?"

"What if all this power changes you? What if you aren't the same Ariane I fell in love with?"

"Is that what all this is about?" He can't be serious. It's not like I'm going to get this power then throw myself on a sword. Or decide to taunt the wolves.

"Partially."

"I think you're grasping at straws. You don't want me to go through with this, and you're trying to find any way to convince me not to."

He peers into my eyes. "I love you, Ariane. I don't want anything to happen to you. You're my everything."

TWENTY-NINE

FORD RETURNS WITH A GORGEOUS WOMAN on his arm. She's tall with the same brown hair as Ford, but hers is halfway down her back. Her eyes are identical to Ford's—a beautiful grey. A slim pair of leather pants cling to her figure. The crimson top she's wearing draws attention to her matching red lips. Rion instinctively takes a step in front of me.

"Calm yourself, wolf. I mean no harm," she states with an air of sophistication. "And if you think for one second my son would bring someone here who would hurt Ariane, you're wrong. I dare say he cares for her as much as you do." Rion becomes rigid. His hands ball into fists. "Good boy. You should block your mind more often. Though it won't do you any good from me." I'm not sure what to do with her comment about Ford's feelings for me. No time to analyze it now.

I move around Rion. His mom is right, Ford wouldn't bring someone here who would want to hurt me. Besides, when he left he said he was going to get his mother.

She smiles warmly, no hint of fangs in sight. "You must be Ariane. I'm Eloise Verascue. My son has told me a lot about you."

"Not willingly," he interjects. "She has a way of getting into your head, block or not."

"It's true," she states as she begins a slow perusal of me. I shift on my feet at her assessing gaze. "When Ford came to me and asked if I'd help a human, well, let's just say I was a little confused. Yes, he's young, but he's never shown interest in one before. I knew you must be special. Then, while doing a thorough examination of his mind, I saw things through his eyes. You, my dear, are quite the extraordinary girl."

A blush quickly heats my cheeks. "I'm no one, really."

"I beg to differ. You're a dream watcher and have a wolf who wants to be your mate. Plus, my son gave you the ability to teleport. And now you're being invited to dinner at a rival pack's home. This dinner has the potential to end the pack war before the fighting begins. Then again, there's also the possibility it could accelerate things." I don't like the sound of that. It's all on my shoulders. I could prevent it or put it on the fast track. Lovely. "Are you sure you'd like more power?" she asks.

I nod. "I don't want to go in there defenseless. A mage has put a spell on the house so no one can teleport in or out. Once we're in there, we're stuck. Everyone else has the ability to shift or heal. They have sharp teeth and plenty of muscle. They aren't defenseless, but I am."

"I told you I would guard you with my life," Rion states.

"I know, but I don't want it to come to that. I want to know that once we're in there, I can take care of myself. I want an advantage. They know I can teleport, but if I get another ability, it will give me an edge. One that could possibly help me stop all this before things get worse."

"Smart girl," Eloise says. "Shall we? I have to meet a friend in Paris and don't want to be late."

I step forward, but Rion grips my wrist to stop me. "I'm doing this whether you like it or not," I tell him and wiggle my wrist free. "This is my life, Rion. I may be your mate, but we are not mated. And even if and when we are, I will still make my own decisions. No one will tell me what to do."

Eloise smiles wide and holds out her hand for me. I take it in mine. "I like you more and more by the second. I'm going to ask one more time, are you sure?" I nod. "Okay."

She brushes my hair off my shoulder to expose my neck. I tilt my head to the side. A sharpness like no other pierces my skin and then is washed away in the sensation of being bit by a vampire. That sense of euphoria settles over me. My head is in a fog. My body is warm all over.

It's just like it was with Ford, but this time, I can feel the raw power being poured into me. It's heady and has me splaying my fingers at my side as it courses through my body. Once it reaches my toes, she releases me, licking my neck, sealing the wound.

I'm dizzy, disoriented. Rion is on one side of me, his hands grasping my waist, walking me to his bed. The soft mattress welcomes me, cradling me as the effects of the vampire bite start to wear off. Seconds tick by, each bringing me back to myself, the fog lifting. Then something else happens. There are multiple voices in my mind, talking to me at once. They get louder. I grip the sides of my head and squeeze my eyes shut, trying to get rid of them.

Delicate hands touch my arms. "Ariane, listen to me," Eloise's voice pushes through the madness in my mind. "I want you to focus on what I'm saying. Tune the rest of it out. Each word I'm speaking, the pitch of my voice, focus." I do as she asks, the voices quieting but not going away completely. They're background noise now. I open my eyes. "Good. You dealt with it quicker than I thought you would."

"What did you do?" Ford asks by her side, concern lacing his voice.

"I gave her a little something extra. She can read minds now."

"This should be interesting," he mutters.

"Yes, it should. You need to learn to control your thoughts around her, my son." Eloise focuses on me again. "You have the ability to heal now. When you're cut, your skin will mend. A knife to your heart will be pushed from your body and healed. Bullets will dissolve in your flesh. The only things that can kill you are decapitation and old age, at least until you're mated. There's no coming back from losing your head, however. You can also read everyone's minds, even with a block on them. You have the power to push past that and find out what they are thinking. You'll grasp how to do this quickly. It will be useful tonight at dinner. You need to get into Travis' head and find out what his plan is. It will help you. But you also have to learn how to block the voices out before they drive you mad. Focus is key. Focus on the voice you want to hear. Let the others fade away. You'll reach a point where you won't hear those at all."

She's right, I hear everything except hers. I wouldn't expect to hear her thoughts. But Rion and Ford's thoughts blend. Ford watches me intently, then throws up a block. His thoughts stop.

"Thank you," I send to him. He nods.

I glance over at Rion where he's standing near the window. Holding out my hand, I beckon him toward me. His thoughts are clear. He's unsure if I still want him, worried I'd rather be with Ford now that I have more powers. He hates that I'm part of this. Wishes we could run away and not look back. Everything he thinks hits me square in the chest, causing tears to pool in my eyes.

When our hands touch, I hold his gaze and speak to him with my mind. *"I only want you. No one else. I have to do this tonight. Paige would do the same for me. She'd walk into a den of lions if it meant saving my life."* He nods and takes a seat beside me.

"You're giving in to your mate bond little by little," Eloise observes. "This is a good thing. You shouldn't jump first and think later. Everything should be calculated. You're not purely human anymore. You're a paranormal. Use your new abilities for good. Don't let them go to your head." She's right. I'm not an average human any longer.

"I can't believe I'm a paranormal," I say in awe.

"The day Ford gave you the ability to teleport, you became one of us." Eloise smiles. "We're not a bad group to be part of. There are those of us who wish to harm others, but for the most part, we're peaceful."

Ford snorts with a laugh. "You can't be serious."

Eloise straightens. "I most certainly am. When you've been around as long as I have, you get a good gauge on things. The situation Ari and the Avynwood Pack are in isn't good, but it's just that—a situation. It's not permanent. Even if the war happens, there will be a resolution and life will go on. Maybe some of the bad will be removed from this world with the war. I don't pretend to be a psychic, but I do know all things happen for a reason." She turns her attention back to me. "Is there anything else you need, dear?"

I shake my head, trying not to read Rion's mind or pushing past the barrier into Ford's. I'm sure at some point my curiosity will get the better of me, but I won't forget what it felt like when Ford read my thoughts. I didn't feel him doing it. It was an invasion of privacy, though, and I don't want to do that to anyone else unless it's necessary.

Peering up from my place on the bed, I find Eloise watching me and smiling. "I made the right decision—giving this gift to you. You're going to be a smart paranormal, Ari. A strong one, too. They won't see you coming."

"I hope you're right. I don't feel strong at all."

"Strength doesn't always come from brawn. It comes from your mind as well."

"Thank you again." Here I wanted to gain one new power and she gifted me with two.

"You're quite welcome. Ford, would you please escort me to the Eiffel Tower? I'm meeting Diane and don't want to be late."

He holds his arm out for her. "I'll be right back." Then they're gone.

Rion peers over at me. I don't hesitate leaning into his warmth as he wraps an arm around me. There's something very comforting about his embrace. Maybe at the end of all this, we'll be okay.

"Do you still love me, even though I can read your mind now?" I ask teasingly, trying to break the tension in the room.

"Yes. I won't shield my thoughts from you. I want you to know every part of me: what I'm feeling, my desires, and my weaknesses. If we're going to be in this together, we have to trust one another."

"I trust you."

"Do you? You're relying on your new powers instead of my ability to protect you."

I pull back to look into his eyes. "This isn't about me trusting your ability to protect me. This is about me being able to fight for myself. You're seeing this in the wrong way. Your goal is to protect me at all costs. I understand that. Believe me, I do. But my goal in going to the Diaminsey Pack tonight is to rescue my friends. Paige is only in this situation because of me. I want all of us to come out of this in one piece."

"And you're in this situation because of me," he counters.

"I decided to be in this relationship with you. You gave me an out, remember? I chose to stay. This is on me. It's my fault Paige was taken, and I'll do whatever it takes so she's safe."

"And I'll do everything in my power to make sure you are."

I smile, knowing I'm not going to get anywhere with him. "You watch my back, and I'll watch Paige's."

Ford reappears. “Mom really liked you.” He doesn't seem to care that Rion and I were in the middle of a conversation. “She'd also like me to fight Orion for your hand and make you mine.”

“Come again?” I ask.

Ford laughs. “Joking, princess.” I breathe a sigh of relief but then catch Ford's true thoughts. He would fight Rion for me. It's more than a friendship he wants from me. He shrugs, realizing I’m aware of his feelings.

“I guess there won’t be any more secrets between us,” I say to Ford.

He turns toward the window, avoiding my gaze. “Guess not,” he mutters.

“What's going on?” Rion asks.

“Nothing. I was relaying to Ford how grateful I am for what he and his mother did for me today.”

The question is, what do I do with this new information? I'm with Rion, committed to him. Ford, while devastatingly gorgeous in the whole bad boy way, is my friend. An amazing friend at that. However, I don't feel the same pull toward him that I do to Rion.

“I know, princess,” Ford says solemnly in my mind. I guess we can now communicate like I do with Rion. Ford did say we share a connection.

“I'm sorry.” It’s all I can offer him. I can’t return his feelings.

This is my life now. Never a dull moment.

THIRTY

ARIES AND CACE ENTER THE CABIN, calling the three of us downstairs to go over the game plan. I honestly don't hear any of it. I'm too busy reading everyone's thoughts. It's distracting. There are so many voices, so many different ways of doing things. At first, I wasn't intentionally doing it. They bombarded me the second Aries and Cace arrived. Now I can't seem to stop. Too much is coming at me at once to get it all to quiet down.

Cace is focused on getting Paige and me out of there safely. Ford is worried about Kiara, but by the same token, he knows she's a strong vampire and will be able to handle herself. His main goal is to get me out safely. And Rion is doing nothing but worrying about me. He doesn't want me to go. He thinks they can find another way to get Paige and

Kiara out of there, without me being involved.

While Aries talks about what we should do, I don't think any of his ideas will work. If there's anything I've learned in my short life, especially during these last weeks with Rion, nothing goes according to plan. You can think your life will go one way, but then you get whiplash by how fast things change. And this—tonight—is going to be a change. I can feel it in my very bones.

The best case scenario is we get Paige, Kiara, and the rest of us out of there safely. The worst is none of us leave alive. Yes, Javen gave his word, but if all hell breaks loose, I doubt I'll be standing without harm. I'm not ready to die, and they don't know they'll have to chop off my head to kill me. I love having this new ability. Advantage: Ariane.

Ford must hear my thoughts because he uses his mind to send me a message. *"No one is getting near you so they can decapitate you. No one."*

My eyes meet his. *"I'm just one girl. There's nothing special about me. Get Paige out of there. She's human."*

"That's where you're wrong, princess. You aren't just a girl. You're more special than you realize."

I blush and duck my head so no one sees me. Ford walks up behind me, his boots clapping on the hardwood floor. He stops at my side and places a protective arm over my shoulders. I lean into him instinctively. No, he's not my mate, as Rion would say, but things are different now. I'm still trying to wrap my head around it. Although, right now, Ford's providing the comfort I need. He's my friend—a best friend. I won't discount him ever.

Rion growls on my other side, his jealous side fully coming out. Taking his hand in mine, I lift it to kiss the back. Our connection flares to life, easing his troubled mind. What am I going to do? I have a vampire for a bestie, who has feelings for me, and a wolf who's my mate. Why can't anything be easy?

"Ari?" Aries says, trying to get my attention. "Have you been listening?"

"Maybe," I reply sheepishly.

"How about the two of you?" he asks Rion and Ford. Neither utters a word. Aries throws his hands up. "Why do I bother?"

"We appreciate your time and direction," Rion starts, "but all that matters is Ari getting out of there safely. I know she wants her friend alive, but once we're in that home, my eyes will only be on my mate."

Aries nods. "I can't fault you there. I'd be the same. Ford, can you focus on Paige and getting her out?"

"No can do, wolf. My eyes will be on everyone in the room and their proximity to Ariane."

Scrubbing a hand over his face, Aries turns to Cace. "What about you?"

"Pack first. That's our motto and has been since day one. Ari is pack. Let's also remember Rion will be in there, and he's the least experienced wolf we have. Those two will be my priority."

"Paige is mine," I say loudly. "I get what the rest of you are doing, but can we all please remember that I'm no longer a vulnerable human? I'm a paranormal now. I can heal instantly. I can read minds and teleport. If you think I'm going in there to talk pack politics with Travis, you're wrong. I'll do my best to read his mind and find out what he's planning. I want my friends out of there, however—Paige and Kiara."

"This is going to be a mess," Aries mutters.

Cace claps him on the shoulder. "This isn't the first time we've had to deal with other packs or this kind of situation. We'll handle it." In each of the books in Lealla's series, there is always conflict. Always a life or death situation. It's what keeps the reader entertained and wanting more. There is one thing we can count on from her books—a happily ever after. That brings another question to mind.

"Has there ever been a couple in your pack who didn't make it? Who were killed before their books could be written?" I ask.

"No," Aries replies. "But that doesn't mean it couldn't happen."

"Don't," Rion growls.

"I'm a realist. You know this."

"I'd rather you don't speak your trepidation when it pertains to my mate." Aries nods.

"We should get going," Cace states. "We're supposed to be there in five minutes." Well, this day flew by.

"Let's get this show on the road," I add.

Ford squeezes my shoulder and sends to me, *"No matter what happens tonight, I've got you."*

"I need you alive, Ford. I don't want anything happening to you. We all need to survive this and bring Paige and Kiara with us."

"We'll do our best." He releases me then strides over to Cace, resting a hand on his shoulder. He sends me a mental image of what the Diaminsey Pack house looks like so I'll know where to teleport. Ford snaps and he's gone.

"Ready?" I ask Rion.

"Not at all."

I don't reply but simply picture what Ford sent me and snap. We reappear a moment later in front of a white stone home beside Ford and Cace. It's not as massive as Lealla's but is grand on its own. Two large, white pillars flank a deep blue door, which stands out in stark contrast to the white home. Turning, I take in the surrounding area. No trees but rather acres of land that seem to go on and on. In the far distance, I make out the line of the forest.

The door opening pulls my attention back to the house. Rion goes rigid beside me. His body is almost vibrating with energy.

"Don't shift," I remind him.

"Easier said than done."

A man steps through the doorway. He's tall with dark blond hair cut close to his head and a full beard. He's wearing jeans and a pair of brown work boots. The red thermal shirt completes the whole woodsman vibe he has going for him. The sleeves are rolled up, exposing muscular forearms. He smiles widely, his eyes trained on me. A shiver works its way down my spine and not the good kind.

"Ariane, welcome to the Diaminsey home. I'm Travis." He walks toward us and extends his hand. I try to get Rion to release me so I can shake Travis' hand, but his death grip on my fingers isn't letting that happen.

Travis' eyes go to Rion. "I mean your mate no harm, Orion. I gave my word that she would be safe. That you would all be safe."

"As long as they don't hurt anyone in my pack," I hear him think. I can't reveal that I heard, but I send the message to Ford so he can say something. Shady wolf. Not that I expected him to be anything else.

"What if I stab your beta in the chest? Will the four of us become fair game to be killed?" Ford asks.

Travis growls. "Don't test me on my land, vampire."

"Oh, I'm real scared," he mocks, pretending to shake.

"Can we get on with this? I have other things to do," I state.

Travis grins. "I think I'm going to like you."

"Goodie for me." Maybe giving the alpha an attitude isn't the smartest thing I've ever done, but I won't change my personality for anyone. Plus, they already know about me, so they probably expect my sass.

"Come inside. Dinner is being served. My pack is already seated."

"Where's Paige and Kiara?" I ask as we walk to the door.

"Right to the point. I like that. They'll be joining us for dinner."

"If you have either of them tied up," I warn. It's taking everything in me not to lunge at him. Of course, if I did that, I wouldn't be able to back it up. Not like I have the strength of Rion or Ford.

"You do have quite a mouth for a human. Then again, you aren't merely human, are you?"

"One point for you for remembering I can teleport."

He laughs. "Yes, I like you a lot."

Rion tugs on my hand, bringing me closer to his side. The word *behave* is tumbling around his head. He doesn't send it to me, though. I wouldn't listen if he did.

Inside the home, we turn left and step into a grand dining room. Two gold chandeliers hang above a long table. There are easily twenty men seated around it. This can't be the whole pack. The females are missing. Well, except for my friends. Paige and Kiara are seated on either side of the empty head of the table chair. Wake isn't anywhere in sight.

We're shown seats at the table on either side of Javen.

Yippee. Rion and I take seats to his right, Ford and Cace to his left. So many thoughts bombard me. It's taking everything inside of me not to wince and cover my ears. I can't do that without giving myself away. Instead, I focus as Eloise instructed. In a matter of seconds, the thoughts drift away.

All heads are turned toward us. A menacing wave of power ripples through the room, causing me to lose my breath for a moment.

"Did you feel that, Ari?" Travis asks from his seat. "That's the power of the Diaminsey Pack. Power the Avynwoods don't have. You see, we've been a pack for over a thousand years. My parents formed this pack with only the most powerful wolves. They all had children. Our fiercest are who sit before you. Our pack is the strongest along the entire East Coast." If he thinks all of this talk of power is going to impress me, he's wrong.

Women come out to serve us. I'm not sure if they are mates of some of the men at the table or staff the pack hires. Everyone is given a plate of meat and potatoes. I have zero interest in eating. I keep my eyes on the head of the table, bouncing from Travis to Paige to Kiara.

"Congrats on your pack power," I say. "But I have no interest in that. I like being a boring high school girl."

Ignoring me, Travis continues his sales pitch. He lifts his arm, pointing in the direction of one of his wolves. "This is Garrison. I think you'll find him appealing."

A man stands across the table from me. His chestnut hair is on the longer side, brushing just past his ears. Between the board shorts he's wearing and the white polo, I guess he's going for the preppy surfer vibe. He's as muscular as every other shifter here. I'll give him that.

It's then I delve into Travis' thoughts. He thinks Garrison could be a mate for me. He's presenting him to me on a platter for my taking. He's lost his mind.

I play stupid. "I'm not sure what he has to do with anything."

Travis laughs and brushes off my comment. "Let's eat."

This has got to be the strangest dinner I've ever been to. What's next? Being shown a room I could live in and a wardrobe of dresses and rubies?

Everyone eats, even those I came with. I push my plate away. "Can I have my friends back now? I get that you want me to join your little band of wolves, but I'm good. I just want Paige and Kiara with me so we can leave."

"I was hoping I could show you around," Garrison interjects. "There's much to see. Much to learn about the pack."

I quirk an eyebrow. "I don't think so. I saw the outside of this place and the grass you have surrounding it. I'm good."

Garrison's eyes flash green and next thing I know Rion is on his feet, his own eyes reflecting the same color.

"Come near my mate, and I will end you," Rion seethes.

Leaning back in his chair, Travis steeples his fingers. "This could be interesting. Do we have a formal challenge for Ariane's hand?"

Swinging my gaze his way, I ask, "What are you talking about? No one is fighting for me. I'm already taken."

"You still have much to learn, Ariane. You see, a wolf can challenge another for you as a mate. It's a battle to the death."

THIRTY-ONE

"EVERY DAY I'M WAITING FOR SOMEONE to show up with white coats and haul me off," I mutter. "You can't be serious."

"I'll make you a deal, Ari," Travis starts. "If you agree to Rion and Garrison fighting to the death, I'll hand over Paige and Kiara, nothing further asked of you."

Rion holds my eyes and sends me a message with his mind. *"Let me do this. It will free your friends and also prove to their pack that I'm the only wolf for you."*

"I'm not letting you fight to the death. He could kick your butt for all we know."

"You have no faith in me, little mouse," he smiles wickedly.

"I have faith. Faith that one of you is going to die, and it's going to be my fault."

"I'm going to agree to it and there's nothing you can do to stop me. I will not have another wolf thinking they can beat me and take my mate. There is more than death on the line—there's pride—and that's very important to shifters. Plus, strength and ability to protect our females." This isn't happening. I don't know what I'll do if something happens to Rion. For him to appear in my life and suddenly be ripped away. No.

"And if you die? Then what? I'm going to live here with this insane posse of wolves."

"No. Ford will get you out of here. He'll die to do so."

"For the love of... I don't like this one bit. I don't want you to die, Rion. Or Ford." I'm near tears, fighting away the onslaught of emotions this entire situation floods me with.

"I won't, Ari. Trust me. Trust our bond and my love for you." Trust him to live and not get killed.

I hang my head for a moment then lift it to face Travis. "Fine. Whatever. They can fight."

"Excellent. Let's move to the battle room." This is such a bad idea.

"You have a battle room?" I ask with a quirk of my eyebrow.

"Absolutely. We have to train somewhere."

"I want Kiara and Paige by my side during the fight. No matter who wins, they leave with me."

"Of course." He smiles. It's the type where he wants you to think it's genuine, but it isn't. I can hear his thoughts. He thinks his smile will calm my nerves and show me he's a nice guy. Ha!

We stand as Travis leads us and the rest of the pack through the dining room to a set of stairs that leads downward. Every step I take, the colder it gets, until we're in a massive room that I would bet runs the length of the house. The floor is concrete with drains spread throughout. I'm assuming so blood is easily cleaned up and washed down them. If that doesn't make me all warm and fuzzy, I'm not sure what will. The walls are bare. Nothing but solid concrete surrounding us.

"Well, this is welcoming," I mutter.

"It's not meant to be," Travis says in my ear. I jump and swirl, coming face-to-face with him. Freaking wolves and their stealthy behavior. His eyes flash green. "This is where we bleed for our pack, Ariane."

He steps aside, revealing Kiara and Paige. I rush at my bestie, slamming into her, throwing my arms around her. "Are you okay? Did they hurt you?"

Her voice and body tremble. "I'm fine. Freaked out to no end but fine."

"And you?" I ask Kiara.

"You shouldn't have added me to your deal, Ari. I can handle myself."

"You've covered for me. Now it's my turn to help you."

Rion is at my back when I turn back around. He dips down to brush his lips over mine, igniting my veins with electricity. "It's going to be fine, little mouse."

I don't hesitate and wrap my arms around him, holding him close. "I don't want anything to happen to you. I've kind of gotten used to you."

He chuckles, his chin resting on my head. "My wolf knows how to win and will do whatever it takes to keep you as our mate."

I pull back. "Wait. Your wolf is fighting and not you as a human?"

"That's right. When we fight, it's always with our

animal." Why didn't that occur to me? Too much is going on in my mind. Trying to block out all the voices, ensuring Paige and Kiara are okay.

"I want to talk to him—your wolf." Rion nods and shifts.

Before me stands an enormous black wolf. His white-tipped ears twitch in every direction, listening to the others in the room while his emerald eyes hold mine. Gently, I grasp either side of his face, his fur soft in my hands. "You win this, you hear me?"

He snorts as if to say, "Of course."

"I need you to survive." Emotion clogs my throat as the enormity of the situation crashes over me again. I might talk a tough game, but inside, the thought of losing Rion is breaking me.

He nudges me with his nose and licks my face. Then he's turning, walking toward the center of the room where a grey wolf is waiting for him. They're equal in height and build.

Travis steps forward. "You know the rules," he speaks loudly. "No one is to intervene. Outside of that, there are no rules. This is a fight to the death. Winner gets Ariane."

I lunge forward, ready to punch him in his smug face, but Ford is behind me, holding my arms in an iron grip. I came here to talk, to get my friends back, not to get Orion killed. This shouldn't be happening.

"Calm down, Ari," Ford whispers in my ear. "Rion can sense your unease." I pause my struggling and focus on my wolf. His hackles are raised, his legs twitching as if he's ready to pounce. "He needs to focus on the fight, not on you. Let him." I relax, but only marginally.

Orion and Garrison both move in a slow circle, their

eyes never leaving the other. Garrison is the first to leap. He jumps toward Orion, but my wolf is faster. He dodges out of the way a split second before he would have been hit. Then he's on Garrison, his lips peeled back, teeth bared as he bites into the other wolf's flesh. Blood coats Garrison's neck. Orion doesn't release him. He shakes his head, digging his teeth in deeper. But Garrison isn't giving up. He drops to the ground and rolls, ripping Orion's teeth from his neck. They both quickly stand and charge each other. This time, Garrison is able to spin around and jump on Orion's back, clamping his teeth down on his spine. Orion yelps in pain.

Tears pool in my eyes; his hurt ringing out in my mind. I can't hear anything he's thinking. He must have blocked me out. I don't have it in me at the moment to break down the wall in his mind. The pain—his pain—I can sense it. His back is on the verge of breaking from the pressure being put on it by Garrison's jaws.

Struggling, I try to break free from Ford's grasp. Nothing I do works. I want to intervene. I want to stop this from happening.

Orion thrashes around, trying to shake him off, but it's not working. Then he kicks out and Garrison is finally jolted off of him. Orion is able to walk, but his movements are slower. It's easy to see how much pain he's in.

Then Garrison is coming back, ready for round two, aiming for Orion's spine again. But Orion has a burst of energy and spins as Garrison lunges. Orion gets a hold of Garrison's neck as the other wolf twists above him. They're rolling around on the concrete, leaving a bloody trail in their wake. Garrison's jaws snap at the air, wanting to get Orion. But my wolf doesn't let up. He holds on tighter.

Now that Orion seems to have an advantage, I search Travis out in the crowd and try to latch on to his thoughts. It's not easy. I have to weed through everyone else's. Travis is as pumped up as the wolves who are fighting are, but his thoughts reveal something to me. Garrison isn't fighting fair. A mage has given him an advantage. He has the ability to kill Orion with his claws. They're tipped in poison. While I was talking to Orion, Garrison dipped his claws in the concoction. He has to sink them into Orion for it to work. Grazing his fur won't cut it. It needs to be in his bloodstream. Travis asked him to drag out the fight. Not to kill him until they've battled for a bit so it wouldn't be suspicious. Oh, no.

Turning back, I focus on the fight again. The two wolves are no longer wrestling. Orion is bleeding heavily from the back, blood dripping from his fur, splattering on the ground below. Garrison is opposite him, his teeth bared, ready to go for the kill. They both run at each other. This time, Garrison ducks as Orion jumps. Garrison slides underneath him then immediately gets on his feet to spring toward Orion's back. Orion is knocked to the ground not far from me, Garrison's teeth immediately go for his spine again. Then the grey wolf rears back, lifting his paw, his claws extended. I refuse to stand here any longer.

With strength I didn't know I possess, I get away from Ford and rush forward before Ford can grab me again. If he were smart, he would have been listening to my thoughts; his focus must have been elsewhere.

I'm at the wolves' sides, neither aware of my presence. They're too focused on each other, Garrison's face turned toward his prey. Ford and Paige are yelling in the background, Ford coming toward me. I have to move fast.

Lifting my foot, I kick Garrison in the side before he can deliver the final blow. Orion is startled for a second before he realizes Garrison is down. He lunges for him, his teeth tearing into his neck, ripping off a piece of his flesh. Fur and blood are flying through the air, Orion winning as he kills Garrison.

There's a growl at my back. I spin to find Javen in wolf form, prowling toward me, Ford on the other side of him. There's no teleporting in here. The only way for Ford to get to me is by walking. I'm left unprotected.

"Call off your mutt!" I yell at Travis.

He smiles wickedly. "You broke the rules of the fight. No one is to intervene. Now, anything goes."

"You cheated! Garrison's claws were tipped in poison supplied by a mage!"

"Is that true?" Cace shouts from my side. When did he get over here? How did he get past Javen?

Travis doesn't reply. Cace shifts into a magnificent red wolf and squares off with Javen, putting his body between ours.

Ford and Kiara rush to me and pull me back to the sidelines.

"You shouldn't have done that, princess," Ford hisses in my ear.

"He was going to kill Orion. I couldn't stand by and let that happen."

"Then you should have told Cace or me so we could have handled it. Now, Cace and Javen will fight until one is killed."

"What?" I scream. No, no, no! Everything is going downhill and it's all my fault.

"Orion killed Garrison," Ford states. "You remain his

mate, but you intervened. Cace can only leave here alive if he kills Javen. He took your place in the fight. You got Garrison killed, now it's up to Cace to end Javen."

My head spins with what I'm hearing. If only I went to one of them, this could have been avoided. I screwed up. But would Orion have died? Would Garrison have gotten his claws in him?

"That wasn't up to you to decide," Ford says, reading my thoughts. "This was a matter between packs. Cace would have handled it. You weren't allowed to fight, Ari."

I bury my head in my hands. I didn't think before I reacted at seeing Orion almost get killed. Cace took my spot. I wouldn't have stood a chance against a wolf. Javen could have ripped my head from my body in one quick movement.

Wait. I came here to get my friends back. But Travis wanted to sway me to their side.

I find him pacing along the sidelines, rooting Javen on as he and Cace go bite for bite and tear into one other. Within Travis' head I find the real reason he wanted me here. He wanted me dead. He wanted the upcoming war swayed in their favor. They wanted to kill Orion and Ford, knowing they'd come with me. Then he'd go for Kiara and Paige.

With us out of the picture, the pack would weaken. Aries would lose another family member. Who knows what that would do to him? Cace is a bonus. The Diaminsey Pack would have the advantage. They had no intention of letting me leave here alive. Once Cace is gone, they'll come for Orion and Ford. Kiara. Paige. Me.

It's evident to me now, I can't prevent the pack war. It's not possible. All that's left to do is leave here in one piece—all of us.

Orion limps toward me, clearly in pain.

"You have to shift," I plead with him as tears run down my face. "You need to heal. We have to get out of here. Please, Orion."

A gurgling yelp brings my attention back to the fight. Cace is on the ground, Javen towering over him, both covered in blood. Cace is barely struggling, blood pouring from his mouth. Javen leans down and sinks his teeth into Cace's neck. His jaw clenches, shaking Cace hard. There's no fight left in Cace. His emerald eyes hold mine as they glaze over and life leaves his body.

"No!" I scream at the top of my lungs. Hot tears pour down my face. I start to run forward, but Ford is behind me again, holding me tightly to his body as I punch and kick the air, trying to get free.

"Cace! No!" I cry. Sobs wrack my body. The scene in front of me can't be real. Please, let this be a dream.

Ford pulls me with him, retreating as far from the fight as he can get. His back meets the concrete as the Diaminsey Pack closes in on us. Orion is back in human form, but he's extremely weak. Shifting once isn't enough to heal him. Ford steps forward and pushes me behind him as Kiara does the same with Paige. We're behind a wall of vampires as I continue to cry. Paige's hand takes mine and grips it hard.

Many in the Diaminsey Pack shift. Wolves bare their teeth at Ford, Kiara, and Rion. Then Rion shifts again and it's game on. He dives toward the closest wolf, regaining a sliver of his strength from the shift. Ford and Kiara jump into the fray, using their vampire strength to rip limbs from the wolves who attack them. But there are too many of them and not enough of us.

Travis enters my line of sight, still in human form, and prowls toward me. There's no one covering Paige and me anymore. We're left defenseless. I can't teleport. All I can do now is protect Paige the best I can. Quickly, I cover her body with mine, my back to her chest, and press her into the wall. Travis reaches forward, grips my neck, jolts me to the side, and pins me to the cold, concrete wall. His eyes are green; his wolf in charge. Those eyes are the last thing I see before darkness consumes me.

Want more of Michelle Dare's paranormals? The story continues in **THE SOMBER CALL**. Also, you can sign up for her YA newsletter to hear news about all things Avynwood.

http://bit.ly/2vBpt9x

Other Books by Michelle Dare

<u>Young Adult Titles</u>

The Ariane Trilogy

The Ash Moon

The Somber Call

The Crucial Shift

<u>Adult Titles</u>

The Iridescent Realm Series

The Azure Kingdom

The Pine Forest

The Fuchsia Lakes

****

The Arrow Falls Series

Where I End

Where I Am

****

The Salvation Series

My Salvation

My Redemption

****

The Heiress Series

Persuading Him

Needing Him

Adoring Her

****

The Ray Point Series

Floating

****

The Vault Series

Uncuffed

Unreserved

****

Standalones

Daylight Follows

The Unattainable Chief

Pleasurable Business

Her Forbidden Fantasy

ABOUT THE AUTHOR

MICHELLE DARE is a romance author. Her stories range from sweet to sinful and from new adult to fantasy. There aren't enough hours in the day for her to write all of the story ideas in her head. When not writing or reading, she's a wife and mom living in eastern Pennsylvania. One day she hopes to be writing from a beach where she will never have to see snow or be cold again.

Newsletter Sign-Up: http://bit.ly/2vBpt9x

Connect with Michelle online at the following sites.
Facebook:
https://www.facebook.com/authormichelledare
Facebook Reader Group:
https://www.facebook.com/groups/daresdivas/
Twitter: https://twitter.com/michelle_dare
Instagram: https://www.instagram.com/m_dare/
Pinterest: https://www.pinterest.com/michelle_dare/
Website: https://www.michelledare.com/

Printed in Great Britain
by Amazon